TRANS HOMO...GASP!

Gay FTM and Cis Men on Sex and Love

Avi Ben-Zeev and Pete Bailey

TRANSGRESS•PRESS

Trans Homo…Gasp! Gay FTM and Cis Men on Sex and Love

CONTENTS

FOREWORD

T his week, I was discussing with a trans woman poet of my acquaintance her frustration at having been recently and unkindly dumped. She is clever and funny and talented and well-accessorized, so I asked why this trifling boy had ended things after just a few dates? When it turned out that his issue was her current genitalia, I burst out—in the middle of a bookstore—in frustration: "What is *with* that? I mean, listen: I have been very…friendly, over the course of my lifetime, and I have encountered many, many configurations and topographies of people's entertainment centers, but they are all, basically, the same stuff. Find a nice spot, pet it; find another nice spot, pet there. Repeat as desired until everyone's a puddle. Yay. The end."

She laughed and shrugged, and I did too, but it's clear from conversations—and from reading many of the stories that follow in the volume you hold—that uncertainty, unfamiliarity, and lack of confidence are the primary reasons that queer trans guys and queer cis guys are not getting it on, and getting off, a lot more often. This is a tragic situation.

In addition to being a friendly kind of a fella, I am also a person who loves to be helpful. It occurs to me that in this regard I have an opportunity to both offer some assistance *and* make some practical use of my experiences, er, doing field research in the area of encountering bodily configurations that are new to me (especially since my dance card is happily very full these days and I have not had occasion to make use of the skills myself in some time).

The first thing I feel prompted to say is that I think we forget: *all* new-to-us bodies are an undiscovered country, which bring both risk and opportunity. It can be tempting to be comforted by the familiar, for sure. The known can be welcoming, especially when we feel vulnerable. But imagine, if you will, what wonders might await if you came to every new sexual partner, however many of them you might have, as though his or her or their body was an entirely new landscape (which it is) for you to explore (with the consent of the landholder) at leisure. What might it mean to consider every part of them afresh, without preconception about what any body part is "supposed to" like—are we not queers? Are we not by birthright ready to make fabulous the ordinary? Address every part of your new partner's body with wonder. Breathe on it, stroke it with your hand, tug it, lick it, kiss it, hump it, roll the softness or hardness of you against it, envelop it, allow yourself to be enveloped by it. Although it may seem like a nonsense "mindfulness exercise" or a platitude, try being refreshed by wonder with every new-to-you body. In time, it may allow any anxiety you might be feeling about the idea of dating or fucking a guy with a different style of hardware than you have to evaporate more easily. Bonus, who knows what new and fun maneuvers you might add to your repertoire. (And in the same vein, gentlemen—and all people, really—it is actually a fantastic gift and a lot of fun for a partner when you are able to say even a little about what you like or don't. I have found it helpful to pair them, historically, especially when giving a hard limit. Like so: "I don't like to be bitten or scratched at all, but I love having my hair grabbed and pulled." It's very possible to be clear about a boundary while also being encouraging.)

It's also worth remembering that, as with anything, the first few forays don't determine overall success. As someone with a lot of experience asking people if they would like to have frolicsome naked time, I have the same checkered record that many 40-ish people of moderately slutty tempera-ments probably do—a fair number of yesses, a smaller but not insignificant number of no thank yous, and a few real assholes. In my case, the numbers are somewhat protective. I know that I can be, and have, fun in bed with persons of any gender, so if someone declines my proposition I can accept it with regret, or even frustration, while still not taking it as a failed global referendum on my sexual desirability as a person. That would not have been as easy if the ratios were different—having, say, 70 people out of 100 welcome my further attentions just *feels* different than if I asked a total of two people and they both declined. In the former instance I have way more rejections. But in the latter, the ratio is worse. The second sample (two people!) is way too small to be predictive. It's incredibly unlikely that none of my asks will be ever be met with a yes. But that can absolutely be how it feels, especially at the beginning. If I were advising past-me, I might give myself a little pep talk before I started wading in to propositioning partners (live or electronically) about the fact that the "no, thanks" answers EVERYONE will inevitably receive are not "you're undesirable," but rather "this isn't a good match," or "I'm still uncertain," or "my dance card is full right now." Not to be a boner-killer by invoking my grandmother, but it is true that my wise Nana has a saying I still return to: there's a lid for every pot. It may be true that some of us are a rather more custom size, and therefore the universal-size pots get covered more, but one good, tight fit is…well, perhaps not all you need, but it's out there and nice as hell to find.

For many gay or queer trans men, the experience of being seen by a cis partner as a man—even while buck naked—to be loved or fucked (or both!) as a man can contribute to the healing of a long and difficult place, a cultural injury that is compounded by everyone who tells us we're not real men. There's also, not infrequently, an ongoing idea among certain cis people that trans bodies are weird or that trans people probably don't get to have much sex and therefore are (or should be!) grateful for what we do get, regardless of how indifferent/fetishizing/dull. Once, on a panel, an audience member asked a long and rambling question—the entirety of which pre-supposed that it was very, very difficult for me to find people to have sex with and wondering how I worked around that? She was clearly startled when I said I didn't find it difficult at all, but her erroneous supposition—that it must be hard for trans people to find love or sex—has been repeated plenty of times within my hearing. I have found it helpful to just remember that when people voice the idea that they can't imagine sex with a trans person or why someone would want that, what they're *really* saying is that they have no sexual imagination whatsoever. Even if I found them appealing in some way before that pronouncement, it immediately wilts any enthusiasm I may have had. It's one thing to feel nervous-but-excited—that describes many of my favorite evenings! But to draw a total blank? No, thanks.

Following these few thoughts are a variety of experiences and perspectives from queer trans men, and the queer cis men who have admired us (some of them from rather close up)—the good, the bad, and the ugly but also the unexpected, the delightful, the reassuring and the affirming. I hope some of them turn you on, that others give you courage, that still others inspire you—they certainly have me.

S. Bear Bergman
June, 2017
Toronto

PREFACE

As trans men who have been dating and having sex with (trans and cis) men in gay male world for quite a while (more than 25 years, combined), we felt a calling to birth the *Trans Homo* anthology. Our driving force was to help demystify, humanize and celebrate what it's like to be a "trans homo"—a trans man who identifies as a gay or queer man—or to be a partner to one. Elders, like Lou Sullivan, paved the way and have brought some visibility to the fact that trans men are, and have been, an integral part of gay male communities. Yet, we trans homos (and our lovers) are still mysterious creatures to many, even within these communities.

Trans Homo is a collection of personal stories, essays, reflections and poems from a diverse range of gay and queer transgender and cisgender men, who come from different ethnic and racial backgrounds, physical abilities, geographic locations, sexual histories and gender presentations. Most books on trans men have centered on the experiences of straight and bisexual FTMs [some, which identify as AFAB (Assigned Female at Birth)]. Very few anthologies focus on the narratives of gay and queer trans men, who primarily or exclusively have sex, date and partner with cis or trans men. Moreover, even fewer have incorporated perspectives of cis gay men who embrace transgender men as equal sexual/romantic partners. This anthology helps to bridge this gap.

Authors' stories and lived experiences help answer questions about trans homo relationships while raising new ones. (Caveat: This anthology is not a manual or suggestive map of trans homo relationships, and authors' opinions are sometimes contradictory—after all, we're a diverse bunch.) So, if you find yourself asking some of the following questions, you've picked the right book!

Trans homo?—Tell me more!

I'm a cis gay male, and want to have/am curious about having sex with a trans guy. I'm excited but nervous: What if I—Say/ Do something offensive? Don't like it? Like it too much? Make him feel like an experiment?

I'm a trans man, and want to have sex with gay cis guys, but not sure how to go about it—How do I find gay men who'd be into me? Carry myself in gay men spaces? Disclose that I'm trans? And…What if I take off my clothes and he no longer sees me as a man?

I'm a queer/gay man (cis or trans) and have already had some (or a lot of) sexual and/or romantic experiences with trans and non-trans men. I'm curious—What have other folks experienced? What are some of the dynamics of being in a cis-trans or trans-trans committed relationship, including welcoming a child into the mix? How can I connect through these stories to others like me, to a larger community?

I am one or more of the following: woman/man/genderqueer/ agender/gay/lesbian/queer/straight/heteroflexible/bisexual/ pansexual/asexual/and even (gasp) heterosexual! I care about the diversity of human sexuality and desire, marginalized communities, social justice, and am a sucker for a good story. What is something new and exciting I can learn from reading this book?

Disclaimer: To protect individuals' privacy, in the autobiographical pieces in this collection, some names and identifying information have been changed. With regard to works of fiction—names, characters, addresses, businesses, places, events and situations—were either creations of the author's imagination or meant to be fictitious. Any resemblance to actual persons, living or dead, or real-world events is purely accidental.

In Part I, *Facing your Fears*, Luciano Sagastume offers practical information and tips for newbie trans men (Section 1) and cis men (Section 2) on how to "navigate, communicate and fornicate with (cis/trans) men safely, liberally and confidently." It's a fun read and chock full of invaluable "how to" pointers—from pickup lines, disclosure, code switching, dealing with rejection, to…how to have the (hot) sex you've been fantasizing about.

In Part II, *Gay/Queer Trans Men*, narratives range from steamy and sexual to soul searching and romantic. Some authors bravely share their angst and doubts, especially as they start their respective journeys into gay male world, while others focus on sex positive adventures, intimacy and growth. The main message is heartening: Coming home to oneself as a gay/queer man leads to greater authenticity, resilience, happiness, self-acceptance and a sense of connection to self and to community.

Trans men stories contain several themes. First, *scarcity beliefs can and should be overcome*. As many of the stories in this collection show, the belief that—"very few if any cis men will desire me"—is understandable but harmful (and untrue) because it can lead to having sex with the wrong guy and to being trapped in bad relationship dynamics. Jonah Elliot realized that he should have known better when he consented to having sex with a cis man who exhibited all the worrisome signs of being a trans fetishist. In retrospect, Jonah understood that the reason he said yes, going against his gut feeling, was based on his then belief that having sex with a cis man meant reaching "the pinnacle of homosexuality." Eventually, Jonah, like many of the other trans men authors in this collection, learned to trust his instincts and to transform difficulty into wisdom. Avi Ben-Zeev overcame the fear of experiencing a "Crying Game moment" (a reference to an infamous film in which a cis male protagonist throws up after seeing his trans woman lover naked). Avi learned that it is not only possible for a trans man to have hot (and edgy) sex with cis men but to also be picky and intentional about who he wanted to date and to have sex with. After all, if we, trans folks, think of ourselves as a low commodity, why would other people see it differently? Instead, if we start practicing radical self-love, and conceiving of ourselves as the catches that we are, possibilities will start opening up.

Second, *overcoming fears takes a willingness to be with and to grow from discomfort*. The payoff is tremendous! After years of being jealous of his cis gay male friends' sexual exploits, Jules Purnell took the plunge and started hooking up with cis men. Through these experiences, Jules found sexual liberation and a welcome membership in gay male community. Pete Bailey was asked to attend a gay cis men's underwear sex party—a situation that once would have felt too vulnerable. Pete said yes, despite the butterflies in his stomach. He found himself wearing mesh underwear, in a swarming crowd of naked and mostly-naked cis men, having the time of his life.

Third, *disclosure can be sexy and empowering*. Initially, Aaron didn't want to make a big deal out of being trans. He thought: "I'm a guy, you're a guy, so what if we have different histories and bodies—everyone does! The guy I'm with will find out once we start getting it on and he'll deal." After experiencing some off-putting reactions from cis men, he decided to disclose earlier, while his clothes were still on. He found disclosure to be an act of empowerment—a way to communicate what he wanted and needed around sex. The when and how of disclosure is a personal decision, as many of the trans men's essays in this collection would attest to. There is no "right" way. The important part is for a trans man to convey how he wants his body touched, communicate around what safer sex practices feel right, and ask for language around his body that feels appropriate and sexy. As Luciano Sagastume points out, different terms work for different folks!

Finally, *trans bodies are desirable and celebrated*. Xander approached his cis male lover, a bit nervously, with the request that the partner fellate him, as if he had a cis penis. "Perhaps move your head differently," Xander suggested. The result was a transformative experience in which Xander felt seen by his partner and more connected to his own body. C.K. Mahdi felt a bit nervous about how the gay cis guy he had just met on Grindr would react to his top surgery scars. Once they got naked, the guy told C.K. that his chest was one of the most beautiful things he had ever seen. That same summer, C.K. found himself at a bar, wearing a tank top to stay cool in the hundred degree weather. An older gay man, who spotted C.K.'s scars, walked up to him and said, "You are doing something wonderful...keep being yourself." These kinds of experiences helped C.K. feel accepted, seen and celebrated by gay cis men. When a hot young pup of a guy hit on Buck Angel at a Los Angeles gay leather bar, Buck froze at first, realizing that this guy was expecting Buck to have a cis penis. After some attempts to give a "heads up," Buck decided to just go for it. He felt encouraged by the hot unfolding chemistry, and the aroused crowd of gay men who gathered around to watch. Buck puts it this way, "I realized that this was my body, and I didn't give a fuck what anybody thought. So, playing with this guy and having everyone be so accepting felt great!" Since then, Buck has proudly proclaimed, "I am a man with a vagina!"

In Part III, *Gay/Queer Cis Men*, narratives range from hot romps to reflections on one's identity, romance and allyship. Many authors confess to initially having had fears of offending trans men, like using the "wrong" language, only to discover that trans men are resilient, and that letting go into an unfolding chemistry can be liberating, sexy and sometimes mind blowing!

Contrary to the belief that gay cis men could never be attracted to trans men, these authors showcase that there are plenty of cis men in gay male community who view trans men as desirable sexual and romantic partners. These stories reflect a growing shift in cis gay men spaces towards becoming more trans inclusive, perhaps due to greater visibility of transgender people in the media, an increased evolution and understanding of trans identities in society, the popularity and growth of dating and social media technology, and a better connection and coalition between gay and trans movements and communities.

Cis men stories include several themes. First, *getting over one's fears leads to real and sexy connections.* Cis men express worries around getting or staying hard, not knowing what to do sexually with a trans man's body, and making him feel like an experiment. As authors attest to, braving these fears is a well worth endeavor. Meeting up with a trans man via a gay male hookup ad, ∂ felt nervous about saying something hurtful or insulting. He wanted to make sure that he didn't invade the guy's boundaries or use language that was inappropriate. His date caught on to ∂'s nervousness and said, "Hey! Relax, just be you…" Shortly after, their clothes were off, and sex was amazing! Moo MuQaribu postponed having sex with trans men for years, because he was afraid to do or say something offensive, to not be "progressive enough," or to inflict damage by not being able to "get it up." Moo concluded that these fears made him stuck in his own head and prevented him from being present with the person in front of him. After giving himself a talking to, Moo decided to go for it with a trans man he had developed a crush on. Their sexual encounter was, "athletic, aggressive, loud, tender, revealing, mindful, passionate and mutually satisfying: It was all of my porn-style and pensive sex fantasies…but better." Moo's, and other cis men's stories, show that working through one's insecurity around not understanding and not knowing how to interact with trans men's bodies, can lead cis men to learn a new map of gender, sexuality and desire that expands their own sense of self.

Second, *genitalia do not a man make.* Yossef Aharon had his first sexual experience with a trans man in his 30s. He enjoyed it tremendously. This encounter lead him to reflect about the nature of gay men's sexuality and to what extent it revolved around genitals, versus other physical and psychological attributes. Yossef found it rewarding (and exciting) to go outside of his comfort zone and to explode assumptions not only about what gender meant but also around differences in how cis versus trans bodies work. AJ Chase realized that his sexual desires revolved around facial hair rather than the kind of genitals a man has. A good friend of AJ's asked him, "If you're fucking a guy that has a vagina does that technically make you bisexual?" AJ informed his friend that he was still very much a gay man, adding, "It's just that some of the men I'm attracted to were born with innies and some were born with outies."

Third, *it's best to question one's assumptions and to follow a trans guy's lead* (after all, he probably has some experience being a cis man's first). Dwayne Treat found himself making the assumption that the trans man he was about to play with would prefer being clothed. He quickly learned that this particular trans man was comfortable getting naked right away. Dwayne realized that his notion, "said more about me and where I was at rather than about him." AJ Chase found that sex with trans men worked best when instead of guessing what would feel good to them; AJ asked what they liked and how they wanted to be touched. He cautions, "So it's good to ask for communication, but be brief about it because you just want to have passion and go for it and not walk on eggshells too much."

Fourth, *trans men can offer a shared sensibility of and healing around being "othered."* Matthew Florence realized that his attraction to gay identified trans men went beyond the sexual—he found that the trans men he was attracted to often held a more radical and inclusive perspective on social issues like women's rights, #BlackLivesMatter, etc. As a Black man and a feminist, it made him feel an affinity to trans men he did not expect. For most of his life, Rev. Daniel Borysewicz believed that he had to be skinny to be attractive to men, which lead him to attempt to lose weight, including undergoing gastric bypass surgery. Rev. Daniel came to realize that not having a stereotypical gay male body did not mean that he had to have sex with just anybody who found him attractive, "I'm not going to do that anymore. I need to be interested in you and find you attractive, because I deserve better than a pity fuck." These experiences made him more attuned to trans men's struggles to overcome body shame and to learn how to demand love and respect on their own terms. Rev. Daniel shares, "With trans men, I sometimes feel that we help each other heal."

Finally, *trans men are partner material.* After Allan went on what he called a "tranpage," and dated and had sex with twelve trans guys in six months, he realized that he wanted to pursue a meaningful long-term connection with a trans man. This realization did not revolve around body parts, but about being drawn to men who had a more thoughtful and intentional relationship with their gender. Sheedu al-Nemmeh has been desiring being with a trans man he would proudly call his 'seahorse husband,' and who would be interested in bearing children. Sheedu says, "In this fantasy we'd build a family with a kid or two and live happily ever after. I know that's a lot to ask, but one can dream!" We wish Sheedu, and us all—May our dreams come true!

In Part IV, *Couples*, cis-trans and trans-trans male couples share their stories. Aaron and Allan met in naked yoga and now live in a house with a white picket fence. Kris and Owen met ten years ago and have been inseparable ever since. They've inspired each other to achieve balance, meaning, and joy, and have recently welcomed a baby into their home. These "… and then they lived happily forever" stories are tender, heartwarming and hopeful.

The ultimate lesson this anthology has taught us is that love transcends labels and happiness comes from embracing and celebrating diversity.

We hope you enjoy!

Part I

Be intrepid:
Tips for newbies

FACING YOUR FEARS

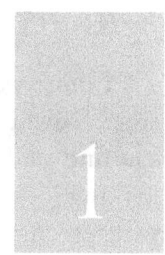

LUCIANO SAGASTUME

If you're a trans man, go to section 1.
If you're a cis man, skip to section 2.
If you're super motivated, read both.
I double dare you!

SECTION 1—TRANS MEN, THIS IS FOR YOU!

Are you curious about exploring gay/queer relationships with men but have never entered the scene? Are you already knee deep in Grindr dates but want to figure out the best strategy to disclose? Maybe you're quite clear on how to communicate your needs as a hard top but need to figure out how to help your male sub talk about his trans daddy to his friends. Both ways, and in all the ways, this first half of Facing Your Fears is all about you: how to navigate, communicate and fornicate with other men safely, liberally and confidently.

HOW TO GET IN

So let's start at the beginning: how to get (it) in. There are many ways to enter the gay scene, and much of it depends on where you live. We'll go over this soon. There is, however, one default: the Internet. Much has been written about the loss of physical gay spaces and the rise of Internet cruising either because of or despite of this loss. See any book on gentrification written by a gay person. For our purposes, Internet cruising is a definite plus.

INTERNET CRUISING

I don't want to bore you with unnecessary information but just to be sure: Download Grindr, Scruff, Jack'd and any other top-listed app you can find under the Google search "gay hookup app" now. Whether you're looking for a hot hookup you'll never see again or the Mr. Gay Husband of your dreams, you'll want to check out what the guys in your area are like, and chances are, they'll be on one of these apps.

Make a profile. For now we'll just go over the basics: Upload a picture. Most men will want to see your face. Yes, even if you're just 6 months on T and look like a prepubescent boy child, take that selfie and put it up. I promise you, there is a gay man out there for everyone. Choose a handle that fits with what you're cruising for: romantic handles (dreamyFTM123, hubby4hubby1) if you're trying to date, hot handles (ready2play, suptonight4) if you're on the hook up vibe.

Finally, you can also cruise on Craigslist, though you run the risk of having to wade through dozens of emails from questionable chasers, the occasional hate mail and many, many bots. If you want to try your hand at it, remember to make a throwaway Craigslist email account. Even if you mask responses with Craigslist's anonymous email function, you don't want to be getting nudes on your work email. Respond only to ads where guys are specifically looking for trans dudes, or where guys aren't explicit about wanting a very specific, and not yours, genitalia. This saves you the trouble of having to educate someone who you might not even meet.

For all online cruising: It is generally safer than what the media and your straight friends might lead you to believe, but there are still some basic ground rules, so make sure you play it safe(r):

> *Meet in a public place.* This is a must. Never send someone your actual home address, nor meet someone at their home before checking them out with the safety of other people around you.

> *Don't waste time.* This is a time honored hookup tradition: we both know we're not here to talk about our day, or what our favorite episode of Arrested Development is. Have a generic script ready to get the action going. For you, it should be something like:

Pickup line: "Hey, you interested in hooking up with a trans guy?"

Some information about your body: "I have original plumbing below the belt."

What you're into sexually for this encounter: "Your fantasy of getting topped hard is something I can definitely deliver; however, I'm not down for a blowjob."

Hosting details: "I live a block away from here and we can go there now."

Phone a friend. Always, and especially when you are first trying out internet hookups, let a friend know who you are meeting, when/where you are meeting them, and have a check in time. This doesn't have to be complicated. Just send a screenshot of the profile, a time and place, and say you'll call in by midnight.

CRUISING THE CLUB

By which I mean, of course, any actual physical space where you might try to cruise gay men. The basic rule applies to you as to anyone else trying to cruise: Look your best. Make sure you keep your hair nicely cut and the clothes on point if you're hitting the clubs. Have nice fitting shorts that accent the booty and nicely cut tank tops for the body if you're trying to find yourself a muscle queen at the gym. And keep up with the latest authors if you're cruising the gay men's book clubs for a hot nerd daddy.

Then, just start practicing flirting with guys. How does this work? It starts with the eyes. Many men check out people they are attracted to. Start paying attention to where their eyes go. Are they following the pretty girl walking across the park lawn, or are they staring at your close cut tank top? Chances are, that man is gay. It is intimidating at first but practice the mutual check out.

First, lock eyes for a brief moment with the guy of your choice, then look away. After a beat or two, circle back. If he's not looking back at you in that moment, don't stare. Just look away again and repeat the circle back. You can do this a few times to determine whether he does the circle back as well. If your gaze is met by his again, hold the mutual stare, and give a smile. If the smile is returned, you're in! He's probably gay and interested.

Now comes the second hard thing you have to practice: the follow up. This will differ depending on how you identify. Tops: try walking over and starting the conversation. You are the initiator, after all. Even just a "Hi, my name is—" will do. Bottoms: invite him over with a small nod. Even after the eye contact and a smile, he'll want to know you actually want to meet him. Switches (and everyone, really): the world is yours! Do what feels right and explore. You might not master the art of cruising on the first go, but over time, you will learn what works for you.

DISCLOSURE

We've touched on it a little, but this deserves its own section because, second only to rejection and violence, knowing when and how to disclose is very important.

WHEN

As soon as possible, really. If you're cruising online, your profile, post or ad should include the words "trans" and "look it up yourself" somewhere. You want potential partners to know up front what your junk is, and you are likely to prefer people who already know what to expect and how spectacularly great the sex can be. You will undoubtedly get messages asking what being trans means, what you were born as, what your real name is, etc., etc., etc., from gay men who are obviously just trying to chat. You don't have to educate them or respond. Real good chances are, you don't want to play with them anyway.

HOW

This is entirely up to you. There are different ways to discuss being trans. It really depends on what makes you comfortable, how you want to talk about your junk and who your potential partners are. Here are some examples culled from real life Grindr profiles, gay trans men my friends and I talked to and some research:

> *Original Plumbing.* This is the most commonly used route
> for trans men who have not had (or will not have) bottom
> surgery. Something along the lines of "I have original

equipment below the belt" is straight forward, without being unnecessarily explicit (if you don't want to be).

Holes. This is the more overtly sexually explicit route. Use only if you are comfortable, as you are inviting people to talk about your body in this way. There are many ways the extra hole can be referred to. "I have a _____"

1. front hole
2. bonus hole
3. extra hole
4. *insert your term here*

Cock. Another explicit way to talk about your body parts. If it is important to you that people refer to your body in a certain way when having sex, it might be best to mention this in your ad or profile, as this will encourage men to think about and talk about your body in this way. "I have a _____"

1. cock
2. trans cock
3. FTM cock
4. silicone cock
5. rubber dick
6. *insert your term here*

The junk. If you're okay referring to your original plumbing by name, then do so. This will inform your potential fuck buddy about how they can talk to you about your body. "I have a _____"

1. cunt
2. vagina
3. pussy
4. *insert your term here*

WHY

Absolutely you want to do this, no matter how uncomfortable it may feel at first. Letting potential partners know about your junk will come easy with practice. However, failing to do so may mean a higher chance of rejection later in your encounter, when the hot new gay man you just met realizes they aren't in for the ride they're accustomed to. It is much better practice to disclose early and often. You can weed out the dummies and get down to it. Believe me, while it's scary at first, it's a much easier ride than holding on to the curtain for a big reveal when you're much farther down the road than either of you bargained for.

REJECTION

Yes, you will be rejected. And sometimes, it will be because you are trans. But you'll be surprised—it won't happen as often as you'd think—and you'll know right up front. No games, no deliberation. Gay men say yes or no and move on. More often than not, they'll be curious when they find out you have different body parts. This is a good thing.

When you are rejected, remember that it is ok and that you were also rejected before you were trans. So rejection is inevitable. It will happen because you're not someone's type, or they're already seeing someone, or they just don't like your haircut. It's sad, but it's part of cruising, and you should move on and try your luck with another guy.

SEX

TOPPING

Absolutely, of course, you can be a gay male top, and there will be plenty of bottoms interested in having sex with you. It might be the case that guys who are more vanilla (versus kinky), and especially cis guys who do not have experience with toys, might not be able to imagine how the mechanics of a trans man topping them could work. Bearing this in mind, just refer to the *How* section above, on how to communicate about your body and sexuality. When cruising, posting online or meeting someone at a bar, it is important to disclose that you have a different type of dick than what they might be used to. Play this up. There are many advantages to having a strap-on dick, including variation, stamina and dependability!

BOTTOMING

Yes, many a gay man will be interested in topping you—in both your front and back holes. There is some interest among gay men in trying out your front hole—especially if they've never experienced it before. It is absolutely up to you whether you want to allow this to happen or not, and you should communicate that early if there's any indication they may want to play that way. But if front hole play isn't your thing, you do not have to let someone play with it just because they're giving you attention. Remember, it's your body and you're there to have fun, not disappear into a dysphoric subspace.

Also, we have heard that many a gay man will ask to bareback in your front hole—this means no condom use. We're sure you are familiar with health risk information and data, so the choice is yours. Barebacking is a long, rich and powerful tradition in the gay community for many reasons, including pleasure, a resistance to the pathologizing of queer sex and just plain fun. However, there are different health risks for front hole sex compared to back hole sex when hooking up without a condom. Make sure to read up on this before making your choice about whether to bareback or not.

Anal sex is also up to you to negotiate. Of course, as you probably know by now, anal sex is what gay men are accustomed to, and you will no doubt be asked to participate. Would you rather only have front hole sex? Say so. This is your gay experience and you can manage it however you see fit. There's no right or wrong way to be gay.

CONSENT

It is no secret that gay men have a very different idea of consent practices compared to other communities, including the straight world, lesbians and queers. Absolutely vocalize your needs and wants before hooking up with someone, and do not allow pressure—peer, sex partner or otherwise—to push you into something you don't want to do. Also, be aware that the gay scene is a much more handsy community than what you might be used to. It is generally agreed that gay men grope, grab and pinch much more often without asking. This does not mean you have to be ok with it. If you do not enjoy such attention, say so.

LOCALE

Finally, locale. While it is true that dating and hookup apps have made it easier than ever to find a hot and willing partner, it is still the case that you will have a much easier time finding gay men to hook up with in larger cities compared to more suburban or rural areas. If you are currently in a less than ideal place, as both a gay person and a trans person, consider moving to or at least visiting a larger populace. You will find many more opportunities to cruise, potential mates to meet, and people who already know all about you and your body and can't wait to explore it. Good luck!

SECTION 2—CIS MEN, THIS PART IS FOR YOU!

Hi cis guys! This is your own section on facing fears. While I'm no clairvoyant and probably will still leave some questions unanswered, and stones not overturned, here's some trans friendly topics we know should be discussed.

NAMING YOUR FEARS, THEN LETTING THEM GO

If you're a decent guy—and chances are that your interest in reading this section is because you're inclusive, open-minded, progressive, and perhaps even (gasp) a feminist—then you will likely have some of the following concerns. Rest assured, you are not alone!

"What if I won't get hard?"

"What if he feels like 'an experiment'?"

"What if I won't know what to do?"

"What if I like it (too much)?"

These worries are normal. In fact, it'd be weird if you didn't experience any of these…So take a deep breath (or two, or three) and think about this: You won't die! Well, eventually you will, but likely not from having sex with a trans guy. I don't mean to be glib, it's just good to keep things in perspective, and also to not take oneself too seriously, don't you think? If you're still feeling anxious, here are some tips:

Say something. You might want to confess that you feel a bit nervous because you're new to sex with a trans guy. As long as you're using "I" sentences—"I feel," etc., the hot trans guy who has piqued your interest will likely be open to hearing you out.

Follow his lead. He might be your first trans guy, but you're likely not his first cis guy, so take cues from him and follow his lead.

Don't focus on being a perfect lover. Heck, who is? Start doing something that makes you hot, and just…go for it. When you get to his junk, ask him how he likes to be touched, or if you're the quiet type and talking during sex kills your mood, then use your intuition, imagination, and start doing things. If he starts moaning, trembling, or flips you on your back and uses your cock for his pleasure, well…you're off to a good start.

If it bombs, it bombs! So what? How many times have you decided that no way in hell are you going for it when a trick opened the door or took his pants off? So it'll get a bit awkward but we're all grown-ups here. It's your job to be a gentleman, and to make your exit gracefully, but it's not your job to take care of him. That'd be condescending, right?

Go for it and have fun! Do I need to say more?

LANGUAGE

Words carry a lot of meaning, and how you talk to your (potential) trans partner is very, very important. It's ok to make mistakes—and do expect to be corrected—but the most important thing is to listen to the trans men in your life, respect their requests, and do your best. Here are a few vocabulary words you'll probably be hearing more often if you're around trans guys:

> *Cis*—This means your gender identity is the same as the one you were assigned when you were born. Literally, your parents announced "It's a boy!" to all their friends in some sort of elaborate gender reveal gimmick (what, they did that in the 80's too, right?) and you're still a man now.

> *Trans*—This means your gender identity is different than the one you were assigned when you were born. Going back to the same gender reveal by parents from our last definition, they screamed "It's a boy!" while blue confetti rained down on them from the heavens and friends did choreographed backstreet boys moves for the camera—and you don't identify as a man.

Front Hole—That bonus hole on a trans man's body. This is a pretty neutral way to refer to a trans man's junk but best to check in with him about how he refers to it. Also, keep in mind that some trans men elect to undergo bottom surgeries and may not have a front hole.

CONSENT

While consent practices in the gay male community may be lax, not every trans man is comfortable with the non consensual heavy petting and groping that happens in gay male spaces. Practice asking before you decide to engage in some type of behavior. This doesn't mean it has to be any less sexy—in fact, having a man say "yes, please do" while making direct eye contact can be sexier than the surprised deer in the head lights look you might get otherwise. Here are some examples:

"Can I kiss you right now?"

"That ass looks so good—may I?"

"Can I take you to the backroom with me?"

RESPECT

Yes, a trans man is a different type of male than what you may be used to. This does not mean you get to decide how to talk about, engage with, or identify the trans man in your life. This is his life, and your job is to respect him. If he wants you to suck his cock, don't choose that moment to ask, "Well, is it really a cock, though?" Follow your trans man's language and lead on how to talk about his body, gender, presentation, and life. Respect is easy and…sexy!

READ ALL ABOUT IT!

The Trans Homo anthology is meant to serve as a resource. In fact, there's a whole section devoted to cis men's experiences with trans men. What better way to know what it's like for a cis guy to have sex or a relationship with a trans guy than to hear from cis men who've taken the plunge? Rest assured, if you haven't had sex with a trans man (yet) and are considering it, you're not alone.

In "What Defines a Man," Yossef Aharon talks very candidly about some of the fears he's experienced before he ended up having (super hot) sex with a trans man.

> I had a fear that…I would not be able to get or to stay hard, and that it would feel both embarrassing for me but also for the trans guy that I was having sex with, and through this I worried I would further stigmatize them.

Check out his essay! Yossef tells it as it is—How he finds the familiar comforting and the unknown scary, how he tends to get stuck in his head, and how getting out of his head and having sex with a trans guy he met on Facebook (!) ended up being different and way more exciting than he could have ever imagined.

In "Spirit and Flesh," Rev. Daniel Borysewicz, a queer cis man, talks about the difference between having sex with a cis woman than a trans man:

> When I had sex with my seminary [FTM] boyfriend, at some point we paused, and he asked me, "Do you really just want to have sex with women, and are using trans men as surrogates?" I told him I didn't think that was the case. Several years later, I had sex with two cis women (after 20 years of only having sex with men). They were both kinky. One of them was androgynous and queer and the other was straight and slender. During sex, the slender woman was straddling my face, and calling me 'Daddy,' and all of a sudden I remembered the question my seminary boyfriend asked. I thought, even though I have had trans men straddle my face in the same position—that in no way was this experience with this woman the same. Her smell, taste, energy, and high-pitched voice, were all very different from a trans guy's. So no, it is not the case that I was having sex with trans men because they were easier to bed than women. There is no correlation between the two. Trans men are men. They smell, taste, and have a masculine energy just like cis men.

In "Like Chocolate? Try Lemon Ganache," Dwayne Treat echoes these sentiments:

> Trans men smell like men! They have the testosterone level of a nineteen-year-old guy that comes out of every orifice

of their bodies and can even be a little addicting. There's nothing feminine about trans men. In fact, sometimes the cutest twenty-year-old man in the Castro is actually a forty-year-old trans man.

In "Love me Some Scruffy Men with Innies and Outies," AJ Chase adds an additional perspective – an attraction to a "type" transcends whether a guy is cis or trans. In AJ's case, it's all about scruff. In your case it's _____ (fill in the blank).

> Society is finally getting to be more sex positive, but sometimes people get confused. My best friend and his wife are a straight couple. They're very monogamous and jealous but they've welcomed my husband and myself into their home, and they acknowledge that we have a relationship that is very different from how they were raised. They say that it's cool that my polyamorous lifestyle works for me, and that they love me. One time, I got a random text from my friend's wife, "If you're fucking a guy that has a vagina does that technically make you bisexual?" I told her the same thing I tell everyone else, "No, I'm still very much gay." I have always been and still am attracted to men with facial hair. It's just that some of the men I'm attracted to were born with innies and some were born with outies.

By reading these essays, you'll get insights on what it's like to be a cis gay man who decides to get over his fears and have sex with a trans man (or two, or more). After all, trans men are a whole other level of hot. Just sayin'.

COMING OUT

So are you still gay if you like sleeping with a trans man? Does Prince William need Rogaine? Yes gurl. If you were gay before, then rest assured that you're still gay after. After all, a trans man is a man. Before telling everyone you're dating/fucking/marrying a cute trans man, check in with him about how he'd like to be talked about. Does he want to remain stealth, and have no one know his business? Don't come out. Is he a trans rights activist who speaks at the rallies and is out to the bus driver, postman, and barista on the corner? It's time to start telling your friends.

How you do so is really simple: "Mom, Dad, Bartender, and dear close friends: I'm dating a trans man." This doesn't change anything about who you are, or how you identify, and it does not mean you have to have some kind of existential crisis where you talk to your confused therapist about front holes and the meaning of life. Relax. Trans man = man, and you're still quite gay. Genitalia, again, does not dictate gender—junk does not a man make. If you're swooning over a particular trans guy you've met, it's probably because of who he is. Very few of us fall in love with genitals. Remember that.

Undoubtedly people in your life will have lots of questions—trans men are not often in the media, and even so, many people have curious and sometimes intrusive questions about below the belt junk, sexual positions, etc. Field these questions for your trans man so that he doesn't have to deal with your bestie asking him whether he's had bottom surgery, or your friends talking about serving fish at the bar (no, this is not a cute joke).

If you don't want to answer something, don't. Tell folks to ask Google. This is the age of information, right? You don't have to educate everyone in your life, and you also shouldn't make your partner do it either. Have fun, love often, and demand respect for him and for yourself. You deserve it.

Part II

Gay/Queer Trans Men

Tranpa Says: Celebrate, Be Safe and Do Something Dirty!*

Buck Angel

I have unapologetically shouted out my truth to the world, "I am a man with a vagina!" to bring visibility and to demystify our sex lives and genitals, in the hopes of reducing social stigmas against trans bodies. I don't feel shame or anger about my anatomy, I love my vagina, and if you have one too, I hope you can embrace yours with confidence like me.

Every day, I receive letters from younger trans men, some that aren't even out of the closet yet, voicing their worries about how to talk about sex. These younger guys tell me that they're afraid of being bullied, belittled, made to feel less than, and all because they don't have a penis but a vagina. So many of these guys are young and inexperienced. They feel insecure about their bodies because of negative messages they hear in community. I want to push the boundaries, encourage trans men to celebrate their vaginas, and to explore and celebrate any pleasure they can get from sex.

I know some of you may be rolling your eyes because I'm referring to a trans man's parts as a vagina, and that's alright with me. I've been criticized by some for referring to my anatomy as "my pussy" and "my vagina." I don't see what all the fuss is about. These are my parts and what feels authentic to me. See, as a community we need to embrace the idea that we won't always agree on words, terms and sometimes experiences, and to allow guys to use whatever words feel authentic to them.

"Pup Love": First Experience of Sex as a Man with a Cis Gay Man

Pre-transition, I had some early unmemorable sexual experiences with cis men; then I began identifying early on as a butch dyke and partnering with mostly femme women. At the beginning stages of transition, I identified (and still do) as being transsexual versus transgender, because my gender identity is binary. At that time, I thought of myself as straight.

When I started taking hormones, my connection to my body and sexuality changed. I began to feel my masculinity, and as I appeared more masculine, gay cis men started to take notice and hit on me. I developed a curiosity, "It could be hot to suck your cock, I could try this." It led me to realize that I could be attracted to men. Initially, that feeling was quite uncomfortable, trying to reconcile my change in desire was somewhat bizarre at first, but I was curious to explore.

It was the late 1990's. I was more androgynous in appearance than I am today. I was bald, baby faced, and projected a very dominant energy but didn't see myself as looking very masculine yet. My body didn't scream manly man.

I spent many nights at a local Los Angeles leather bar, a place where I felt safe and accepted. I'd show up wearing leather pants and a motorcycle jacket, and would hang out, smoking cigars and taking in the cisgender masculine energy. One time, a handsome young pup of a guy approached me. He was smooth, very skinny, wearing only a black jockstrap with boots. I found him to be cute.

"Hello, Sir. How are you tonight?"

"I am well," I replied. We quickly fell into some light conversation. Talking felt easy and I could tell he was interested.

"Can I lick your boots, Sir?" he asked submissively.

I raised one of my boots onto the bench beside me and he dropped down to his knees and began licking it. As I watched him, I could also see, in the periphery, men kissing, rubbing chests and grabbing cocks. I felt so turned on.

The young pup started running his hands up my leg. I knew something was going to happen, but I wasn't sure what, or how. This was going to be my first time with a cis man as a man. He started kissing me, and I was into it, but I also felt overwhelmingly nervous. This was quickly surpassing my previous experiences. I worried about what to say. If things went much further, he'd discover that I was not like him. I was not one to pack, I've never really been, so if his hand moved to touch my dick, he'd likely be quite surprised to find my vagina.

"Sir, would you like to go to the Dark Room?"

"Yeah, I would…but I have to tell you something."

"Sir?"

I froze, thinking of what, or how, to tell him about my vagina. I couldn't think of a great way to say it. We stood there for what felt like an eternity, but was likely only a few seconds, staring at each other, while I found the words, "Well, I have a pussy."

The young pup looked at me with a puzzled expression, but didn't say anything.

"I was born a woman and had a sex change to become a man," I explained.

"I don't understand, Sir."

"I was a woman and became a man, so, you're not gonna find what you're looking for down there. I have a pussy."

"I still don't understand, and I really don't care."

He led me to the Dark Room, a backroom that was dimly lit, smelled of a mix between cum and bleach, and you could hear men fucking all around. The walls had little cutouts so that others could peak through and watch, some holes big enough, you could put body parts through. We started making out in a sort of a passageway, just outside of view. But there is no such thing as privacy in these kinds of places. A small group of men gathered around us, stroking themselves while watching us make out.

As the pup kissed me, he slid his hand down my pants and started to feel and touch my vagina. He just went for it! It felt really good, so I pulled down my pants. He started sucking on my pussy. The group of men were still watching us, stroking themselves and looking aroused. Young pup made me cum. I dropped to my knees and sucked him off.

That was my first real time being with a gay cis man as a man. It was in public and I was accepted as normal. Having all those gay men standing around and watching me suck his cock and him sucking on my vagina was empowering! I realized that this was my body, and I didn't give a fuck what anybody thought. So, playing with this guy and having everyone be so accepting felt great!

My guess is that I was welcomed in this space because it was a leather bar. In my experience, the smaller niche communities—faeries, bears and leather community—tend to be more accepting than men in broader gay community. All of my early experiences with gay men were validating and supportive of my identity. I wouldn't be the man I am today, without the early support I received from cis gay male communities.

GOING FURTHER WITH GAY MEN

With increased confidence, I started to go out to more clubs and to experiment further. I didn't have a lot of sex—mostly just blowjobs and jacking guys off—because I was always partnered with women. My relationships with women were somewhat tumultuous because my gender was in constant evolution, and I had been partnering with lesbian identified women. After a few failed relationships, I stopped dating and was single for about a year. That's when I started to get deeper into the gay men leather scene. As I started to build emotional connections with men, I was more willing to invite them home with me. Around this time I was gaining visibility as a public figure.

I became concerned about my safety as people started to recognize me in the bars. I started escorting to feel in control with cis men and to experience actual fucking with them. I was able to control the scene, choose who I wanted to see as a client, and get paid for it. It was a lot of fun at first.

I had this one very wealthy client, who would fly me out to different places to meet him. The last time we were together was in London. I arrived at the hotel, dressed head to toe in leather, with heavy boots, carrying a big duffle bag of clothes, dicks and toys. With every step I took, I felt the eyes of the other guests and staff watching me. Self-conscious, I continued to the elevator. His room was on the top floor of this extravagant hotel. I knocked on his door lightly, and to my surprise, it was unlocked and opened slightly, so I let myself in.

"Come in," I heard him shout from another room, trying to project his voice over some porn he was watching.

He had been busy shopping. In plain view were several jockstraps, a few harnesses, and at least a dozen pair of brand new boots in my size.

"Take all your clothes off and put on anything you want," he yelled.

I put on a sexy jock strap, and some boots, and walked into his bedroom. He was in his sixties, totally gay, very well groomed and stocky.

He sat kneeling on the floor watching porn, also only wearing a jockstrap and boots.

"Hi Sir, thank you for coming. Can I get you a drink?" he asked in a kind tone.

"I'll have a coke."

He got up from the floor, fixed us drinks; a soda for me and a Jack Daniel's for himself.

"I hope you don't mind that I'm drinking alcohol, Sir."

"Not at all."

"What would you like to do, Sir?" he asked, as he handed me the soda.

"I don't know," I said, standing silently for a minute. "Go sit in the chair."

He did as I instructed, and I followed him. Things shifted from me giving orders and him following them, to a more organic dynamic. I sat down on his lap and started kissing him, making out, rubbing him all over.

I got off his lap and started sucking his cock. Things got hot and passionate, we were both really into it. We got in bed, he moved my jockstrap to the side and started sucking my pussy. The whole time, porn was playing in the background, as usual with this client. As the intensity built, I took off my jockstrap, and he fucked me in my pussy. In the end, he came by jacking off while sucking me off again.

"You know what, Sir?" he asked.

"What?"

"I always put on porn in the background because I get bored halfway through my session, but I never get bored with you. I never once looked at the porn the whole time we were having sex."

"Thank you, that's awesome," I said, feeling good. As a transsexual man, I provide a different experience than other men, which can be very exciting to some people.

TRANPA'S TIPS FOR TRANS MEN

I've been having sex with cis men for seventeen years, and the best piece of advice I can give is make your decisions about what you are/aren't willing to do before you enter into a situation. There have been several cis guys that have wanted to have sex with me without a condom. For me, a condom is a must and I am not willing to negotiate about it, but I know that barebacking is a longstanding tradition in some gay communities. It is hard for me to relate because I have different anatomy, but I can see that some of it is about pleasure and some of it is political—gay men's sex should not be pathologized.

Trans men need to be thoughtful and intentional about their sexual health. I worry that younger or less confident guys enter into dangerous situations, because they desperately want to experience sex with men. I want you trans guys to know that you will find a partner, and that it is important to find someone who will listen to you.

If you want to have sex with your vagina, do it! If that's not your thing that is fine. You can take it in your ass, your mouth or you can fuck someone however you want. The most important thing is that you decide what and how you want to do it. So, if you want to use condoms, confidently say, "I won't let you fuck me unless you put this on." That is it! It really can be that easy, and I guarantee you that more guys are willing to fuck with a condom on, than not fuck at all. I want you to know that you have power, you are fuckable, and you have the right to state your wants and needs. No one else is going to take responsibility for your sexual health and safety. This is a big deal and you need to be ready to talk about it.

When you approach conversations about sex, be careful with your words, try to embrace some sex positivity, and don't criticize or make someone feel bad about their decisions. Often sex will be a compromise, make sure you are stating your needs.

Also, as we grow older, testosterone makes our bodies change, our vaginas can start to dry some, causing some of us to experience pain while having sex, and even tearing. This is real, and we need to speak about it. Lube is your best friend! You want to make sure that you are using enough and preventing injury. I am currently working on manufacturing a lube that will meet your needs. Keep an eye out for it!

As a former porn star, I wish more than anything that I could tell you how to have an amazing sex life, but I can't. I can only speak about my experiences, how I find pleasure, and about what I know. There is no guarantee that we will agree, or that you will like what I like. My favorite sex position is missionary, because I like the way it feels and how my parts get stimulated by fucking. There are many other ways, so find your own. The best advice I can offer you is to start being willing to put yourself out there. If there is something or someone you want, then you have to try and get it.

Many guys write and tell me that they want to have sex in their pussy or front hole, but are afraid that cis men won't be attracted to them. That seems ridiculous to me. Men are not attracted to the asshole, they are attracted to a person. So, if you want to meet a man, you need to start pursuing men and being honest about how you want to fuck. Remember, regardless of whatever you think you should want sexually, you are the one that ultimately chooses what kind of sex to have. Never let other people tell you how you can have sex or what you should like. That is really dangerous.

At the same time, I also recommend that you stay open to new experiences. You may not know that you like something until you try it. Sex should be fun, so feel free to experiment. Try different ways of masturbating and see what feels good. If you know how to get yourself off, then you can show someone how to do it too. It's a win-win.

You can be slutty if you like, but own it, and don't criticize yourself. Sexual confidence is sexy, it's what really allows you to enjoy what you're doing, regardless of what that is. I developed my confidence by putting myself out there. I had to experience things firsthand to be able to be confident. Just like in the story I shared about having sex with the young pup at the leather bar. I opened up and was honest about my vagina and it was more than fine! It worked for me, it will likely work for you! Even if the first, second and third times feel uncomfortable, trust me, you will learn and you will become more comfortable.

The best thing to do is to focus your attention on how you are feeling, instead of what others are thinking or saying about you. In the end, I've learned that I can't stop people from talking shit. But, I'm able to care less about their judgments and to live my life authentically and safely. I choose to focus my attention on the positives. Remember, any judgments people place on you, are really more about their own insecurities, than anything about you.

Also, it is important to know that the type of sex you have—top, bottom, in your pussy, or ass, or any way really—does not define your sexuality. A gay cis man can have sex with a trans man in his pussy and not be any less gay. Anatomy and sex position do not define sexual orientation—that is solely left up to the individual to decide.

TRANPA'S FINAL THOUGHTS

I have built a satisfying life that allows me to live in my truest form. I did this by liberating myself from the judgments of others. Don't let others tell you how to speak about your life, body, sex, anatomy, or anything personal about you. You are in control of your decisions—write your own narrative, and use the words that feel accurate.

A big part of transitioning for me was learning to feel present in my body as a man, sexually. When I was finally able to announce to the world, "I am a man with a pussy, big deal," it felt like people were able to move on from focusing on my parts. There are so many cis men out there creaming in their pants for us. This is our opportunity to educate, take out the mystery, and start having frank discussions. The more that we shy away from questions people are curious about, the longer they will have these questions.

When you feel intimidated by a situation, don't run from it, confront it. You are the only one that can manifest a totally awesome sex life for yourself. If you feel like you are missing out, then you need to start taking chances and going for it. The only person who can make your desires come true is you. Happy hunting, be safe, and do something dirty! You've got Tranpa's permission.

Interview-turned-essay, conducted by
and in collaboration with Pete Bailey.

Top/Versatile Trans Homo in Search of (Gasp) Intimacy

3

Avi Ben-Zeev

P re transition, during what I now fondly refer to as my "passing drag queen phase," my sexual and romantic relationships had been with hetero cis men. I used to zoom out during sex, and enjoy the scene as if I were watching amateur smut on a large, crisp but far away screen. Once I started transitioning, and coming home to myself as a gay man, I couldn't wait to become more of an actor than a spectator in my own porn; to be present, in my body. Witnessing my physical appearance change to align with how I felt on the inside, my dick growing and throbbing from testosterone, fueled vivid fantasies of fucking, and sometimes being fucked by, bearded hairy men with thick bellies, large pecs, and broad shoulders.

I was constantly horny and hard but the prospect of acting out my desires in real life, with flesh-and-blood gay cis men, felt daunting. I worried that once I took my clothes off, they wouldn't see me as a "real" man. Worse, I was terrified to experience what I thought would be an inevitable "Crying Game moment." If you're unfamiliar with this reference, it's to a movie that you can check out on IMDB. Be warned (spoiler alert), it contains a dreadful moment when the protagonist—a hetero cis dude who falls in love with a gorgeous trans woman—throws up after seeing her naked.

> *"Jon, I have a confession to make." I'm trying to be articulate but I can feel a sinus headache coming on. Perhaps it's from the dankness of Jon's office, situated in an in law unit of an old Victorian, smelling of mold and the comforts of a bygone home.*

"Tell me," Jon says, with an encouraging nod. He doesn't look like your typical therapist, with his multiple facial piercings, faux hawk, tattooed arms, and black leather motorcycle boots.

"The homework you gave me, I still haven't done it."

"Ah," he says, therapist like. "Why not?'

"What happens if I take my clothes off, and this guy gets repulsed by my body?"

Jon looks at me with great empathy, "Avi, I hope someone will barf at the sight of your naked body one day and sooner than later!"

"What kind of therapy is this?" I exclaim, my eyes big like a bug's.

"Well, chances are that it won't happen, and even if it did, I trust that it will only make you more resilient."

Disbelief and betrayal must be written all over my face, because Jon adds, in an extra soothing voice, "Now, now, someone's disgust won't kill you."

I agreed that vomit did not equal cyanide, but I worried that experiencing this kind of explicit visceral rejection would damage my psyche (maybe even kill my soul, a little). I trusted Jon, so despite the voice in my head that screamed, "I'm not ready yet," I took the plunge and went on sexual and romantic adventures with cis gay men. I'm happy to report that a literal Crying Game moment never happened. My experiences have ranged the gamut, from a few hard-to-stomach encounters that made me question, at first, whether a cis gay man would ever see me as the man I knew myself to be, to mind blowing, affirming and meaningful. Over time, I got what Jon was trying to teach me: A guy's reaction to me being trans was about him and had very little to do with who I am or what being a man means.

Well over a decade since I started my foray into gay male world, I'm still very sexual, but I don't hook up as much. Right now, sex + connection = hot! I'm emotionally available, and ready for intimacy and exploring a committed romantic relationship. Instead of waiting for my bearish prince charming to knock on the door (I wish!), I've crafted an OkCupid profile (filter set to gay identified men only, so unless you are one, the scoop's right here):

> I'm a social scientist with an artist's soul who loves my work and enjoys spending time with my friends/chosen family, among many other interests and activities, like yoga, meditation, reading and traveling. I love being sexual— am top/vers and a Dom if it comes to BDSM play—and looking for more than just a casual connection or a friend with benefits.
>
> I'm attracted to men who enjoy exchanging ideas and sharing thoughts and feelings, without taking themselves too seriously. The guy I desire is passionate about _____ (insert topics of choice here), an honest, direct, yet gentle communicator, and a person with a big…heart. I welcome "emotional baggage," as long as you're introspective and tend to be amused by and curious about your neuroses. I'm Jewish—so I understand.
>
> I was born and raised in the Middle East to a construction worker family. Contrary to the odds, I grew up to be pro-Palestinian, army defector and gender outlaw (thank you, Kate Bornstein, for this term). Growing up, I learned to be tough. After living in San Francisco for over 15 years, and practicing mindfulness meditation, I have come to understand vulnerability as scarier, stronger and sexier. While I'm not flying around with angelic wings in a full Lotus position quite yet, mindfulness has been a helpful tool for contending with the "what ifs," "shoulds," inevitable life changes and loss, and for cultivating joy and presence. I've never felt more alive, happy and at home.
>
> I'm a gay man who is transgender (FTM). I've come home to myself (in more ways than just gender-wise) and am grateful for this rich and rewarding journey. It's ok if you're somewhat nervous about having little to no sexual experiences with trans men, as long as you're open to exploring what that might be like if the chemistry is there. Sexually, I like to take control, so happy to show you the ropes, metaphorically and literally.

So far, OKC has delivered on some wonderful friendships but not so much in the way of a romantic match. I've met some quality guys on there who were interested in pursuing sex and dating, but had a common denominator that scared me off: a U-Haul-ish desire of wanting an "insta hubby." Most of these guys liked hiking, dogs, discussing their emotions, vanilla-ish sex with a sensual aromatherapy massage-like sensibility (the thought alone makes my body hair stand on end), monogamy, and held a deep disdain for gay male scenes, clubs and bars.

Don't get me wrong, I'm seeking some of these granola qualities in a potential partner (especially the love-having-dogs part), but need him to have some kind of an edge. After all, as my OKC profile hints, I'm a kinky guy. In lieu of starting a gay male dating site for kinky prudes (you in?), I've expanded my search for a romantic partner to include hook up apps. I see you rolling your eyes at me. I choose to be optimistic. Woof. On Recon, an online site for gay men into BDSM, I get more explicit about my sexuality and desires (if you're single and curious, my handle is SMtop4intimacy, and, FYI, I like guys who are a bit awkward, so if you're a smooth operator, "swipe left").

> Sadistic Dom looking to play with masochistic subs with strong personalities. My biggest turn on comes from playing with a man who wants to please me—Someone who is eager to be a good boy and to explore his limits while building trust.
>
> I give instructions well and enjoy when you inevitably "fuck up," despite your best efforts not to, so I can discipline you verbally and physically until you earn the privilege of being called a good boy.
>
> I like the men I play with to have well-rounded lives. I'm open to some casual encounters, but am mostly excited about getting to know someone well and developing a hot dynamic over time and actual intimacy. How kinky is that?

There you have it! This trans homo wants a house with a white picket fence and a dungeon in the basement.

"So?" You might ask. "What's the response been like, and more importantly, the action?" Guys' messages fall broadly into three categories: good, bad, and straight up ugly. I'll start G-rated, but not to worry, I'll progress to R and even X.

THE GOOD

One chilly summer's day in San Francisco, I opened my Recon app, and found a message from Like2DOMboyz that put a sweet sadistic smile on my face. Late 40s, handsome in a clean-cut way, just add facial hair and tattoos and he'd be my ideal physical type.

> The thing I'm currently seeking the most in a partner is the connection that you described in your profile. I haven't yet gone deep into pain play as a sub, so I don't know how well I would do. I recently had a couple of men dominate me and opened up my hole and I've enjoyed bottoming for them. I like to sub so I can learn more about how things feel from that end, so when I'm a Dom I know better what I'm doing to the boys I'm with. I've been dominant with a few FTM guys, but I have yet to sub for one. I'd like to meet you if you think you'd be interested in meeting me.

It was clear that Like2DOMboyz actually read what I had to say. He also addressed the trans angle in a factual and straightforward way. On top of that, I confess to enjoy flipping top-leaning guys. Check, check and check. All in all, my gut told me that he was openminded, not a trans fetishist (I can't even), and that at the very least we'd have a good conversation over drinks.

We met up at Hole in the Wall, a gay bar in South of Market, with a Blade Runner theme. I'm not a big drinker but I love grabbing a beer from time to time at an off-the-beaten-path gay bar, surrounded by scruffy sexually charged men as a backdrop to conversation and making out. Like2DOMboyz turned out to be a touch nerdier and shier than his profile suggested, a total turn on. We ended up having a fantastic rapport, and play was intense, connected, and left us both wanting more. It's not that section where I go into sexual details yet. Sorry. That will come later, if you're very, very good.

THE BAD

Read it here! Fresh of the press, this time from GROWLr, the gay bear app, and courtesy of HairyOtter75 who described himself as sweet and as having a big heart (and after a few getting-to-know you back-and-forth messaging, including unlocking private media):

"Your profile says you're transgender. Is that true?"

Some of you get why this question doesn't feel good, so feel free to skip my explanation. First, why would I be lying about being trans? Second, regardless of HairyOtter75's intention, his question made me feel "othered" (there's an implication one can tack onto the end of his question: "but you seem so normal"). It's not devastating to get these messages, just disheartening sometimes, especially after building a rapport with someone, however brief, that seemed to have humanized us both.

This next specimen came from ManlyPoet69 on OKC. I'll let you form your own opinion, before I interject my reaction.

> I am looking to date gay cisgender men. It is just where I am in my life. I fully appreciate and respect your personal journey, yet I also wanted to get that out in the open. If you would like to meet for drinks on a platonic level, I am all for that as I think you have a great profile.

I respected ManlyPoet69's honesty. At the same time, it didn't feel good. I couldn't imagine responding to his invite with, "Why, yes, that'd be lovely!" I'm still not quite sure why I felt that way. I get that some men only want to date non-trans guys. So what was it about ManlyPoet69's message that made me file it under "bad?" Maybe the blatant rejection of I don't date "people like you" said to my face? Was I being too sensitive?

The final part of this section has nothing to do with how cis guys write to someone trans and is more about generic come-ons.

> Hey

> How are you?

> How's it going?

Sometimes a simple one-phrase message is the perfect way to indicate interest and start a conversation rolling. After all, it's not worth investing in writing someone who might not write you back. Believe me, I've been there. Still, if a guy was bold and said something about why he was writing me, that'd be refreshing and sexy. "Would love to meet up to check out our chemistry, and, btw, have not been with a trans guy before," works. Even better would be, "Hey, I'm single, love to sub selectively to a Dom I click with, and care about social justice/politics/art/_____. Would love to meet up for...a date!" Told you, I'm a bit old fashioned underneath the tough exterior. I'll spank your ass (only if you begged nicely for it) and then hold hands at the movies.

THE UGLY

LoveBIGdick&balls' message on Recon doesn't qualify as a devastating experience. Still, I consider his to be one of my favorites in the uglies genre:

> Don't understand the F 2 M thing and then being a gay male. I find that confusing. I'm not judging you just verbalizing. So my big thing is balls and I am to assume you don't have those or a functioning penis. I'd be interested if you did. Seems like a cheat to go from FTM and not get functioning male parts. Unless you have a never had a pair of balls a huge part of the male experience is missing. I'm sure it would be interesting to talk with you.

My idealized self didn't care about LoveBIGdick&balls's message—"off with his transphobic head"—it exclaimed, emulating the Queen of Hearts in Alice in Wonderland. My real self hurt. I felt queasy by the implication that a trans man who identifies as gay is a cheat and can't experience what it's like to be a man unless he has cis balls and a "functional" penis. After I sat with this need-a-psychic-shower feeling for a moment, what Jon had taught me in therapy kicked in, and I snapped right back out of it. This guy's message wasn't about me, or about any of us trans guys trying to find a place in gay male community. "We're here, we're queer, deal with it!"

Take heart, my trans brothers who are new to gay male world. The good far exceeds the ugly. In fact, I'll show you an example of good by actually talking sex. Ready? Here goes. (Finally!)

His handle was AuthenticWerewolf, so I'll call him Wolfie. Our exchange on GROWLr was short and sweet. We decided to meet up for drinks at Lone Star Saloon (aka Bear Bar USA). Yeah, that same place that Matt Rice used to bartender at back in the day.

Wolfie arrived on time, which was already sexy. Early 50s, buzz cut, vintage 70s Aviator glasses, long beard Bandholz style, firm round belly, thick curly chest hair sticking out of small gaps in a plaid shirt that was on a tad too tight. His "Avi?" had a gay lilt to it that made me instantly hard. Wolfie's masc fem combo was mail order rent boy hot, at least for my taste.

We started off having this warm if slightly awkward conversation. I asked way more questions than he did—"Oh, so you're from the South, what was it like growing up there?" "Columbia School of Journalism? Cool! What kind of journalism?"—Wolfie's responses were short, witty, with intermittent bursts of booming laughter that made some people turn their heads with raised eyebrows. When I tried to meet and hold Wolfie's gaze, he'd stare sideways or down at the ground, which only intensified my stare. At times it felt like an interrogation scene, with hard-ons.

Wolfie asked "What?" a lot, and at some point, with reddish cheeks, confessed that the year before while performing in a (bearded) drag show, he fell off his high heels, banged his head hard on the concrete floor, and lost most of his hearing in one ear.

The music at Lone Star was loud, so we gave up on conversation. I put my hand on the back of his thick neck and squeezed. His body slouched to my touch, chin tucking towards his chest. "What a sweet sexy boy," I whispered to his good ear, "I can't wait to fuck you." He smelled woodsy, like freshly chopped Oak, with a hint of poppers. I slid my hand down his strong back and rested it on the small of his back. Taking in a deep sip of breath, I reached for his large muscular thigh. His dick was protruding from his pants, a wet spot forming from his precum.

"My pussy is so wet, Dad," Wolfie said, his head still hanging low to his chest. His use of 'Dad,' versus the more typical 'Daddy,' felt wrong and exciting.

"That makes me hard, but I need to get going, so you'll have to ache for my cock." I leaned over, brushing my hand against his bulge, and kissed him sweetly on the lips.

"Look at me," I said.

Wolfie raised his eyes. I felt surprised by how much younger he looked underneath his long unruly beard, which at that moment seemed like a mask. Did it hide a weak chin?

Holding eye contact, I placed my hand on his bulge, and squeezed, feeling it swell in my hand.

"We're gonna have fun," I said.

Wolfie nodded, "No doubt, Sir."

Fast forward, and a week later, Wolfie materialized at my place. Play was fairly scripted at first—"Look down at all times and don't speak until spoken to," "Undress, put your clothes, folded neatly, on the stool to the left of the door," "Face the concrete wall, then lean into it, ass sticking out." "I'm going to use you for my pleasure." "Say, thank you, Sir!" This prelude was followed by bondage and impact play (and if you're into the hankie code, add the colors dark pink, yellow and purple into the mix). Just what the pervy doctor ordered? Absolutely, and at the same time nothing out of the kink unordinary, at least in my twisted BDSM book, which is quite a bit more intense than 50 Shades of Gray. What came after play, took me by surprise.

We cuddle on the sofa, the black leather cooling our overheated bodies, still revving after over two hours of play.

"Did you cum?" Wolfie asks.

"No, but that's totally fine. I'll jack off after you leave."

"May I blow your cock and make you cum, Dad?"

I stare at his chest, my cock getting hard from the sight of his juicy nipples sticking out from the mussy fur. I feel this intense urge to flick my tongue, suck on, and bite down on their tender flesh, till they get even more erect and raw. Spanking, caning, pissing—sure, no problem, but this need to molest Wolfie's man boobs feels strangely verboten. Fuck it, he's too sexy.

"Play with your nipples, for Daddy."

Wolfie obeys, pinching and twisting his nipples, tugging on them with so much force, his hairy tits start wobbling. "Is this what you want, Dad?"

My cock throbs so hard I could cum without touching it. "Harder," I command, "I want it to hurt."

"Yes, Dad," he says, his breath getting louder, faster. "Ouch, this hurts so bad, Dad! Can I please stop?"

"Not until I tell you to." I slide my hand down to my groin, grabbing my cock at the base. I start stroking it, moving the foreskin up and down the shaft. My dick's so engorged I'm about to explode.

"Listen very carefully," I say slowly, with an emphasis on each word. "If you're very, very good, you'll get to suck my dick. Stop what you're doing, lay down on your back with your arms by your sides, close your eyes, and don't move."

Wolfie submits, following my instructions to a T. I lay myself on top of his perfectly still frame, the heaviness of my body pressing against his rough and warm flesh, feeling his heart beating fast against mine.

I slide my body down till my head is level with his chest. I rub my head against it, pausing to burrow my nose in his salty, sticky fur, inhaling his man smell. I reach for his tits, squeezing them together with both hands, giving him a hint of a hairy cleavage. His nipples are raised and red from all the tugging. Possessed, I start sucking on them, moving from one nipple to the other, till I settle on the one that makes him moan the loudest. I reach for a clothespin to clamp the nipple's raw sensitive flesh between its prongs. Biting down on the clothespin with my teeth, flicking my tongue on the swollen tender flesh caught in the clothespin's grip, my cock grows in my mind's eye till it's thick and 10-inch long.

"My pussy is so wet, Dad. Fuck my pussy! Please, Dad."

"I thought you wanted to make me cum," I scold him, with my best impression of a disappointed parent (I was raised by a Jewish mom after all), "How the fuck did this become about you?"

"No, I…" *Wolfie opens his eyes wide. Relieved to see me smile, he smiles back. We both break character and burst out laughing. Perhaps it's the effect of the endorphins, or of waking up from a shared dream, relishing in an innocent, child-like trust that we will keep each other safe from harm no matter how carnal and perverted we get.*

"Dad? Can I confide in you?"

"Sure, my sweet, sexy boy, what's up?"

"I want you…I want you, to call me 'girl.'"

I draw a deep breath and take a good hard look at this grizzly, beast of a man, with his long beard and big throbbing cock. Shazam! As though a sorcerer with a quick unflinching flick of the hand cast a gender-bending spell with a sparkly wand, I see her materialize, my quivering girl, a tantalizing bearded lady.

"Hi my sweet girl," *I say softly, looking into Wolfie's eyes, turned from amber into smoky coal.*

"Hi, Dad," *she giggles.*

"I'm gonna teach you something really important today.

"Please, Dad."

"Remember, in Snow White, how the prince kissed the princess awake?"

"Yes."

"Well, before he did that, he kissed her somewhere else. I'll show you, but you have to lie there very quietly for Dad, like you're a sleeping princess.

"K', Dad, I'll be very, very quiet."

I start licking Wolfie's clit, from the base all along the shaft.

"Does this feel good?" *I whisper.*

"So, so good, thank you Dad," *Wolfie whispers back.*

"This is going to feel even better."

I straddle my girl and slide her engorged clit into my front hole. Claiming

Wolfie's dick as my own, I ride her, thrusting slowly, then gaining speed, swept into what feels like the centrifugal force of a Graviton. The desire to fly, to defy gravity, is so exquisite it borders on agony. There's no getting off until the ride is done on its own terms, obeying the laws of physics.

"I'm about to…"

"Cum for Dad," I say.

Thrusting my thighs faster, harder, my front hole starts spasming. Wolfie screams out as she shoots a heavy load, filling my insides with warm wetness. I rub the thick dripping liquid on my cock, and after just a few strokes, I cum so hard I'm gasping for air.

Wolfie lets out a deep sigh, her face flushed, "Wow, Dad."

"The spell worked! My princess woke up!" I say with a big smile, wiping the sweat dripping from my forehead.

We laugh and, poof, we've reached THE END of a deliciously warped fairy tale. Wolfie's back to being a man, whatever being a man means.

Wolfie and I played a few more times (for one of our scenes, he surprised me with a set of pastel colored women's underwear he bought at Target that looked wholesomely sexy, who knew?). We even started dating for a little while, until we realized that we were more compatible as friends. He left me with a weakness for bearded drag queens, but I assure you, I'm open to many other types. For the record, feminization and (oye vey) sleeping princess play aren't my usual preferences. These scenes hit the proverbial spot because Wolfie and I vibed off each other and allowed ourselves to go to deliciously wicked and healing places that neither of us could have foreseen.

In exploring my sexuality and desire, both kink and (yes!) vanilla, I've become more and more versatile. For topping, I have a collection of shapes and sizes to choose from. My favorite is a thick 8-inch silicon dick with ridges down the shaft. It presses just right against my cock as I thrust inside a guy's ass or front hole, feeling energetically and physically connected to him and to my own body. It never gets soft, so if I'm fucking you, I'll go as long as you can stand the intensity and pleasure. Stamina is sexy. Regardless of the exact physical acts, I'm finding that letting go into a naturally unfolding chemistry, versus coming from a pre-determined script, connects me to my dick and, more importantly, my heart.

Sex aside, I'm emotionally available and wanting to find my one-and-only (primary/open/monogamous+ or even, ahem, monogamous) lover. My life is full. I'm lucky to have a job that's rewarding, where I get to see my students grow, learn from them, and do research on how the mind works with implications for social justice. I love, love my dear friends and chosen family, the beauty and openness of the Bay Area, and my sweet dog. Life would be even better with that special bear/otter/wolf. So this next part's for you, my elusive future lover.

> I'm mixing the ingredients in my cauldron for a love spell, knowing that whatever shape you'll take, it'll be more than their sum. You're…uniquely you, much better and more flawed than any script I could conjure; a script, by the way, I hope you shred to pieces.

> Waking up in the morning, I reach for you (or my iPhone). Sometimes you're there sleeping soundly and sometimes you're at your abode, where you live alone or with your pet _____ (dog, cat, parrot, iguana, rock). You need your alone time.

> You're a bearded, hairy and tattooed gay man. When you were born, the doctors shouted, "Congrats, it's a _____ (boy, girl, baby). Growing up, you knew you were attracted to men. You may have tried having sex and even a relationship with a woman (or two), but eventually realized that yes, you're a feminist, have respect for women, appreciate their aesthetics, but are not sexually attracted to them. You think dating is contrived but you enjoy the process of getting to know a man who has piqued your interest and to be seen by him too.

> We're equals. I look up to you. I love that you see meaning in what you do. We laugh a lot. We're not afraid of honesty. Being real, warts and all, is an aphrodisiac we both crave and get off on.

> Write me (transhomo13@gmail.com).

Snapshots

Pete Bailey

I have no real memory of my life before the age of eight, due to complications from chicken pox. But that is not what this story is about. Without memories to reflect upon, I rely on the stories told about me and the person I see captured in family photo albums.

The preemie photos are terrifying; I came out looking more like an alien than a human boy or girl. I was missing the nonessentials: eyebrows, fingernails, tear ducts and eyelashes. My skin shone bright red, a result of being brought into the world too early.

As the pictures progress you see a young white girl with eyelashes and nails grown in, dressed in a pretty pastel or white dress. She is wearing white gloves up to her wrists or elbows, tights, dress shoes, and dons a bonnet atop her head. But she frowns, her bottom lip protruding. Standing slumped back, her belly poking out, she looks thoroughly uncomfortable in all these photos.

Flip forward a few more pages in the album, and you see the first Halloween where I broke gender norms. I'm maybe eight, a proud Charlie Chaplin, dressed in a black and white suit, sporting a black cropped wig, a narrow mustache, and carrying a cane. I looked happy.

These images of my gender play pop up repeatedly as the album moves forward in time. There's a gender neutral/boyish clown and then the Mad Hatter. Wearing these costumes provided a space where I could comfortably live.

As we move forward there are images and sweet love notes from my first girlfriend. We met when we were both thirteen at summer theater school. She walked up to me and a friend as we sat on a cold linoleum floor holding hands and rehearsing lines for a scene later that day.

She stood before us, sizing us up and said, "Why are you two holding hands? You're clearly a gay boy and you're a lesbian."

No other thirteen-year-old I knew had ever spoken this way. She was different from my peers, probably due to growing up in California. She chain-smoked cigarettes, even at home with her parents. She wore cut-off jeans trimmed extra short, her pockets showing below the fringe.

Memories of that summer are sweet. We had sleepovers where we lay in each other's arms, shared fleeting kisses, and had funny conversations about who we thought the other queer kids were at theater school. Then, the summer ended and she returned home to Los Angeles.

My next vivid images are from high school. School was rough in the mid-nineties. The pictures are of a very awkward, pudgy, sloppily dressed sort of hippie, with a greasy face and general look of unhappiness.

The school hallways were echo chambers for mean call outs from the jocks and preppies. I was being mooed at in the hallways, called a "carpet muncher," and told that I "lick a lot a puss." This was a common experience in my city's schools if you were perceived to be gay, lesbian or remotely different.

My sister, several other high schoolers and I started a Gay Straight Alliance (GSA) chapter in 1995 to bring visibility and support to our friends and ourselves. At the time my sister identified and was out as a lesbian. In contrast, I was always careful not to label myself because when I looked at dykes and lesbians I did not see myself reflected.

After word got out about the existence of our club it became the focus of public debate. First it was discussed in the schools, then the school board, and finally went to the state legislature. This created a whirlwind of media attention. We were contacted by Oprah, the BBC, the Today Show and Rolling Stone magazine. Most of the attention was focused on my sister Kelli, as she was the official founder and spokesperson of our club. But as her younger, participating sibling, they focused on me too. Stories would appear in the paper, "Kelli Peterson, lesbian, and younger sister, Holly, to speak at school board hearing tonight," and alluded to the ambiguity of my sexuality.

After one of these stories was printed in the local paper the next day a correction appeared. In the bottom, right hand corner of the Local section, it read, "In the article published yesterday quoting Holly Peterson about the GSAs, she was misrepresented as a lesbian, and is in fact a heterosexual."

I had no idea how to reconcile the idea that both identities, lesbian and heterosexual, rang untrue.

My father was an editor for the Salt Lake Tribune, the nonreligious alternative to the Deseret News, owned by the Mormons. He ran the correction without consulting me first.

My friends enthusiastically joked, "It must be true—it's in the paper!" They teased, "What are you going to tell the girlfriend?"

"I guess she'll just have to know our truth," I said, feeling a knot form in my throat.

I went to local support group meetings at the Utah Stonewall Center, a local non-profit founded to provide resources for the gay, lesbian and bi community. The concrete building was small and dimly lit, with a modest library and several open spaces for meetings. The organization clearly had little funds and was primarily operated by volunteers.

The front desk worker was a tall, thin woman, with light brown hair, that flowed down past her broad shoulders. She wore a conservative navy skirt, with a breezy white blouse. Her voice was a little low, but she spoke in slow, breathy tones that had a singsong type quality.

She greeted me, "Hello. Here for the group? It's in the small room in back."

"Yep," I smiled and walked past.

"Let me know if you need anything else," she said kindly.

"Will do. Thanks!"

I entered the group room, and poured myself some soda. There were a few men sitting alone, waiting for the group to start, and a couple stood away talking to each other.

I overheard the bearded, husky bear say, "Did you see that man in a dress?"

"How could I miss him?!" A sassy twink replied.

"I know, those he/she's, they're not a part of our community. I think it's perverted for a man to be parading around in a dress."

The subject of their mockery was the first transgender person I had ever met.

When I turned eighteen I moved in with Matt. He was a timid boy with long, strawberry blond, sun-damaged hair, and skin covered in freckles. He was a virgin who'd had a fleeting relationship in high school but really had no sexual experience to speak of.

On a severely cold night in Utah the two of us attended my coffee shop's holiday work party. We had a great night drinking beers and hanging out with my friends. The night ended, with the two of us, stupidly deciding to drive back home. Together we navigated two flights of stairs, staggering toward our apartment. We both found comfort on the couch, draping our bodies across the cushions and one another.

"What a fun night," he said, as he lay his arm on my stomach.

"Amazing!" The only words I could muster.

We sat quietly, comfortably nestled together. Slowly, Matt leaned in toward me, pressing his lips gently into mine. I kissed him back, somewhat unsure of what this could be. I had not kissed a boy since seventh grade. He moved his hand toward my boobs. Suddenly the sweetness of the moment left. I launched myself off the couch, standing up quickly.

"I can't."

I walked away, leaving him there perplexed, retreating to my room for the night.

The next day I went on the lam with a best friend to process what had happened. We stayed in a cheap motel. The view from our window was a giant billboard that read, "You cannot hold hands with God when you are masturbating." Taking perspective from the confusing moment with Matt, it became clear there should be no more kissing between roommates, and that was that.

Shortly after, I moved to Eugene, Oregon, a small town filled with hippies, dykes and anarchists. A utopian city for white America, filled with one-way streets lined by Red Alder trees, where the speed limit rarely exceeded 25 mph, and the dwellers complied.

This small Northwestern town felt safe to me as a young white hippie. The rents were affordable and it would allow me to successfully transition from a life of partying in the comforts of my hometown to the life of being a student in a town far from home. As I entered this new world it was with a fresh slate, anonymous and without a history. No one knew about the GSA, my family or my dating history. I could rewrite my story and no one would know to question me. I introduced myself as Pete to every person I met.

A year after moving there I had thinned down some. I had hair that landed just above my shoulders. Every day I wore a bandana and dressed in a crunchy granola type of style. I met a handsome, successful young man— the type my parents would want me to marry. He came from an affluent family. He was cute, with brown hair neatly trimmed, generally wearing nice pants and a button-up. Together we looked like an odd couple, but we enjoyed talking politics and got along well.

One evening, I went over to his house for dinner. I remember the rooms were cold because the pilot light of the heater was broken. We sat in the kitchen on barstools in front of the oven eating tomato soup and left the door cracked to provide us some warmth. We discussed whether Al Gore or George W. Bush would win the upcoming presidential election.

He changed the conversation from politics, "You know you're cute and smart, right?"

"Thank you," I said, feeling squeamish. I wasn't used to men saying these kind of things to me.

"Can I kiss you?"

"No," I said in a firm tone.

"Why not?" He said. It seemed like he had not heard this before in his privileged life.

"It's complicated, I've done all this gay activism, and people think I'm a dyke. If I kiss or date a man I lose everything." These words made me realize how trapped I felt, but simultaneously the fear of losing the gay community terrified me. It would be like giving up oxygen. The gay community had always been a place where I could be me. Even though I still didn't see my image reflected within the gay world, I had always found people who accepted me for me.

"I get it."

We finished our soup and our friendship faded away, but I was left with a sense of curiosity, wondering what it would have felt like to kiss him.

Not much later I met Del. She was a "straight" girl who would slowly transition into her own form of butch. She was strong, athletic, sarcastic and kind.

We fell into the stereotypical lesbian U-Haul love story. We were a complimentary pair who could pass hours going on adventures and finding fun wherever we were. Near the end of our relationship I was trying to uncover who I was and had started to share this process with Del.

"So, there's a talk at the university tonight. Some trans people are going to be speaking…" I waited for her to say something. "Want to go?"

"Huh, ok," she replied in a neutral tone.

At the lecture, there were three speakers—two trans men and a trans woman. They talked about their lives, how they dated, where they got hormones, how they came out as trans and what life was like for them since transitioning. I caught the first glimpse of what my life could look like.

Their stories reassured me that I wasn't a total oddball. For so long I'd been confused about who I wanted to love and have sex with. I did not find these answers in what they shared, but inside I knew that I had taken a step toward finding myself.

On the drive home that night, when we stopped at a light, I took a deep breath in and said, "I think I might be…trans." I reached out and grabbed her hand, giving a gentle squeeze. It was my way of saying, "Thank you for going with me," silently.

"I know," she said as she squeezed my hand back.

In 2003, I moved to Oakland, the biggest, most diverse, city that I had ever lived in. I was exposed to new and diverse types of people, cultures, subcultures and countercultures. I witnessed people from all walks of life living together, negotiating space and community. The best thing about living in Oakland was joining a thriving community of queers. For the first time in my life I saw trans people, living happy, ordinary, city lives, with friends, lovers and community. I felt an increased freedom to be myself.

I started to open to the notion of finding a person, not a gender, while cruising for a date. At first, though, I exclusively dated and had sex with women. They were mostly femmes, which made me uncomfortable because it often felt like I was engaged in a heteronormative type of gender play.

As my transition progressed and I appeared more masculine, I transitioned to dating masculine women—butches and sporty dykes. Still, I never found the connection I wanted; the dating energy with women, regardless of their presentation, felt wrong.

I stayed open to possibilities and met a kinky trans man I'll call Mykel at a party hosted by a mutual friend. He was shorter than me, stocky with thick, strong, muscly thighs. He had a cute face, deep brown eyes and a wide smile. He lived in an apartment building around the corner from my house.

I picked him up for our first date, feeling nervous as he got in the car. This was my first date with a man. Before, I was worried about losing my gay card, if I were to date, kiss or fuck a man. Now, with transitioning, it was no longer a threat. I was viewed as the man I saw myself to be, which meant that an affair between two men would allow me to retain my place in queer community.

"Hi, thanks for driving," he looked at me with a bright smile.

"You're welcome. Nice to see you." I leaned in and kissed him. I felt like I needed to set a clear tone that this was a date and not a friend hang out.

He kissed me back.

"That was unexpected, but nice," he said, with a surprised look on his face. "So, what kinds of things are you into sexually?"

"Oh, well, I like making out, giving and getting oral…I like to fuck people with a cock strapped on." I was a little taken aback by his question.

"Do you do anything dirty or kinky? Or, you're just pretty vanilla?" he asked, looking underwhelmed.

"I made a sex tape once. Is that what you mean?"

"Not really. If we go back to my place tonight, I'll show you."

At the restaurant, we talked more about the usual things in life. After paying the check, we headed straight to his home. In the elevator he gave me a mischievous look, chuckled and said, "I'm curious what you'll think."

His small one bedroom apartment was crowded with furniture and decorations. After walking through a narrow path to his room, we arrived at what looked like a sex shop, with all the merchandise on display. My eyes scanned his personal collection of BDSM gear and toys consisting of whips, paddles, floggers, canes, ropes, crops, quick ties, nipple clamps, collars, anal beads, candles, latex gloves, leather gloves, blindfolds, gags, butt plugs, cocks, spreader bars, chains, handcuffs, safety pins, pinwheels, vibrators and clothes pins. At the time, I did not know the names for many of the things I was viewing. I was shocked.

"So, what do you think?" he said in a devious tone.

"Wow, I don't know what to say." I felt so naïve and in over my head. "I've never seen things like this before. I have questions."

"Do you know what a bottom is? I'm looking for a good boy that will gladly take my beatings. Do you want to be that boy?"

"Yes." My response surprised me. This room looked like a possibility, like it might bring me closer to who I was. I now understand that saying yes, came from wanting to do right by, and find, myself.

I finally let myself follow my desire to start dating and having sex with men. The similarities of Mykel's and my body assured me that I would be seen and respected. He showed me how to push my limits, open up to experiences, and how to appropriately say yes and…no.

To keep meeting gay men I turned to technology, using websites and apps to message guys who might be interested in me. I had become accustomed to passing as male in my daily life, which gave me hope that I could enter gay male spaces and be seen and treated as an equal.

Initially, I sent weird messages to desirable profiles because I didn't know yet how men flirted or how to pick up a guy online. As time went on I started to learn their language and how to approach someone. I found lots of men willing to go out with me. Some were friendly guys and some were outright asses. Either way, I rarely saw them more than once, often feeling like our connections were as superficial as the messages we had sent.

When all hope felt lost, a dashing gentleman showed up in my Scruff account.

"Hi. I like your profile. Want to get a coffee sometime?"

His photo was a black and white image, featuring a man with longish hair that swept away from his face. His profile sounded genuine. He talked about having wonderful friends, a great job, and that he was very close to his family. He expressed in no uncertain terms that he was looking for more than a one-night stand. This profile sounded like boyfriend material and I was ready.

We met for a cocktail. I was uncertain what to expect but felt hopeful. He arrived a few minutes late, looking a little flustered, sharply dressed, wearing designer jeans, a crisp button-up and a well-tailored suit jacket. He was clean-shaven with perfectly styled hair and smelled of aftershave.

I approached him, "Hey, are you Max? I have seats up front."

"Yes, can I get you a drink?" He gave my forearm a quick squeeze and walked hurriedly toward the bar.

I returned to our seats and waited, wondering what made him feel so uneasy. Was it because I was trans? Was he instantly repelled by my appearance, and was already looking for a way to leave?

"Here you go. Sorry I was late, I was coming from work and traffic was terrible," he said breathlessly and took a big sip from his drink.

"It's ok. It's nice to meet you." I reached my hand out to gently touch his thigh.

"You have amazing eyes. I'm sorry I was late, that's not like me," he said, taking another sip.

We made friendly conversation. I felt a spark. He captivated me as he shared about himself. He hung on my every word as I talked about my hobbies and goals. As the conversation flowed he relaxed and seemed more comfortable with me. Sitting on our barstools, we seized every opportunity to steal a touch or lay our hands on each other.

"You're sexy," he said, leaning in to kiss me, pulling me toward his body.

Electricity surged through me. I was oblivious to the existence of the straight hipsters surrounding us at the bar. "Thanks," I said, our bodies still pressed against each other, "you're sexy too!" Another kiss and then we started talking again.

"When I saw your pic on Scruff I was attracted to you right away! Then I read your ad and saw that you were trans…I thought to myself, "Why not?" Even though I've never done this before, you were handsome and seemed nice."

"I liked your pics too."

He pulled me close, pressing his hips into mine. He kissed me again. I felt him grow hard against my body.

"Want to go back to my place? It's about three blocks from here."

"Let's go."

His apartment was clean, classy and well styled just like him. "Do you need some water?" he asked.

"I'm good."

I kissed him. He pushed me against the counter and kissed me back. We held each other close as we kissed deeply, grinding together and shoving our hands beneath clothing. Quickly, we started unbuttoning and unzipping our pants and shirts.

"Is this ok?" he asked, while walking me to his bedroom.

"Definitely ok."

As we entered we walked past a full-length mirror. I kept walking and he said, "Wait—come back here!"

I back tracked a couple steps and stood next to him. He placed his arm firmly around me, squeezing me tightly.

"We look good together," he said, looking at our reflection. His gaze made me feel seen as a gay man.

We got in bed, our bodies overlapped as we kissed. He turned his mouth, "I've never done this before. Let me know if I do something wrong," he said quietly.

"Don't worry, I know what I'm doing," I said, climbing on top of him. I grabbed his wrists and pushed his arms down into the mattress. I kissed him, forcing my tongue deep into his mouth. Then I lined up our cocks and rubbed them together, still holding him down. I pulled back, released his wrists, and looked at him intensely, "Is this ok?"

"Yes, god yes!" He said, pulling my head down to kiss again.

I slid down his body and started sucking him off. He shoved his cock deep in my mouth, and I happily swallowed it. Things heated up from there! I showed him how I got myself off, and then he happily offered his skills. When both of us reached the edge of euphoria from our oral ecstasies, we escalated things by wildly fucking. We were like high schoolers again, trying out a bunch of positions, stretching open all of our holes, and telling each other, "You're so fucking hot," over and over again.

He stayed around for several months and our relationship showed me that I could be seen as a gay man by a gay man. He was cis, fifteen years older than me, and had exclusively had sex with cis men. From our first to our last date he always made me feel like a sexy ass gay guy.

"So, what are we doing tonight?" Jameson asks, as we finish our traditional dinner of nachos in San Francisco's Castro neighborhood.

"I don't know. What's going on?" I sip my water and wipe the grease from my fingers.

He pulls out his phone and starts flipping through his apps. "Well, it looks like The Sons of Sodom are throwing an underwear party. Want to go?"

"I definitely didn't wear the right underwear tonight," I say.

He looks me in the eye, bats his eyelashes, and flashes an enthusiastic smile, "Umm, we are in the Castro. We can buy some underwear. That's the least of your worries." He gives me a more serious look, "So, do you want to go or not?"

"Ok, let's go buy some underwear."

The streets are full on Friday nights. Gay men, walking arm in arm, searching the streets for dinner or drinks as we go on an underwear expedition. There are three stores within a hundred feet to meet our needs. We scour the racks for the unicorn pair, the one that will be magically right for the situation. I have never quite had to make a decision like this before.

The stores are filled to the brim with briefs, boxer briefs, trunks, boxers, jockstraps, bikinis, long underwear and G-strings. Too many styles to choose from!

"I don't know what to choose. What do you think is best?" I have been trying to imagine what the men in the club will look like and what they will be wearing. I expect to stand out for being trans, and I don't want my underwear to add an additional spotlight.

In the end, I buy three pairs of underwear: one black jockstrap, a pair of blue and white striped boy shorts that had a few cartoony bears printed above my crotch, and a riskier pair of black mesh boy shorts.

We go back to Jameson's house to clean up for the party. I wash myself like one would in a gas station bathroom, using the sink to clean my pits and freshen my private parts. I try on all three pairs of underwear. I cannot imagine going into public in any of them.

"I can't do this. I feel ridiculous," I yell from the bathroom.

"Put on whatever makes you feel sexy and let's go," Jameson yells back from his bedroom as he finishes getting ready.

I slide on the sexy mesh pair, conceal them with my clothes, and we set off for the club. As we drive, I worry about what it will be like to go to the club as a trans person. Will they make me feel unwelcome? Unsafe? What if they don't let me in?

"Are you sure this is a good idea," I ask timidly.

"Like, what do you think is going to happen? What are you worried about?"

"That's the problem, I don't know what to expect."

"Ok, so let's try and go in and check it out." He looks at me compassionately. "If there's a problem, though, what do you want to do? Do you want to leave, or do you want to go all Stonewall Riots on their asses? I'm down for either but just want to know what you're hoping for."

I start laughing and Jameson joins in.

"I'd probably just want to leave," I say, feeling a bit more relaxed.

We pull up to the bar in an industrial part of town on a wide and dimly lit road. Luxury cars and Ubers continually arrive on the scene. We follow the parade of handsome gay men into the club. They walk confidently ahead of us, pay the fee, and begin disrobing in the lobby, as they wait in line for the clothing check.

"Are you doing ok?" Jameson asks, with a soft smile.

"Yeah, but I don't know if I can take my clothes off yet." I scan the lobby of muscly men—all tanned and waxed. I am not one of them. My heart is pounding; I can feel it beat throughout my body and hear it's rhythm in my ears. My legs are shaky and my stomach is churning, I'm unconsciously holding my breath as we walk down a long hallway to the main room.

As Jameson and I wander the bar together, I do a safety analysis and feel more at ease. I see imperfect bodies, more poor underwear choices, and men looking nervous and drinking alone. Yet, I still wish more than anything that I could teleport myself back to the underwear store and change my purchase. But, we are already walking toward the line for the clothing check.

"So we're doing this?"

"Yeah."

I gulp in air and begin to undress. We exchange our clothes for a number written in black sharpie on the inside of our wrists (no pockets). As we head back toward the bar I am internally cheering myself on with every step.

I order a drink and watch how men navigate the room. Some men cluster together drinking and laughing. Others are cruising the room, gently caressing an arm, belly, ass or package. By observation I learn the silent code: If you are interested then just let things keep going, if you aren't then simply brush the arm away or ignore the advance. I can do that!

I stand, trying to put out a receptive vibe while talking to Jameson.

"So, do you feel good enough that I can go wander and see what kind of trouble I can find?"

"Sure," I say, feeling somewhat nervous, but also excited to explore the room and see if I can pick someone up.

Jameson walks out of sight. I see a big stocky man wearing black and white boxer briefs across the room. He is standing alone and I decide to slowly approach. As I walk toward him, I feel hands on my ass and arms. My confidence rises; their touches make me feel welcome.

Standing next to the bearded man, I smile and slide my hand down his chest, then further down to his cock, constantly holding his gaze. He is smiling back, as I continue to rub him over his underwear. I pull it out, "Can I suck it?"

He nods permissively.

"I'm trans."

"I know…your underwear," he looks down.

"Right."

I start sucking him off. Adrenaline surges through my body and I feel alive and fully present. I know others can see us and I like that, but I also like that no one seems to see me as out of place.

He taps my shoulder to get my attention, "Wanna fuck?"

"Sure."

He leads me to a bench, "Bend over!"

I comply.

The sex was fine. But the experience was amazing. I felt like I had moved a mountain, and in a way I had. This had felt terrifying to me up until now! This was where I wanted to be—seen as male partaking in the dark underbelly of the gay male world and learning a new language of consent.

The images of the disdained girl who I don't remember and the unkempt teen I do remember are safely stored in my albums. While these foundational moments shaped me, my life's journey has been more complex than a simple linear path. Some moments set off a flash, capturing a moment, permanently stored in a bounty of memories.

Reflecting on my life thus lived, it seems that it was easier to find myself by figuring out *what I was not*, instead of what I was. For much of my youth I felt this push/pull between being attracted to men and being repelled by the notion of them touching me. This dissonance continued until I could reconcile my body and mind.

I changed my body from a place that was rented, to a place that's a permanent home. By loving and accepting all of my parts, I stopped having to apologize for its imperfections or differences. I've created a warm dwelling to share with those who love me.

In pursuit of love and desire, I had to be brazen, push myself out of my comfort zone and remain open to possibilities. Only in this way could I find my place in gay male community. A place where I can stand proudly in mesh underwear, socks and sneakers and little else, having the time of my life.

Queer and Loathing in Ohio: On Transmasculinity and Sex with Cis Men

Jules Purnell

I grew up queer in Ohio. It's not the most hospitable place to try to find oneself, particularly when that self happens to be transmasculine and androgynous. My father lives only a few exits off of I-71 from where transgender teen Leelah Alcorn took her life, only a state away from where Ky Peterson continues to rot away in jail for defending himself against his rapists. I was on the receiving end of more than anyone's fair share of homophobic bullying in high school, and while I was a good decade away from knowing and naming myself as trans, I was policed enough for failing to appropriately "do girl" that I stuffed whatever inklings I may have had of my own transness deep down, and didn't begin to untangle that particular bundle of Christmas lights until well after graduation.

All of this becomes infinitely more complicated if you're a person of mixed race and therefore possess some sort of tantalizingly indeterminable ethnicity. ("Let me guess, you're Greek! Italian!...Latino?") I came out as a bi, chubby, quasi-goth fourteen year old long before I had fully cemented my gender identity. I was attracted to boys, and by and large these boys were the ones who subverted the seething masculinity the sporty homophobes in my high school pretended at. I liked my boys femme, which often translated to gay. I supposed this made me gay, too, at least in some capacity, and further assumed this meant that I should date girls as a girl.

But dating *anyone* as a girl was complicated. I hated being foisted into the "girl" role, and though I presented quite femme myself, I preferred taking the "dominant" role in my relationships, irrespective of my partners' genders and/or bedroom positions. Still, the gender "A-ha!" was elusive. I knew I felt uncomfortable changing in the girls' locker room. I knew the ballooning curves of my body felt foreign and I became increasingly self-conscious. But hey, don't all girls feel that way? I wore my hair long and my push-up bra high, perhaps in an effort to do away with any concerns anyone had about my fledgling gender confusion, or perhaps in a kind of parody of hegemonic femininity as I understood it. I was something of a drag queen in the way that Dolly Parton or Tammy Faye Bakker are drag queens—so hyperfeminine that the performance has come full circle and become queer. All of this masquerade stemmed from a very real sense that I could not do what was expected of me, and so I rebelled in the ways I knew how. Rather than let myself fully succumb to self-loathing as a result of this glaringly apparent failure, I found solace in the queers and fellow gender rebels I had available to me as friends and lovers in my para-rural hometown. But the only trans people I knew or had even heard of were trans women; I'd never heard of someone like me. These feelings were puzzle pieces I simply couldn't put together.

I eventually reconciled my body's first transition, from lithe tomboy to pin-up proportioned teenage girl, learning to feel at home in the form that attracted the attention of horny boys and men. And, like them, I liked to fuck. My weight and my gender dysphoria never kept me from fucking boys, and my sex drive often far surpassed theirs. I always felt that being physical with men was easier somehow. I didn't know the rules of engagement with girls, and their hesitance to make the first move was disappointing and confusing. Boys flirted. Boys fucked on the first date. I loved being fucked in my front hole; I loved sucking their rock hard dicks and the way they sucked and licked mine. I loved their muscled backs and the way they smelled. Everything about the raw, rough sex turned me on.

At the same time, I didn't totally hate being a girl. Being girl-reared made me considerate of others and put me in touch with the beautiful aspects of my emotional being. I was fortunate enough to be allowed to cry, to be sensitive and sweet. It was okay to care about animals and the environment. I was never told to "man up" as a child: was never told that my affinity for pink, sparkles and princesses was bad or sinful. I was also lucky enough to live in a world of relative societal acceptance of masculine girls, where I could climb trees, catch frogs, and engage in a lot of the activities synonymous with boyhood without being punished. I was seen as a girl, but I palled around with the boys. I inhabited a soft space between genders and stayed there happily until puberty.

As I grew older, however, I recognized that women and men were treated differently. When my body began to mature, I was encouraged to be smaller physically and psychologically, to be increasingly palatable to the male gaze and to be non-threatening to the male ego. I experienced sexual violence, I had an abortion under fucked up circumstances, and I became more and more relegated to a world where being read as female meant I was expected to be subservient to men. These experiences brought me to feminism and to social justice. These things made me aware of the nuances of consent and of the scaffolding of interconnected forms of power and oppression.

This was supplemented by my undergrad education, where I formally studied the works of my queer, sex positive elders who came before. Foucault taught me about systems of control and subjugated sexual histories. Butler spoke to me in complex soliloquies about the subversive powers of drag and questioning the stability of heteronormativity. And then, of course, there were Leslie Feinberg and Aunt Kate. Feinberg and Bornstein were the gender transgressive auncles I could have used as a young queerling. If I had known their existence was possible as that confused fourteen year old, it would have cleared up almost a decade of heartache and frustration.

Their words spoke to me, breathed life to me directly from the bound pages of their books; their works were so honest and unrelenting that the hair on my arms and neck would stand at attention as I read. I compared the tales of their sexual exploits to my own, the intersection of my own sexuality and gender confusion reverberating through their voices. Feinberg's protagonist in hir seminal *Stone Butch Blues* grappled with non-binary identity in a way that felt pulled from the pages of my own story. Ze made a space for bothness, neitherness, and at the "end" of the tale, settled on not settling. Slogging wearily through account after account of rape and violence was immensely triggering, but also connected me to the stories of others who had been through what I had, and I felt less alone in their company. Bornstein's *Gender Outlaw* was more of a diary, an intimate whisper into my ear from someone who had known the desires of my heart long before I did. Bornstein's playfulness and saltiness mixed with her undeniable braininess made me fall for her, and, in turn, I fell for the parts of myself her words saw in me.

My second transition from female-to-who-knows-what coincided with the beginning of my college experience. I moved away from home and sequestered myself in the loving arms of a vibrant, artsy New England town. I studied at a small state university under still more amazing, queer, feminist elders. I had the support of a trans community that now overwhelmingly included Assigned Female at Birth (AFAB) butch and transmasculine folks. I missed the presence of my trans women friends and lovers, but feeling included for the first time ever, feeling truly known and seen was indescribable.

Still, something was amiss. Despite being ever more comfortable in my body and readily accepting the designation of genderqueer, my opportunities to date cis boys who actually saw the boy in me was limited at best. I had my glut of women and fellow transmasculine folk as potential partners, but in my mind, the "holy grail" of sexuality was getting to fuck cis boys as a boy. It felt like uncharted territory. The biggest part of me that feels male is that which desires other men. As time marches on, I find that I am read as male more and more, even by gay men, but it's not yet something I feel in my bones. It does make me wonder if the perception of others counts for some aspects of my gender. If I am treated as male, am I male in that moment? Does the attraction to me as a man *make me* male? After all, who is a better authority on what is male than a man who is attracted to men?

This is something that has been so difficult to articulate and has been the source of so much shame for many years. Am I only pretending to be trans so I can fuck gay men? When I was living as a girl, I developed what were seen as inappropriate crushes on (and protracted longing for) my cis male gay friends. I felt awful, as though I were the stereotypical fruit fly who falls for her gay bestie, making him and his sacred, gay spaces feel unsafe. The phrase I used at the time to explain my predicament was "always the fag hag, never the fag." As a trans person who has been on the receiving end of so much transphobia for not having a "male" body, I also questioned my ravenous desire for cis men. Was I placing their value as men above trans men and, if so, what did that say about me? These things have plagued me, making me feel like a bad trans person or a bad feminist.

Prior to transition, I had not made any meaningful connections with trans men or other AFAB genderqueers. This was partly because of lack of opportunity and partly because of my own internalized transphobia. I didn't know trans men could be sexy. I worried that my own socio-sexual capital would wane if I were to begin any outward physical changes. But that wasn't the case; in fact, my sexual dance card flourished post-transition. I've since learned that sex with trans men and their adjacents (my fellow oddball gender offenders) can be just as raw, raunchy and scintillating as sex with cis men. Yet, there is something a bit different in our approaches with one another. Perhaps many of us built the pathways of tenderness in our hearts and our hands as we grew up, knowing the disappointment of not being on the boys' team, yet never quite feeling like we were "one of the girls." Perhaps it's a shared culture: for instance, I can play "I have that book" bingo with my trans friends' bookshelves.

It helps that the AFAB queers I've fucked have been, like me, interested in social justice and have worked in non-profits devoted to ending intimate partner violence and systemic poverty. These feminist boys and bois have been the ones who emulate our fore-parent Les Feinberg in our class consciousness and our understanding of the capitalist disease that has permeated our generation's struggle. When we fuck, we hold not only our own sexuality, but we pass our fingertips over the brown and pink smiles of our top surgery scars, kiss with full, hot mouths the invisible wounds of our shared traumas. We suck each other off, strap each other on, carry over the lessons we learned when many of us spent our time as the hot butch dykes of our respective scenes. We know each other's bodies. We know the pain of our dysphorias as keenly as we know how to get each other off.

Sometimes, this is too much to hold. Sometimes I merely want to come, and that level of intimacy and connection is almost too much to bear. My heart can't always take it. As my transition has progressed, I have noticed myself increasingly garnering attention from the gay cis men who are becoming more openly vocal about their proclivity for my kind. It reminds me of my first puberty all over again. I am aroused by the arousal of those who set their sights on me, who chase me and eagerly receive my advances. After the end of a particularly traumatic relationship, I decided to give myself the gift of what I had always wanted. Without shame, and without eternal agonizing over my own motivations, I allowed myself to hook up with cis boys, satiating the sweet tooth that had patiently waited for so long.

I made my foray onto dating apps, discovering that flirting and hooking up via Scruff and Grindr was actually a lot of fun. Even the occasional Craigslist or Fetlife connection could provide the kind of queer gold rush I'd always dreamed of. I met up with a sexy turquoise-haired boy in Bushwick for an age play scene while staying with a friend, savoring the 1 am walk of shame back from his apartment. I fucked a chiseled, tattooed god with a dick that actually hurt (been years since that had happened) during a Thanksgiving trip back home to Ohio. I had boys over to my apartment that I barely knew, and had a fine time having exciting sex with total strangers. After having spent years jealous of the exploits of my cis gay friends, I felt as though I was part of the club. I popped my little boy cherry and it felt like hot, gay magic. Each of them was tolerant or enthusiastic about my safer sex requirements, putting to bed my imagined awkwardness of having to ask what I need. The HIV/AIDS mass genocide of the 1980's and 1990's has perhaps made my generation keenly aware of the need for safety—at least for us gays and queers. Straight men are a different story however.

Through all of this, my ambivalence about my body has been ever present. While my peers and lovers post fundraisers and navigate the ulcer-inducing red tape of insurance negotiation for top surgery, my desire to alter my chest remains merely a fleeting consideration. In truth, I have no problem with my body. My tits aren't a drag. They remain an erogenous zone, if only a little hairier and differently shaped than they were a few years and several hundred T shots ago. Likewise, my cock/clit/whatever as it stands today (pun intended) fills me with little to no desire for alteration. I like that it is a small mouthful. I like that it gets visibly hard and rigid, making it easier to meet up and grind against the engorged dicks of my trans male lovers. I often fantasize about being able to penetrate, but honestly, it's not the biggest goal in my life. If a dick could be grown out of stem cells and installed, without having to graft any skin from any other part of my body or cause potential nerve damage, I might consider it. But frankly I'd rather get more tattoos. Yet, perhaps I shouldn't be so dismissive. After all, the technology is improving every day. Bottom surgery options for trans folks like me are being refined as demand increases, and many surgeries are more successful and satisfying for patients than even a short time ago.

If I personally could see one thing improve, however, it would be the misogyny of some gay cis men that turns off so many trans men and AFAB genderqueers and how internalizing this misogyny makes us hate ourselves and our anatomy. My body shouldn't have to be changed to please anyone else. Just as I have come to accept my curves and my weight, and have put away the need to hide behind a façade, I refuse to believe that any part of my body is ugly or lesser. My dick is amazing. No, it really is. It's as amazing as any dick out there, and my front hole is just as good of a fuck as any cis guy's ass. While the gay male community has a long way to go, I am pleased by the increasing acceptance of cis male attraction for trans men. Quick scans of personal ads and trans guy/cis guy porn indicates a better future for all of our sex lives. I truly hope this is the case for the next generation of teenage trans boys or trans-whatever coming into their own in places like Ohio. I also hope that someday as an elder I can give back to them by telling stories that will ignite their imaginations and give them permission to fully be themselves.

GAY FOR DAVID BOWIE*

XANDER

I consider myself to be bisexual/queer. I've always been attracted to men, consistently, and because of understanding myself as a girl growing up that felt normal and straightforward. When I found myself attracted to women, I initially wrote it off as aesthetic appreciation—after all, women are amazing—but ultimately realized that most straight girls don't think that way, and recognized that I was queer. I continued to date men, and all my major sexual and romantic relationships have been with cis men, trans men and genderqueer folks.

COMING OUT AS TRANS

I didn't figure out I was trans until I was twenty-going-on-twenty-one, about two years ago. In the beginning of my junior year of college I found myself wandering in and out of men's departments and clothing stores but not admitting to myself why I was there. I would meander in, put on men's clothing, then leave and not think about it. I developed this almost super power of not thinking about questions starting with "why."

I also decided to cut my hair short, which I had wanted to do for a while. Shopkeepers and other folks started calling me "sir," and I was like, "Hmmm…this makes me really, really happy, I guess I should figure out why." I also remember a particular evening, after I cut my hair, sitting down to dinner with my immediate family and some of our distant relatives. At some point the people sitting near us started talking with my parents and trying to guess which kids were from which side of the family. It went something like, "That girl's the daughter of x, that guy's the son of y," and so on. Then, the focus shifted to be on me. Before anyone ventured a guess about my side of the family tree, a man looked at me and said politely, "I'm not sure what gender this person is." That comment really stuck with me.

I thought, "I'm pretty sure it's not normal to be reacting so positively to this."

Soon after, I paid a visit to the queer center at my school, and asked for books about transmasculine people. I tried to pretend like it wasn't a big deal, but they saw right through me. They handed me the material, and I said, "Thanks, I'll see you later," like everything was fine and dandy—and got out of there as fast as I could! It took a lot of reading and thinking before I came out to myself as trans. I think that for so many trans guys, their understanding of transness came from pain, but this was not the case for me. Mine was a recognition that came from joy.

Once I came out as trans, I realized that I was suffering from chest dysphoria without knowing it. I had to literally look in the mirror to determine the size of my breasts because I had used my "super powers of avoidance" for so many years. My chest dysphoria has taken the form of dissociation rather than a more specific emotional pain.

You might imagine me as this butch looking person, but in reality, I'm pretty damn femme. If I had been born with a factory-installed dick, and the whole deal, I would probably have been one of those cis fellows going around in skirts and lipstick (which, as a trans man, I still totally do and love).

Reconciling femininity with my trans maleness was something that took some time. I needed to conceptualize my body in a way that made sense to my own mind. I'm a pretty curvy person, and as a girl, people complimented me, "Oh my gosh, you have a fantastic ass; you have these sexy hips." At first, as a guy, I felt like I couldn't enjoy having feminine attributes anymore or wearing lipstick; that I couldn't feel good about that. I had to contend with my own sexist bullshit and to remind myself that gender isn't real, and that it could be whatever I wanted. So I started presenting more femme again, but only indoors, among my closest friends. I knew that if my curvy self went outdoors in a dress there was very little chance that I'd be gendered correctly. Later, once my beard started growing in, I began wearing lipstick in public again and it finally felt right. Femme is an authentic expression of who I am.

ON PRESENTATION AND DEFYING HARRY BENJAMIN

In part, what delayed my realization I was trans was that growing up, there was no gender role conformity I needed to push against. I was one of three girls (at the time, anyway) and it was clear to me that a girl could grow up to be whatever she wanted. My mom was made to wear skirts to school because her father demanded that she be "ladylike." She never pushed this on us however. All three of us were athletes, and the mentality was to wear whatever you wished, go play in the mud, and do whatever the fuck you wanted. On top of that, I'm a very aggressive and blunt person in a Jewish family that values argumentation. Perhaps if my family had a different understanding of what it meant to be a woman or man, I would have found out earlier that I am trans. Instead, it was totally fine to go around in skirts, wear lipstick and shit, and still be "boy like" by many social standards.

I've never been butch, so that means that I don't fit the Harry (Fucking) Benjamin standards, right? Honestly, one of the most uncomfortable parts of my transition was at the very beginning when I felt like I had to dress in a masculine way and "perform" masculinity: that there was no other option. I have this vivid memory of going to some fancy ass event in a suit and just before leaving the house, thinking, "Fuck it! I'm going to make this as gay as I can." So I added this little pink pocket square and wore a gold dangly earring in my right ear. These small changes to my outfit made me feel comfortable again.

GAY FOR DAVID BOWIE

The first time I was attracted to a guy in an explicitly queer way was to David Bowie (shocking to nobody, right?). I watched "The Labyrinth" at a summer arts camp in high school, surrounded by lovely queers and fab weirdoes. This wouldn't have been possible at home because my parents are great people but fairly politically conservative.

So there I was, watching "The Labyrinth" and drooling over Bowie in his ridiculously tight pants thinking, "Oh my God, he is so hot!" I still thought I was a girl at the time, so I didn't quite know what category to put my attraction to him in, like, if I was a straight girl just crushing out on a hot dude. Also, at the time I knew I was attracted to queer men and how they love to fuck, but because it was normalized for straight women to openly profess attraction to gay men, my finding Bowie sexy did not lead to an immediate, "Aha, this means I'm trans" type of realization. In retrospect and having watched the movie again, as a trans guy I realize that, "Holy shit, I was gay for David Bowie!"

My Queer Relationship with My Lovely Straight-ish Cis Male Partner

Right now I'm in a relationship with this lovely "cis-ish" guy, Daniel. He's the same person that I was dating when I came out as trans over two years ago. I met him through the guy I was dating before him, in classic queer fashion; the two of them were (and still are) good friends. I was very attracted to Daniel from the get go. I asked him out three different times before he eventually said yes. So here I am, having a wonderful relationship with this guy, and six months later I'm like, "Shit, I'm trans!" Up to this point, during his whole life, Daniel identified as straight, except that the partner he had before me also transitioned from female to male, so this was his second experience.

Still, I was nervous coming out as a guy to my cis-straight boyfriend, wondering how it was going to go. I didn't expect things to be perfect, certainly, but Daniel is an extraordinary person. The entire time since I began transitioning, I don't think Daniel has misgendered me more than three times, all by accident, which any trans person will tell you is a big feat. Even I can fuck up on pronouns. He has been the most supportive person throughout my entire transition.

One of my favorite examples of how incredibly tender Daniel has been with me was when we were arranging a foursome with this couple, Shmuel (a queer cis guy) and Miriam (a queer woman), both good friends of ours. Ultimately, Daniel wasn't into the idea and we canceled the date. Afterwards, Shmuel took Daniel aside privately and said, "Hey, I just want to know, were you reluctant to go through with the play date because I'm a man?" To which, Daniel responded, "Shmuel, I've been fucking a man for a while now." What stands out in my mind is that Daniel never told me about this. Shmuel did months later. When I first started dating Daniel, Shmuel told me that Daniel was not good enough for me, that I needed somebody "more special." But after that, Shmuel changed his mind. How fucking amazing is that? Daniel never told me. I can't get over it. I love him so much.

After I figured out that I was a guy and started declaring it publicly, Daniel asked if it was okay if he still continued to identify as straight. My mind went to the kind of conversation in the lesbian community where a butch person comes out as a trans man and their partner questions whether they can still identify as a lesbian. So I told him that he could of course identify as straight, and he didn't need to ask my permission to name himself, but I did say that "ours is a queer relationship and you've got to call it that." After being around lots of queers, and hearing the way we talk about gender and all this stuff, he eventually came to the conclusion that he is less straight and less cis than he had thought. We've been together now for over two and a half years and it's been wonderful.

SEX, SEX, SEX!

This is the story of the best (and queerest) blowjob I've ever gotten. It was from Daniel, who identified as straight at the time. At first, we were both struggling with how to accommodate my transition into our relationship and our sex life. Like, how I wanted my chest touched. I had been a sexual health peer educator in college, so I knew that the clitoris is a shaft. I asked Daniel if he could try giving me a blowjob on my clit. "How?" he asked. "I don't know," I said, "maybe move your head differently, so I can imagine you're sucking a cis cock." He figured out a way to suck my clit in and out of his mouth and move his head up and down at the same time, such that it completely felt and looked like, well, like I had imagined it all along. It was profound. He was able to make me feel this way even before I went on testosterone and there was not a whole lot there to speak of. I swear to God, I wish this guy could teach classes on how to do this! He's so talented, it's ridiculous. It was one of the most spiritual experiences I've ever had. I felt so connected to my body, enraptured. It was absolutely incredible and I've never forgotten it. It was also such an interesting example of queer sex, of how we create things with our bodies that defy cultural conventions. We can create something beautiful with whatever we have on hand.

These days, I am also dating Clyde, a genderqueer, transmasculine butch person. I love how hy goes around in skirts in summer and am also tremendously jealous, because it takes so much guts to do that. It's funny to say but sex with Clyde feels both queer and masculine and I don't get that queer-boy feeling about sex with Daniel. It's possible that I've known Daniel for so long that our bodies have configured to having sex regardless of gender dynamics. I'm not sure.

Clyde and I are both tremendous nerds, and as our initial attraction began to grow, we talked a lot about queer theory and masculinity. We flirted by talking about our mutual adoration for Sinclair Sexsmith's writing and sharing our favorite erotica. One thing that's been very striking is that strap-on dildos have taken on a whole different meaning for me. I used to think of them as just fun toys. I knew that some folks felt them as extensions of their bodies, but it hadn't quite clicked for me before meeting Clyde. For Clyde, it *is* hys cock. Seeing the connection to hym, feeling the pleasure pouring off hym when I play with hys cock, I've finally started to get it. The heat and the intimacy, queer magic, transmuting your own body! With hys encouragement I've been strapping on, too, when we fuck. It hadn't been part of my desire before and I still have a hard time doing it on my own.

Before Clyde, I'd had a few strap-on blowjobs in my life and generally they were like "Okay, cool, but I mostly can't see what you're doing with your mouth and I can't actually feel it..." I wasn't particularly interested in strap-on play. It might have been because of some dysphoria or my own perception of my cock as already existing in the form of my clit. I didn't even desire going there. But Clyde completely turned me around. Hys connection to strap-ons was so clear that it crackled. Hy makes me feel it when hy sucks me, it's ridiculous. So the fact that with Clyde I can feel connected to a dildo is mind blowing, and makes me realize how much energy and intention are important to sex! I used to dismiss all of that as woo-woo shit, but boy have I been proven wrong by Daniel and Clyde.

I feel like I'm growing in new directions. My partners constantly teach me about connecting to and with my body and how important intention is for sex. The brain is the best sex toy you'll ever get.

Interview-turned-essay, conducted by
and in collaboration with Avi Ben-Zeev.

10 Years of Transitioning: Finding my Place in Community

C.K. Mahdi

Pre- Top Surgery/ Hormone Therapy

Eleven years ago when I was eighteen years old, I came out as transgender. Although I lived in liberal Northern California, medical laws required a step-by-step sequential diagnosis in order to transition. My identity did not fit into a two-gendered system, so I was unsure of how to move forward.

I identify as an androgynous male, comfortable with both masculine and feminine qualities. This may seem more acceptable in transgender and queer communities in the present day, but eleven years ago, my identity did not fit into societal expectations of what "transgender" was.

Medical laws were rigid at that time, and left no room for grey areas. Psychiatric laws stated that a trans male must go through six months of therapy and live "as male" in order to start testosterone. Only after nine months on testosterone could a person become eligible for gender reconstructive surgery, which was not covered by insurance and had to be paid out of pocket.

Although I knew I identified as male, I was hesitant to transition physically from one gender to the other. The sequential transition laws were too binary for me and did not allow me to transition into being my authentic self. At the time, I decided against hormone therapy because I did not agree with the societal or medical expectations of who a "transgender male" should be.

As a result, I spent the majority of my twenties being an "undercover transgender." My expressions and characteristics, both feminine and masculine, would often confuse people, even in the small transgender community I grew up around. The trans men I knew validated trans identity by being hyper masculine and telling people such as myself, to "man up" and start hormone therapy. Luckily, the medical laws changed in 2015, and I was able to start my transition at my own pace and by my own standards.

EXPERIENCES OF TRANSPHOBIA IN LESBIAN COMMUNITY

I have always been attracted to both men and women. Prior to transitioning, I had limited sexual expression because of my invisible transgender identity. Although I have always been sexually attracted to men, I would find it difficult to date them because of my fear of being trapped in a heterosexual relationship and being viewed as a woman. Therefore, I mostly dated cisgender women at that time. However, those relationships and dynamics ended up invalidating my identity in other ways.

Coming out to cisgender lesbian women was a struggle, their reactions and replies were often transphobic and not accepting of my identity. They would automatically assume I identified as a woman, even though I looked masculine-androgynous.

When I would explain to them that I didn't identify as female and didn't know if or when I would like to physically transition, they'd say things like: "I'm a lesbian, I don't want to date a man," "You're too pretty to be a man," "I can't call you 'he' or 'they', you look too much like a 'she'," "I don't get it, you wear mascara sometimes," or, "I don't see you as male— you have sex like a woman, because you let me fuck you." I felt like these women's lesbian identity made them reluctant to acknowledge my gender identity.

Some cisgender women accepted my trans identity, but as a fetish, or something to brag about (liking the idea of dating someone different or "trans"). Their support was often gone once I seriously expressed wanting to start hormone therapy and having surgery.

Ultimately, coming out as transgender without a time frame of when, or if, I would start hormones caused me to experience displacement in lesbian and transgender communities. No matter what I explained, it seemed like each community wanted me to be one gender or the other, or not one gender at all, which kept my identity and full sexual expression subdued.

TRANSITIONING AND FINDING ACCEPTANCE IN GAY MALE COMMUNITY

I chose to have top surgery before starting testosterone because of my hesitation to adhere to binary gender standards. After surgery, I was finally able to physically see myself as male and not just think it in my mind. My attraction to gay men became more prominent, and gay men were attracted towards me as my body transitioned to being more masculine. After surgery, I felt closer and safer with men, both cis and trans. Thus, my identity shifted to a queer male, which allowed me to blend in the gay community. I started a Grindr account and actively began flirting with men.

I wanted to appear more physically masculine but continued to resist full transition, so I began a low dose of testosterone therapy. As I became more comfortable with my body a monumental thing happened: My attraction to humans who identified as male, grew stronger, and I experienced a greater sense of acceptance and belonging from cis/queer male and trans male subcultures and communities.

As I further transitioned with hormone therapy, my male status became accepted in gay male communities, especially on dating sites, which has been extremely validating of my identity as a trans genderqueer man. Surprisingly enough, I have felt the most support from gay men.

Having gay male dating accounts, such as Grindr and Surge, has validated my identity as male. Guys who message me generally use the right pronouns and rarely ask about my genitals and surgery status. I have not had to defend my gender, as there is a mutual understanding that I am a man and that I am attracted to other men.

Dating and sleeping with men relieved the anxiety of having to explain my transgender identity, pronouns, and that I have no breasts. The only thing I find myself explaining at times is that I was not born with a penis. Ultimately, I choose to sleep with men who are queer, bisexual or gay, rather than men who identify as heterosexual, because it validates my identity as a queer man.

The first cisgender man I slept with after my top surgery was someone I met on Grindr. I was only six months post-op top surgery, and was very nervous about my top surgery scars. I was ready to explain myself before I took my shirt off, since that was a habit I'd developed while navigating previous experiences.

Once he looked at me naked, he stated that my six-month, post-op chest, was one of the most beautiful things he had ever seen, "You're like the perfect catch. You're beautiful, you have no breasts and you have a vagina."

I will remember that moment for the rest of my life. Finally, I was accepted for who I am.

Since surgery and taking low doses of testosterone, I have received more positive attention from cisgender and transgender gay men than from cis/trans women. On dating apps and in person, most gay cisgender men compliment me and state their attraction towards me and don't seem to care that I am transgender.

I've also had instances in public places where I've felt a great amount of support. The summer after my surgery, it was one hundred degree weather. I was at a bar by myself wearing a tank top, which made my scars partially visible. While I was sitting down, an older gay man walked up to me with his husband. He smiled, shook my hand and said, "You are doing something wonderful…keep being yourself." He gave me a hug. "Our community needs more people like you!" he said and went on his way.

I smile when I think of my experiences with men and feel a sense of belonging in gay men's community. I used to worry that I would not be accepted as a queer male because I wasn't born with the correct genitals, but that has not been a problem for me. I often wonder why I don't feel supported in other communities, or why it is that gay men have embraced my identity more.

For the first time in my life, I have found a community that accepts me. I have spent years in limbo between the L, G and T communities, and ultimately, I have felt an overwhelming support from gay cis and trans men who I have flirted with, dated, fucked and loved. Gay men embrace my body and accept it for how it is; they respect my pronouns and don't question my level of masculinity or gender. They see me as male, and we have a mutual respect towards one another. There is a sense of equity— with no need for explaining my identity in depth. With gay men there is no need to prove that I am who I am.

EYE OF THE BEHOLDER*

T

I was born in the Central Valley of California to a couple of very straight vegetarian Jews, Sephardic on my dad's side and Ashkenazi on my mom's. I grew up attending public schools that were racially and ethnically diverse—roughly a quarter white, a quarter Black, a quarter Latino, a quarter South East Asian, and with a lot of Vietnamese and Cambodian folks. The Central Valley is wonderfully diverse in this way, and because of that, it was weirder that we were vegetarian than Jewish, and I was teased accordingly. Since as far back as I can remember I've always been interested in both men and women, but primarily men.

I assume based on random street harassment that when people look at me, more often than not they can't quite guess what my gender is. I'm slender, have short black and blue hair cut in a side-shave "queer haircut" style, and despite efforts to the contrary, mostly dress like a teenager. I've been on and off testosterone over the years, partly for medical reasons, so there have been some permanent changes to how I look and sound. My voice is low, I have stubble on my face, and my jaw has squared off. I've also had top surgery, so my chest is flat. About half of the time I'm read as a guy and the other half as a woman. It's like I'm a gender Rorschach that reflects social beliefs. This is both exhausting and also where I'm comfortable.

How my gender is read also affects how my partner's sexuality is perceived. We can be walking down the street looking like a het couple or like two gay guys, depending on who is watching. Any man who would consider partnering with me would have to not give a shit about being seen as queer or straight, regardless of his identification. It's been an issue with dating in the past.

My cis male partner and I have been together for 10 years and recently bought a house. I've been unpacking and sorting boxes of photos, stuff from my parents' attic that I deliberately have avoided looking at for over 20 years. This project of sorting what to keep, scan or discard, has been intense. When I look at my childhood and adolescent photos I see a kid who was fairly happy until I was six years old. It took me about twenty-five years to be happy again.

AIN'T NO PRINCESS LEIA

When I was maybe eight I told my therapist (I was the kid who got therapy at an early age) that I didn't like playing with this other kid, a son of my parents' friends, because when we played Star Wars, he would make me be Princess Leia. I wish I could go back in time as an adult, eavesdrop on that therapy session, and be like, "So what did you make of that, lady therapist?" Diagnosing trans children was not a thing back then.

Around that time, I came home from school one day and asked my mom what a lesbian was because somebody had said that word on the playground. Her answer was actually pretty great in retrospect. She said, "Sometimes two women decide that they love each other and they wanna be together and we call these women lesbians, and also sometimes two men fall in love and they wanna be together and we call them gay men." I remember thinking, "I'd like to try that, to be a gay man. Or a gay woman." Life is funny, I did grow up to try both.

I'm realizing now that I've always been a bit of a femme. As a kid I was interested in "girl stuff." I was a ballet dancer for a long time, from childhood all the way through my first year of high school. Puberty hit me really hard. That, combined with discovering the joys of making out, meant that dance went by the wayside. Back then I was really trying to conform, to be a "girl." I had no idea that I could be trans. I just thought, "I was born as a girl, so I kind of have to be a girl." I tried to be one, I really did. Now that I'm almost 40, I have a newfound compassion for the person that I was all this time ago.

Revisiting all these photos of myself back then, I not only have nostalgia for skin collagen, I realize that I wasn't nearly as ugly, awkward or unattractive as I felt at the time. I was trying to be something and someone I just simply wasn't meant to be, which was the source of so much pain.

FINALLY…SAN FRANCISCO

In 1998, I went to San Francisco State University and majored in Photography and Anthropology. I took side classes in gender studies and human sexuality. Students were mostly cis women and a few cis gay guys, and probably a ton of fellow trans people just starting to realize what might be going on. The writer and activist, Jamison Green, came to give a guest lecture to one class I was in. It's a bit of a cliché, but he was the first trans guy I'd ever really seen, and this little voice inside me started going, "fuck, fuck, fuck!" My heart literally sank a bit because I realized that now this was an option, I couldn't not explore it further.

At the time I was dating a kinky, cis, goth poly dude, and we checked out an FTMI meeting. You have to remember that back then we didn't have Tumblr, or nearly the same level of online support or exposure to any of this information or community. People were a lot more isolated, and we'd have to send away via mail for newsletters or use a newspaper for a hook up ad—Paper Tinder.

My boyfriend and I had been doing a lot of role-playing and dressing up at the time, with me as a boy and doing kinky games around gender play and stuff. I also would wear latex dresses, but increasingly all the boy/boy role play just felt a lot more fun and comfortable. I'd always fantasized about being male during sex, but I was never willing to actually do these kinds of games and role play with someone I was dating. My boyfriend was also into being penetrated and even fisted as a bottom, so I was learning a lot about sex and doing things I'd only ever kind of dreamed up.

We were also going to some play parties at the 14th Street house, which was this legendary Fairy house in the Mission that threw parties where everyone would go. At the top floor, there'd be an orgy of straight folk and swingers, and down in the dungeon you'd see queer action: women topping men, women topping other women, and gay male couples having sex. One night I saw guys doing sounding (putting rods in the urethra), some leather dykes doing cutting and play piercing, and lots of fisting. It was a great scene where all kinds of people would go and play side-by-side, lots of diversity. I don't think that really exists anymore. Even in San Francisco, parties and people are a lot more separated into groups, which is too bad. It really made for a sense of freak community that was incredibly special.

FTMI had a local group that did monthly meetings, so we went to one to try to meet other trans/cis couples. There were a lot of very binary trans guys there with their female partners. Many of these trans guys identified as straight, even if they had been part of a lesbian community in the past. I'd never considered myself a lesbian, so I felt less connection with that group than a lot of other guys did. But I know they helped a ton of people.

At the time, there was a lot of frustration and anger in the lesbian and gay women's community, a general sentiment that "all of the butches were becoming boys." Butch women were also upset because they felt like their identity was being erased and lumped into a masculinity that they weren't comfortable with, which is totally valid.

I came from such a different world. After trying to be a straight girl for my teenage life, I didn't realize that what I was really seeking was to be a trans man in a gay male context. I just couldn't see myself reflected in any of the narratives or paths these FTMI guys were on, which included multiple surgeries, growing beards, etc. I have nothing against all that, but at the time I wasn't there yet. My boyfriend and I walked out after the meeting and didn't go back.

PERFORMATIVE FEMININITY AND TRANNY FAGS

I'd always enjoyed the trappings of performative femininity, probably because being a woman felt like a false front. I was goth, kinky, and liked wearing wigs and makeup. Still, once I found out that hormones and transitioning were options, I had to move forward. There started to be more of a community around gay identified trans guys, including workshops for "Tranny fags," one of them literally called, "All About Dick," to educate people on safer sex as applied to trans guys with cis guys. So many trans guys came out of the lesbian world, there wasn't a lot of good knowledge about safer sex with cis men.

There was a lot of unsafe sex happening. Places like Magnet and other MSM organizations in the city were offering HIV and STI prevention and treatment but only to cis men. This was well before PrEP, so trans people were especially at risk. Given that I had been having sex with cis men most of my adult life, I found myself teaching trans guys how to use condoms, and how you insist that your partner wears condoms, and things like that.

"YOU'RE HOT, I LOVE YOU, BUT I'M NOT A GAY MAN"

My boyfriend dumped me right before my last semester of college and that was incredibly hard for me. My parents were convinced that it was because I had just come out as being trans, but I think this was a fear they projected onto me partly due to their own discomfort with my being trans. Yet, they weren't totally wrong. It was a combination of a lot of factors, but I know that he became increasingly uncomfortable being seen as a gay guy and worried what his own parents would think. He was an artist who had been called queer and bullied in high school, so he carried some trauma around that.

The more the reality of my gender identity sunk in, playing gay men scenes no longer worked for us because it was no longer "play." The pressure of walking around being seen as a gay couple was not something that he could take on. This is just my theory, because he's never admitted this to me. I'm pretty convinced it's the case, because after I started medically transitioning and had begun being read as a male was when he became really uncomfortable. It was less about me and more about him; he didn't like it that I made him gay.

IN AND OUT OF BEING STEALTH

I understand why people avoid medical transition or choose to do it and then go stealth. Telling everybody you're trans is like wearing your secret on your sleeve. As soon as people find out that I am trans, especially cis people, they never ever see me as anything other than trans again, ever. I have trans male friends with full beards, and as soon as cis folks find out they're trans, they start misgendering them.

It's like something in people's brains goes automatically to what they think they know is between your legs, and that's somehow meaningful for them in determining your "true" gender. For this reason I don't like to tell people that I am trans.

Meeting new people is always fun. At some point they lean over a table and say something like, "Hey, I don't wanna be offensive but can I ask you a question?" I think, "Shit here it goes again…"

I think my gender identity starts once I leave the house and start interacting with other people. It's not when I'm home brushing my teeth, petting the cat, reading Facebook, or gardening. In the outside world I have to be okay with total strangers coming up and asking me what pronouns I use. I know that sometimes that comes with the best of intentions, like wanting to be respectful of me, but every single time it takes energy. Even when I do say, "I prefer male pronouns," people get it wrong half the time anyway.

MY ROCK

It took me over a year to come out as trans to my current partner. When I realized we were falling in love, I became petrified that disclosing my identity would mean losing him. I'd lost two really significant relationships partly due to being trans. I'd also been on and off testosterone for a while and was scared to admit that I wanted to go back on it. I thought, "What's the point of having a relationship if I am lying about who I am?" I was trying to be more empowered than fearful, mostly faking it but needing to be honest to both him and to myself. When I finally told him, his response was a mild "ok." That's really how that went. As a white cis guy, my partner has so much privilege that he doesn't care what other people think. That's one theory. Whatever it is, I've never met anyone who cares less about what other people think of him.

That said, I do realize that his "I don't care if people hate us because we're gay," response, was also because he genuinely loves me as I am. My gender is a non-issue to him. It's taken me a long time to actually believe him, because I'm an insecure artist that has always dated other insecure artists. I've learned a lot about my own confidence from him.

After I finally came out, he confided in me that when we first met, he couldn't tell if I had been born male or female, or how I currently identified. He was living in the Castro at the time and identified as bisexual (still does), so not knowing my gender until after our first date was a non-issue for him. That's why I married the guy. If he can put up with all the feelings, stress and ambiguity that being with me entails, I can put up with the fact that he leaves his underwear on the floor. Our relationship is solid now after being so long together. He works a full time job and makes a lot more money than me right now, so I end up doing more of the cooking and cleaning, even though he's much better at baking than I am.

My partner is tall, cis, white, blonde, and writes software. He knows that his life is on the easy setting, especially in the Bay Area, and he admits it. He's aware of his privilege but to me it's very obvious sometimes that we're very different, in great part because of how we were socialized as children. I grew up trans and queer and soaked up all of these messages that who I fundamentally am is deviant, wrong and embarrassing to my family, and that I don't deserve to be happy. Toxic shit that I've spent years in therapy trying to unlearn. So sometimes being with my partner is kind of rough. He doesn't know or understand a lot of things I've been through, but he has compassion. That division can sometimes be challenging in a partnership. We're poly, so sometimes I wonder what it would be like to date somebody more queer, and who, frankly, would understand certain aspects of me better than my partner ever can.

BEING POLY AND GROWING FROM MISTAKES

We're working out being poly. I like it but it also freaks me out. We are married now, have bought a house together, and the stakes feel very high. For me, if this relationship falls apart it's gonna be catastrophic on every level, personally, logistically, financially, like…everything. So when he started dating a woman last year, who is tall, skinny and pretty, it brought up a lot for me. It hit some kind of nerve; a lot of that has to do with seeing his sexual and romantic interest in a woman with a body type I was trying to have for a really long time, and with the gender that I was trying so hard to be.

I had top surgery about a year and a half ago, although I wish I had done it twenty years ago when I was younger and hotter. So this also brought up a lot, like being worried that he would feel differently about my body. He's admitted that he misses my breasts. What he actually said was, "I don't miss your breasts, but I do miss breasts." I get it! I don't know if I would worry any less, though, if he wanted to be with a cis guy. That would probably open a whole other can of worms.

This situation has brought up and triggered old fears, that maybe, he's really only attracted to women after all, which is clearly not logical but that's a lizard brain for you. I get that he wants variety. Anybody would after a ten year relationship, so I don't blame him. I want him to be happy. Trust is a challenge because right now he wants to date women, and a lot of women in the poly scene are straight, and that is not a community where I feel welcome, comfortable or understood.

As for me, I don't necessarily want to spend the rest of my life sleeping with just one person, as much as I love my partner. I've had a more adventurous sex life in the past, which is partly why I'm not actively seeking more of that out now. He and I have a wonderful relationship, great sex but we've been together so long that interjecting other people into the mix, honestly does keep things fresh. It reinvigorates us both, brings in a different energy, and helps us to appreciate each other in new ways. Being poly helps remind me why he and I are together, and to continue being intentional about our commitment. As a neurotic Jew, who overthinks everything, I am working on letting go of trying to (over) control life. I have been working a lot on that, especially around acknowledging and honoring my fears.

The nice thing about stability is that it allows me to work through stuff, and let go of some of what's not useful. I feel like I'm at a place in life where I've spent a while processing all my mistakes, growing and learning from them. Maybe in another year or two, it'll be the right time for me to go out and make some new mistakes.

Interview-turned-essay, conducted by
and in collaboration with Avi Ben-Zeev.

On Instincts

Jonah Elliot

When I was nineteen, I came out to the world and embraced the classic heterosexual trans man fantasy. I thought I knew myself, finally, after years of discomfort, confusion and guilt. It only took a single rainy Monday night in October to set off a reaction that would ultimately obliterate my sense of identity in the best way.

That night, I offered to drive a classmate home so she wouldn't have to walk the half mile from campus to her house in the rain. I took a few extra turns, enjoying the sound of a heavy rain rumbling against my windshield. The asphalt seemed to roll in wide waves alongside us, reflecting the city's lights in a blurred darkness. I rounded a sharp curve and found a murky shape directly in front of me. I jammed my foot into the brake pedal and pounded my fist against the horn.

The shape tumbled onto the sidewalk just as my car slid through the place where it had stood. My head pounded so hard I couldn't see clearly.

My passenger already had her door open, yelling, "What the fuck, dude?" She slammed the door, and I locked it behind her.

I watched her confront the shape, gesticulating wildly. When she knocked on the window to be let back inside the car, the vaguely human shape glided away—on what I could then see was a vintage bicycle—in the direction I had been driving.

"I work with that asshole, but I felt sorry for him, so I invited him to hang out and warm up for a few minutes," she informed me.

We sat on the splintery floor of her rickety Victorian home, drinking tequila straight from the bottle and playing "Never Have I Ever." The guy was shivering, and his cheeks had rosy blotches from the cold. He leaned against me to warm up, and I caught myself checking him out. I attributed it to the tequila, but our hostess conspicuously winked at us and made her way into the kitchen. As soon as she was out of sight he climbed to straddle me.

"You know what I want?"

I didn't want to push him off. "Hm?"

He leaned close and put his lips on my neck. "I want us to fuck like rabbits right here," he whispered.

Warmth spread down from my stomach. He licked the length of my neck and wrapped his arms around me. I heard a crunching sound, and he pulled away. He reached down beside my thigh and pulled his mangled phone from under his knee. The moment passed quickly, and I regained my composure.

Later that night, as I ushered him out the door, he turned and said, "You should come by my house sometime. It's the one on the hill at the end of Rosewood."

"Maybe," I said. "I'll try to make it up there."

A few weeks later he invited me to a party. I was promised wine and Martha Stewart quality food, so I accepted the invitation without a thought. When he opened the door, I could hear floating notes of slow jazz and silverware clinking against dishes. He was tall and lean, a ballet dancer, with sad brown eyes and shaggy hair. I knew he was gay, but I had no idea the party was exclusively for non-straight men.

The living room was decorated with twinkle lights and framed charcoal drawings of human bones. A sugar-white Persian cat lounged on the back of a spotless white sofa. The space was scattered with men in pastel cashmere sweaters and dark sport coats with glinting gold watches and suede loafers that looked brand new. I was out of place in my scruffy oxfords and black t-shirt emblazoned with "Let's Get Weird" in neon pink. My red hair was tangled in an unruly fauxhawk that one of my slightly older trans friends had carefully shaved and taught me to style over his dorm room sink.

Movement in the corner of the room caught my attention. There was a group of five or six men on a Kelly green velvet sofa. They were kissing and fondling each other like horny teenagers. My face flushed, and I couldn't stop gawking. They bit one another's necks. One man in a blue sweater unbuckled his belt as another slid off the sofa and onto his knees on the floor. I tried to avert my gaze, but it kept sliding back to the group of men who were taking turns going down on the guy in the blue sweater.

Watching a private moment acted out so openly filled me with a sense of shame. I made my way into the dining room, despite the heat sliding down through my belly that urged me to stay.

I felt embarrassingly young. I recognized some of the guys from pictures of my older friends, and I could recall some of their names from the stories I'd heard about their escapades. Among them were an attorney, a well-known cellist and a nationally-renowned professor. I was just a kid in my first year of college. I was only learning what it meant to be a man. I hadn't started medically or legally transitioning yet, and that party felt far beyond my league.

I hid out on a rickety stool in the tiny kitchen. I heard moaning and the staccato beat of furniture banging against the wall from the living room. My self-consciousness ate at me while I tried not to listen in on what I thought was a private moment. I was chubby and awkward and my voice felt wrong, even in my mind. I had a blue thrift store mug brimming with merlot that tasted cheap, although I knew nothing about wine. I looked around the kitchen and wondered if I could escape through the back door.

Just then my host ran into the kitchen, sliding across the linoleum in his expensive navy socks. He slid towards me like a gangly puppy. He asked, "Do you like it? The party?"

I refilled the mostly empty Mason jar in his hand with the nearest bottle of wine and nodded. He was as drunk as I wanted to be in that moment. I hesitated, and he leaned closer. He sensed my nervousness and ran a lithe finger along my soft, hairless jawline. I wanted to pull away, but I froze, trapped under his slightly unfocused gaze. I looked at his soft, full lips, and the heat in my belly began to burn again. My heart pounded a drumbeat against my ribs.

He plunked his wine down, splashing some on the white tile bar. He leaned in. My entire body prickled with adrenaline. Even the hairs on my arms stood at attention. I shifted backwards on my creaking stool, but his mouth caught mine easily. The kiss was ferocious and sloppy, and it electrified my body. It felt good. I pushed my tongue into his mouth and kissed him back aggressively. It felt right. I wanted to feel embarrassed when the only woman at the party slipped into the kitchen to smoke a joint, but I only pulled him against me more tightly.

Afterwards, we went outside to share a menthol Virginia Slim 120 in the rain. I sat on the porch railing and smoked while he stood between my legs and kissed my throat, rubbing his hard-on against me. We did that many more times until he moved to New York to pursue his dreams of dancing on much larger stages. By then, I was hooked. I searched for that same sense of euphoria on the lips of countless women after him to no avail.

What followed the dancer was a parade of serious relationships with women. I grew into myself more with each failed partnership. I had a new beard, new legal documents, and a defined sense of my gender identity. The more I came to understand about myself, the less I wanted to stay with the women I said I loved. After each relationship met its demise, I created a new profile on a dating website and immediately deleted it as soon as the next partner came along. That was how I met the couple.

After a painful, extended breakup I created my usual online profile, and I eventually received a message from a pink-haired nonbinary person. They asked if they could get to know me. I wasn't attracted to them at all but I ignored my instinct and acquiesced. They were a fat femme with a love of liquid eyeliner and bright nail polish. I had dated plenty of femmes before, but I wasn't interested in having sex with this femme at all. At the time, I couldn't identify why I wasn't attracted to them, so I assumed it was because they were fat. I chided myself for allowing a society obsessed with thinness to influence my sexuality that way and determined that I would give them a shot.

They were part of a polyamorous couple, and their husband was a heteroflexible cis man. When we finally met in person, I was instantly more interested in him than the femme. He was just an average white guy with a gorgeous cock and a collection of dragon t-shirts. The two of them were dedicated nerds who loved board games, *Star Trek*, and *Dungeons and Dragons*. We had very little in common. My hobbies at the time were reading and working so I could afford to go back to school. Neither of them had jobs, and I wasn't entirely sure how they survived. I constantly made up excuses not to let them move in with me.

A year after we met, we were quickly approaching our first anniversary as a triad. During that time, they moved out of state and started trying to have a baby. I became their out of town boyfriend who drove up for a long weekend of board games, drinking and kinky sex. I still wasn't attracted to the femme partner.

I knew the end of our relationship was quickly approaching when the femme turned to me in bed one Sunday afternoon when we were alone and asked, "Are you more attracted to my husband because he has a penis and I don't?"

I lied. "Of course not, babe. I'm more emotionally attracted to you. I feel like we connect better."

They both accepted that as truth.

On the five-hour drive home I relived the moments when the husband fucked me and I sucked his cock. I thought about how I let him cane me and cum in me.

He had put his hand around my throat as I was looking for my car keys. "You know you can't leave until I'm satisfied," he's growled.

When I got home, I found blood in my underwear.

I had loved every second of it, but I quickly realized that in all my memories from the weekend, the femme fell into the background far behind their husband. I couldn't even remember where our partner had been while he fucked me that last time.

I relegated the hollow, ugly feelings of having sex with someone to whom I wasn't attracted to to the outer reaches of my mind. I put them in a cobwebby box to unpack well after the hickeys, caning stripes and handprints peppering my skin were gone. Without the throbbing, erotic ache of those marks across my body, it was easier to forget the hot sex and consider the reality of our relationship. When that time came, my discovery was startling.

I didn't think of myself as a trans man anymore. I was just a guy who had a unique body type, and who wanted other men to touch that body. Having partners who wouldn't leave me behind allowed me to change myself. I grew my beard out, started going to the gym, stopped eating meat, and spent a lot of time pursuing my unexplored interests like quilting and cooking. I stopped existing as a person who wasn't a man trying to be masculine, and I became a man who didn't care if I was masculine, as long as I was myself.

I ultimately lost total interest in my nonbinary partner because I couldn't identify with the bad body days, dysphoria and gender anxiety anymore. Those things drained me emotionally and created unnecessary stress in my life. I couldn't relate, and I certainly didn't want to force myself back into a headspace of self-doubt and anxiety. I couldn't pinpoint when I stopped thinking about my gender every day, but it was somewhere in the midst of our thirteen-month relationship.

I realized that gender no longer dominated my thoughts, and the way people perceived me seemed to have changed. This was when I realized

I was stealth for the first time. Despite that, my sexuality wasn't exactly a secret. My coworkers constantly asked if I had a boyfriend or if a certain male customer was my type. I managed to successfully evade their questioning for a few weeks, while my polyamorous relationship neared its end. Ultimately, I told my coworkers when I became involved with one of our patrons.

I was at work one morning shelving books in the college and career section, when he approached me. He was fresh out of an unhappy marriage to a woman and cruising at the library. We had virtually nothing in common, with more than a twenty-year age gap between us. I wasn't attracted to him, but he was extremely interested in me. One Tuesday morning, he approached me, despite the headphones I wore to ward off unnecessary chatting with the public.

"Nice tattoos, brother. Can I see?" I showed him my arms in that way all tattoo-bearers do when strangers ask to see the rest of whatever's peeking out from their shirtsleeve. "Those are cool, man." He looked me up and down, licking his lips. "So, uh, have you ever had a man behind your body before?"

I was stunned. I had never been approached for sex in such a blatant way. The alarms in my head were ringing with ferocity, but I ignored them.

After listening to me stammer noncommittally for what felt like hours, he asked, "Can I get your number?"

I wasn't thinking logically when I said, "Come back later and try again." I knew I was in the final weeks of my triad relationship but I wasn't sure whether I wanted to fuck a stranger that soon. I didn't expect him to actually come back.

About a month later, I was organizing knitting books in the stacks when a rough hand landed on mine from the other side of the bookshelf. His touch startled me into knocking over a row of quilting manuals, which he didn't offer to help pick up.

This time he said, "It's good to see you. I thought maybe you were just fucking with me when you told me to come back. Do you, uh, do you have a minute to meet me in the bathroom?"

My head pounded from anxiety. "No, sorry. Security checks the bathrooms all the time to keep that shit from happening."

"Aw, man. I just saw the security guard check the bathroom on this floor."

"Sorry, I have to be downstairs in a few minutes."

"C'mon, man, it won't take long. I just want to wrap my arms around your body and feel you."

"I really have to get downstairs for a meeting."

"Well, uh, can I at least get that number, then?"

My organs felt like they were twisting themselves into knots, but I gave in. The wave of instantaneous regret that hit me as soon as I listed the last digit was impressive, even for me. He gleefully took my number. Before I could escape into the staff elevator, he texted me, "Hey, sexy."

Once I was out of sight behind locked doors, I responded. "How's it going?"

"My dick is so hard thinking about you right now. I haven't got to fuck since before my divorce."

Silently berating myself for giving him hope, I attempted to execute several efforts at boring or offending him into disinterest. I first explained the nuance of grad school, and then I tried to make him angry by asking what he did to make his wife leave him. Nothing seemed to bother him, so I finally decided to do the big reveal as a last-ditch effort.

I texted him, "I need to tell you something, and if it turns you off that's fine." I tried to do it as bluntly as possible, hoping the surprise would send him reeling away from me. No such luck.

The patron was still in the building when I told him this, and he came down to say goodbye to me before heading out to catch the bus. He had a look on his face that I'd seen before. Cis gay men who fetishize trans men always have a devious version of Christmas morning excitement on their faces when they find out a guy is trans. I should have known better, but it was unusual for a man to be so interested in me. For a moment, it made me feel like I had reached the pinnacle of homosexuality.

He was unlike anyone I had slept with before. By forty-something he had been married three times, spent a few years in prison for selling drugs, and lived at a men's shelter because his most recent ex-wife had gotten the house. He had an old bullet wound on his right forearm that I could never bring myself to touch or ask about. Everything about him seemed sharp and intimidating.

The first time we hooked up was at his friend's apartment. I almost bailed but managed to convince myself that it would be an adventure I could write about one day.

He was hard and half naked before I got in the door. He couldn't keep his hands off me as I examined his friend's two pet turtles with legitimate interest in the living room.

He sucked on my nipples as I asked, "Are the turtles okay? They look kind of hungry. Maybe they need some fresh water or a little snack."

I climbed the stairs to the bedroom with his fingers inside me from behind. He waited just long enough for me to ask him about his STI status and make sure he knew we were going to use condoms.

After he said, "Let me see those fat pussy lips," I felt a little uneasy with him, but I didn't put on the brakes. Afterwards, we had a conversation about naming my anatomy. I told him I preferred words like "cock," but he could never seem to stop himself from saying words that felt diluted and unpleasant for me, like "boy-clit" and "man-hole."

Even though I was no longer attracted to him after only two awkward encounters, his set of skills in bed really impressed me. He enthusiastically went down on me for record amounts of time, and I had never been touched with so much precision and understanding of the mechanics of sex. Still, I was uneasy with the way he talked about my body. We hooked up a few more times.

It took me a few weeks to understand why I felt this way, but I realized that he didn't respect me for who I was—a sexual equal. He only wanted to use my body to live out the fantasy he saw in grainy videos on free porn sites. I was a sexual object that allowed him to stay in the closet and feel good about it. He seemed to think our sex couldn't be gay if I was pre-op and let him fuck me in the front.

One day in June, he texted me, "I want to see you."

After a few hours, I responded with the truth, "I can't. My friend died last night. I need some time."

He ignored me, "Oh, I'm sorry. You want to split a hotel room?"

I finally ended it. For once, I listened to the alarms in my head, though their clanging was quiet after years of being ignored.

I just sent him a text that said, "I can't believe you. I'm done."

When I finally acknowledged those feelings, my lungs felt full to bursting, and my heart felt lighter than it had been in a long time. I realized that being strong enough to say no was profound for me. I was finally enough all on my own.

I spent years of my life unhappy with women and unhappy alone because I grew my sense of self-worth from the desires of men. If a man wanted me, I thought I owed it to myself to fuck him because I never knew if another man would ever want me again. But suddenly I felt free enough to say no.

Nothing would change about my desirability if I chose not to sleep with any guy who was interested. Another man's hands on my body were no longer what defined my self-worth. I was a gay man, with or without other men's love and interest. After all those years of searching for myself in the eyes and mouths of strangers and lovers, I ultimately found myself in my own instincts.

The G Word

Brian George Bernstein

I was fourteen when I had my first wet dream. To this day I remember every last detail. I could feel the sweat beading off our backs. His taut muscles tensed underneath my fingertips. In my dream, I was a man topping another guy. I thrusted inside him. We moaned in unison.

Up until that point, all I knew about sex came out of a few flustered flips through my friends' hentai comics, which I snuck home in my backpack, sex education courtesy of the Florida public school system (complete with PowerPoint slides starring close-up shots of gonorrhea nodules), and a few awkward chats with my mother about where babies came from. I'd never seen porn, so for the life of me I couldn't trace where the sex scenes in my wet dreams came from.

As far as I knew, I was an otherwise "normal" girl—albeit, one who used to smoosh my breasts under my palms after a shower and stuff socks in the front of my panties to simulate a bulge. I didn't know much about transgender people or that being a man was a possibility. I was a depressed teenage girl with no real sense of self, who spent the morning after that dream both trying to catch my breath and wrap my head around it.

I started dating my first girlfriend, Madeline, right out of middle school. I told myself I loved her. She was naturally blonde but constantly changed her hair color using Walgreens' bargain dye, favoring shades like an anime-esque green. She developed early, towering over most of the boys in our class. To boot, she'd been gifted with broad shoulders and a husky voice.

I'd often picture her walking down the street with guys catcalling her. Butch, and confident, she'd flex her biceps, leaving them perplexed and cowering. With my ungroomed eyebrows and sharp jaw, I was more masculine looking than most girls in my class, but next to Madeline, I looked like, well, like a girl. I tried not to think about it.

We dated for a grand total of three years. In that time we only open-mouthed kissed once. I was ashamed to let her see my body. I didn't know why. I did what I could to force myself to feel attracted to her, think of her breasts when I rubbed myself, but I could only ever sum up the sort of affection one feels for a close friend, which she was. When Madeline finally ended things over text, I found myself sighing with relief.

Throughout high school, I didn't know how to feel about men. A part of me gazed after them longingly. I would fantasize about being able to touch them, run my fingers down flat, muscular chests. I would lock my gaze onto the giddy giggling girls standing at their sides, hips meeting hips. Trying to imagine myself as one of them felt wrong.

It was the gay couples I envied. Though most of the gay men at my school and in my town couldn't walk down the street holding hands without jeers, I related to two rough, powerful bodies joining together. It was the only kind of relationship I saw myself in, but being a man's boyfriend seemed impossible.

At sixteen, I felt like I had to do something, so I decided to come out to my parents. They were sitting across from me at my mom's craft table. Mom choked up as I muttered, "I'm…a lesbian. I guess." At that time, I thought of lesbians as women who eschewed makeup whenever possible and had a serious case of penis envy (regardless of any fantasies they might have had about dominating men). My father, who while far from stoic was not one for letting the waterworks flow, teared up. It was one of the only times I would ever see him cry. Even at that tender moment of speaking my then truth, I felt as though I'd done something wrong and deceptive.

Everyone always asks me how I knew I was transgender. I guess, I've never known how to really answer that. It was never one specific moment but a dozen little ones bubbling under the surface: like how I seethed with jealousy when my brother got a basketball for his birthday and I got stuck with Polly Pockets. Or that time when a guy called me, "Sir," when I was boarding a bus, and I kept smiling for the rest of the day.

When I was eighteen years old I finally came out to myself. I'd never really met another transgender person until then, at least not in person. What little exposure I had consisted of movies like Ace Ventura, where I'd been lead to believe that trans people were deceptive drag queens. The reality of the transgender experience didn't dawn on me until I stumbled upon trans writers and video bloggers online.

I discovered men who described their experiences growing up as girls and wondering why they felt wrong and out of place. I found myself imagining what it would be like to bind my chest, inject testosterone in my thigh, and shave fuzz off of my cheeks just like they did. It was then that it finally hit me. I was one of those men.

Just as I was figuring out how I was ever going to come out to my friends and family, I met a girl online. Danielle had long brown hair that she wore tucked behind a bandana. In every single picture she pressed her round lips into a heart-shaped smile. She'd text me frequently, with messages featuring dozens of exclamation points, hearts and smileys.

"You know, I've always wanted to date a trans boy. You're going to be handsome." Her voice ran together like a breeze.

It felt validating but empty.

We never once met in person over the two and a half weeks that we dated over Skype and text. I tried and failed to imagine myself even getting undressed with her in the same room. I couldn't summon up any lust for her. The idea of having sex with her, especially with my pre-op body, befuddled me. The only time I ever felt like I wanted to be with her was when I'd imagine her transforming into a man, with biceps bulging from her pale arms and hair exploding over her chest. That's when it clicked.

I broke up with her over text and never again dated women.

I'd been out of the transgender closet for about a year before the subject of my virginity began to pain me. I was sure I reeked of virginity and inexperience. At nineteen years old I was desperate to finally start passing as a man and not as a little boy (on a good day). My friends were still calling me adorable.

I was still far too young for the sole gay bar in my small Oregon town but not too young for the hookup apps. It didn't take me long to land my first guy through Grindr.

Steve was old enough to be my father, but I told myself it didn't matter. He was either a professor or a principal. We traded a few below-the-belt pics and met up at a café downtown. We both wanted the same thing, sex. He needed to scratch his itch of experimenting with a trans guy. A win-win situation, really.

"So, uh, I'm a virgin," I confessed.

"Fine by me."

On the way to Steve's place, in his Jetta, Pat Benatar screeched over the radio. We traded awkward small talk. I tried to force back second thoughts.

"God, I remember when 9/11 happened. I was sitting in my office watching the news," he sighed. "You?"

"Oh, I was in the first grade. Teacher turned on the TV."

"Ah."

We kept sitting in uncomfortable silence for a while, until we finally rolled up to his house. As we got out of the car, he warned, "Keep quiet. My boyfriend's home."

"What?" I asked, confused.

"Open relationship."

I didn't believe him but I followed him inside anyway.

Steve's bedroom was dimly lit. The bed was set low at the foot of a wall length mirror. He lay down first, immediately stripping off his clothes. His chest was broad and lightly covered with salt and pepper hair. Pleasantly plump, faint lines of muscles protruded from underneath his tan skin. I pulled down my jeans and boxers but left my t-shirt and binder on—one more thing that would separate our bodies—I didn't want my breasts to flop around while we had sex.

With a deep breath, I got on top of him, brushing away the emptiness between my legs.

Steve was a gentle and patient lover, guiding me carefully throughout each position, giving pointers and offering techniques to try. He guided my thighs apart and thrust inside of me. After we both came, me by his hand,

and him by my mouth, I rolled next to him and wrapped my arm around his chest. A sheen of sweat had settled on us both. I inhaled the smell of his cologne.

"Wow," I said, my heart rattling in my chest. "Can, can we do that again?"

Steve laughed.

"God, you're cute," he tousled my hair. "Maybe."

We never spoke again.

I hold onto that memory. Brief as it was, it would be the last time I would have positive sex for a couple of years.

I was raped by the next guy. Still trying to pick up the pieces to this day.

I did what I could to leave it behind me.

I settled for running off with a bisexual guy, I'll call Ryan, going so far as to move down with him to Sacramento. I met Ryan on a Facebook group for self-described admirers of trans men. He was blond and rail thin, with a patchy beard that edged over his jaw.

When Ryan and I were together, I was out as male but hadn't yet started taking hormones. I was broke so I didn't have a doctor to prescribe them. On birth control, which I started so he could give up condoms, my hips and chest began to swell even further. I became a depressed mess who stress ate to cope, which in turn only made my feminine curves grow bigger. He, of course, loved it. Ryan made it no secret that he wanted me to avoid top surgery, which was, in his words, "mutilation." All the better to ensure there'd be breast milk handy when he inevitably knocked me up. He promised he'd share with the kid.

I'll give him some credit. He never misgendered me or used my old name. Still, I never once felt like I was his boyfriend.

"Gay men don't like pussy," he often said. "Grosses them out."

"How do you know what every single gay guy likes?" I replied.

"If they liked you, they're not really gay."

"So you're saying I'm not a man?"

"Of course you are," he choked. "It's just that you're…"

"What?"

"You're different. That's all."

Ryan took a long draw off of his cigarette. "Your body's just female. Nothing wrong with that."

I turned away, like usual, and put an end to the conversation. Like clockwork, he apologized, called me handsome, and we fucked exactly how he liked it. This ritual repeated itself almost weekly.

The night before I left him for good, it got worse. We argued. I had a panic attack. He left me alone for most of the night until just as I was about to drift off to sleep and then he came into bed.

"Come on baby, don't do this," he slid a hand between my legs.

I closed my thighs together like a vice trap.

He yanked them apart. "Let me make it up to you."

"Not tonight."

He got on top of me. Lying still, I let him do what he wanted so he'd leave me alone and let me sleep. I felt dirty and sick the next morning. I threw up bile and couldn't keep anything down.

I tried to let it go. I even took him back not long after I moved back to Oregon, and we dated long distance, but I couldn't forget what he did. I tried to summon up some kind of grief when I blocked his number. All I could do was sigh and try to figure out if it was wrong to enjoy feeling relief.

Sometimes, I'm hesitant about the reality of dating again. The pool of gay and bi men who are willing to date a trans guy like me feels limited to nonexistent, especially because I'm still unsure about bottom surgery. I've had hookups and friends with benefits but as far as a long-term relationship, I'm not expecting much.

As of now, I'm on hormones, in therapy for my PTSD, and coming closer to having top surgery. I'm doing what I can to get through the days. Eventually, I figure I'll feel confident enough to open up to another man, whether he is cis or trans like me.

BLUE COUCH

JACK WHACKER

I was twenty-seven years old, less than a year on testosterone, when my sex drive revved up, feeling like it was pushing ninety mph every hour of the day. Taking "T" changed how I thought about sex; it went from a want to a need. I could be at work, sitting quietly at my desk, doing a mundane task and then it would happen, my underwear or pants would shift and my growing cock would cry out for attention.

I would sit there in my rolling office chair, crossing and uncrossing my legs, leaning forward, to the back, to the side, holding on tightly to the plastic armrests in attempted resistance, only making it worse. Every shift made my cock grow larger. It felt like it gained a tyrant's impatience, demanding touch. All I could think was, "Can I really jack off in the bathroom?" I never did, for fear that one of my coworkers would figure it out or somehow catch me—both unlikely scenarios.

The first step to releasing the mounting wave of desire was to invest in a collection of sex toys. My first attempt to satiate my cock's desires was with a new vibrator. The new gadget provided a brief respite from this overwhelming need, so I purchased more pleasures. I bought a small butt plug, then soon after a medium sized one, and then finally a large one. Over time, several new cocks of different shapes and sizes were added to my collection, some with vibratory capabilities. I explored sensations, and my body celebrated every moment that it was allowed to finally release the sexual pressure that had built during the day. I became fixated on how to get the most sensation all at once. I learned that I could take a cock up front and in my ass and then stimulate myself—pure, powerful, pleasure.

This process of masturbatory exploration launched a full-on sexual awakening that necessitated finding anonymous sexual partners. This was prior to dating apps, so I was on a one-way road to Craigslist. I decided to be bold, reach out to the world, and announce that I did not know anything about dick, but was more than ready to learn. In a Casual Encounters post, I shouted to the San Francisco Bay Area as loud as I knew how, "I'm ready!"

> FTM 4 M: Looking for someone to teach me how to give a blowjob.

> Super horny, non-op on top (still have boobs), on t, have a giant t-cock (hormonally grown clit), hairy legs, some facial hair. I'm tallish, dark hair, average body. I am looking for a nice guy, to tell me how to suck his cock, and fuck around. Not sure about sex, limited experience. I only have safe and sane sex, condoms are a must! Must be willing to meet in public first! Must send face and body pic! I will trade pic for pic. Must know what FTM is and have some experience! Can host or travel.

Not surprisingly, my inbox was flooded by men that would love to teach me how to suck their cocks to their liking. I sorted through the emails, eliminating the ones that didn't follow my rules right away. If they wrote nothing about themselves and only wrote, "Suck it," they were trashed, as were the ones who failed to acknowledge that they in fact had any previous experience with, or even knew, what FTM was. The ones who unfortunately said something like, "I've always wanted to meet a guy with a pie," were gleefully discarded. Once the upper crust of anonymous sex candidates was identified, it came down to their looks: both face and dick pics mattered in my assessment. In the end, there were a scant few who seemed like they met my specifications enough to maybe fuck.

I met one guy who followed all of my basic rules. He sent a face, body and dick pic; he expressed having knowledge of and confidence in working with men's bodies, both cis and trans; he was willing to meet in public; endure random "get to know you" questions; and was eager to provide dick sucking tips and tricks! He told me a little about himself: He lived nearby, worked early mornings, and enjoyed cooking on the weekends. He did not show any early warning signs of being a serial killer, so I agreed to a drink and conversation, with the hope of a blowjob.

We met at the dive bar down the street from my house. The sun was shining brightly and the wind gently blew on a late summer afternoon. I nervously stood in front of the bar waiting for this mystery man to arrive.

I had seen a picture of his face, but feared I would not recognize him in public.

He arrived and I thought he was handsome, but horribly dressed. He was a little shorter than me, with thick brown hair, a short, well-kept beard, a warm smile and a paunch. He was wearing baggy jeans that barely stayed up when he walked with an oversized, gray, Oakland Raiders t-shirt and dirty, untied, whitish sneakers. He winked and said, "You're Jack?"

I smiled back and reluctantly offered my hand to shake. He countered my move and offered a hug. We sat down at the bar and talked about our jobs. He worked in construction, which I thought was hot. I told him about my job at the coffee shop. We both related to being tired from our early morning schedules. He seemed friendly, but not someone whom I thought would be a friend.

After two drinks and a shot of whiskey I asked, "Want to go back to my place?"

"Yeah, great!"

He paid our tab and we started walking towards my apartment. The sun had dropped in the sky while we were inside and the breeze had started to roll in from the ocean. My skin was chilled, partly due to weather and partly in anticipation. I was terrified I would let him down.

"So, I know I've told you this, but, I've never really done this, you know, given a blowjob before…but I want to."

"It's ok, it's really not that hard."

We walked into my apartment and I started to take him on a brief tour of my small, one bedroom home. As we passed my bedroom door I refused to open it. I worried that if we went in there we would automatically fuck, and I wasn't ready.

We sat down on my blue couch, arm to arm, making out with just our necks and heads turned towards each other. It was like I was thirteen again, trying to kiss my boyfriend in the movie theater without fully turning my body, separated by the hard armrest of the theater chairs. His hand ran up and down my thigh, getting closer and closer to my cock. I felt the burning desire, but for what I was unsure.

I decided to change the scene. I took off my t-shirt and underwear, still wearing my binder, and knelt down on the wood floor in front of him, "How should I start?"

He unzipped his pants and revealed a small, soft, penis, laying on a thin bed of pubic hair. "Put it in your hands and just feel it for a second, then lick the tip." I followed his every direction.

"Open your mouth and let it slide in…good."

I slowly and cautiously ran my mouth down his cock and I felt it grow and become hard. He let out a groan and then forcefully slid his cock far in my mouth, hitting the back of my throat. I gagged, coughed and my eyes watered.

"Sorry!" he said, "I got carried away."

We stopped for a minute and I got a glass of water for each of us. During our blowjob intermission, I asked, "Is it going ok? Does it feel ok?"

"Yeah, ready for more?"

I knelt down again and put his dick in my hand; he was soft again, so I tried to lick it, but nothing happened.

"I don't know what's wrong…" he said.

He played with his cock some more, but wasn't able to get it hard again. "You're so sexy, I don't know what's wrong. This never happens."

After each of those comments I thanked him, or reassured him that it was ok, and even chuckled, because I had nothing to compare it to.

He left my house in a somewhat somber mood. "Thanks for having me," he said. I thought I would never see him again and fretted about him leaving unsatisfied by my inadequate skills.

I regained my confidence when I received an email from him, "Hey, what ya doing tonight? Want to give it another try?"

"Of course! Cum over!" I was grateful to have the rare opportunity of blowjob redemption, while receiving some hands on sexual education.

That night went down similarly to the last time we met. But this time I knew the first steps. Play with his cock gently in my hands to wake it up, then lick the tip. After that, open wide, curl the lips around your teeth and gently bob up and down.

The intention of the first date was to provide formal education, with clear direction, on how to perform a blowjob. He was happy to let his preferences be known. While I was sucking his cock, I looked towards him to try and gauge his pleasure. He was smiling, watching closely, and said, "Try running your tongue from my taint," he leaned back on the couch and spread his legs apart. He pointed to the spot where he wanted me to start, "to the tip of my penis."

"Ok." I slowly dragged my tongue across his skin. He exhaled a low, slow sigh. I resumed to sucking him off.

"Now get my cock really wet, sloppy." I let the drool spill from my mouth.

"Now put a hand near the base, be firm, but gentle. Never too hard." I practiced swiveling my hand around his cock. "Now try sucking it and stroking it." I did. It felt complicated, like it would require practice to get all parts working together, perfectly in sync.

He moaned as I awkwardly twisted and jerked on his cock, while taking him shallowly, then deeply in my mouth.

I took a break to catch my breath, looked him in the eye and said, "I like your cock!"

"I like you," he said, staring straight at me.

I went back to my blowjob lesson. He breathed in deeply and then said, "Never forget about the balls!"

He laid back on the couch, again with his legs spread, with one hand he stroked his cock, and with the other he cupped and gently squeezed his balls.

Blowjobs started to feel like a choreographed dance—forward, back, slide, pause, spin! I then added the ball cupping to the base holding, tongue licking, and mouth sucking dance routine. While following the choreography he stated with a small chuckle, "I like tea bagging, it's one of my favorite things!"

"We've got to keep something to learn about next time." I smiled, then happily resumed sucking his cock.

He came, squirting a liquid medal of honor on my ass cheek.

"Hope to see you again. Next time it won't be all about me," he said.

"Ditto. Sounds fun."

We kissed good night. I felt relieved and proud. On my second attempt I had successfully brought a man to orgasm using only my hands, mouth and tongue. I felt like I had magical powers. Little did I know, how easy it can be to make a guy cum, if you are willing to try.

Anal sex entered my mind, by way of a certain type of magic in my early

twenties. My partner was a light sleeper who was plagued by insomnia. I was a restless sleeper, sleeping heavily, but continually tossing and turning in bed, and narrated my nightly dreams, as she lay awake.

One morning over coffee, she cracked a smile and said, "You'll never believe what you said last night!"

"Tell me!" I said with anticipation.

"You said, and I'm being real, 'FUCK ME IN THE ASS!'" *She yelled this out. "You sat straight up in your sleep and joyously yelled,* 'Fuck me in the ass!' *Anything you want to tell me?" She leaned in and gave me a kiss on the cheek. We had never tried anything with our butts, so I assumed she was quite surprised.*

"Dreams are crazy, I have no idea what that was about. Sorry, if I kept you up."

The next time I saw the construction worker I was determined to have ass sex. I was a connoisseur of ass fucking. I had taken tons of dildos and an occasional small fist of a trans man, but I had never done it with a cis cock. Unexplainably, I was more intimidated by a cock being propelled by at least two hundred pounds of a cis man.

He arrived at my house wearing baggy jeans, a plaid flannel and well-worn, brown, workman's boots. I had prepared for hours by not eating lunch, doing four fleet enemas, trimming and shaving pubes, and then tidying up the place. He arrived and I was so nervous. We made light conversation, but I was distracted by my mounting desire to, and irrational fears of, him fucking my ass. I sped things up to reduce the conversation. As he spoke, I started to undress myself and him, rubbing on his chest. "Do you want to go in my room?" I asked.

He followed me and we shed our remaining clothing. As we entered the room, he dropped to the floor to suck my cock. I got hard and horny. I let him suck me until I could no longer wait to feel him inside me. I looked down to him and said in an authoritative tone, "I want you to fuck me in the ass."

He stood up and I turned around. He stroked his hard cock, slathering it and my ass with lube, and he pushed into me. At first, I was too tight. I reached back and fingered myself, and my ass relaxed. Then his cock gently slid into me, inching forward, until he rested to let me accommodate his full size.

He laid me flat on the bed with a pillow under my stomach, angling my butt up toward the ceiling. He lay on top of me, his beer belly fit the curve of my back, and he thrust deep into me. He played my body like a cellist would play a perfectly strung cello. He curved his body around me, pulling me closer to him, pressing into and releasing my strings, and leaning in for deep strokes and powerful vibratos. My body was the instrument, with curves, rigidity, movement, and the ability to release deep tones and vibration. I came with his cock deep inside me.

This began our sexual liberation. What had been one hot ass fuck for me became one giant ignition switch, to boldly go where neither of us had gone before. He and I both had histories of being in mostly monogamous relationships, with some periods of casual sex in between them. We both had been sexually active, but neither of us had done things that were too outside of the box.

We started to explore things we had never done before. Initially, we started out light with some 69ing, a blowjob on a hiking trail, and having sex at other people's homes. I was perpetually house sitting to make extra money, he would often come and visit, allowing us to have local sexcations. As time passed we got more confident, explored more positions: standing up, upside down, me fucking him, in every angle. We tried it all. Then came the glory holes, the threesomes, the sex on the sidewalk, and my first double penetration. The two of us together were insatiable.

Around our one year fuckaversary, we were still in our stride. He had been over twice that week already, and we had been passionately pressing our sweaty bodies together through the heat wave. I was on all fours, looking toward the wall, he was stroking my cock and fucking my ass, "Ah, Jack, you feel so good." He would thrust into me more, kissing me on my back or biting my neck. Sometimes he would get tough on me and pull me back by my shoulders, or force my neck back by pulling on my short brown hair, always pushing further into me. "Ah Jack, I love your ass." He continually said my name, as he thrusted, "ah Jack, yes, Jack, oh, ya, so fucking hot, Jack!"

I couldn't focus. The truth is, I had never learned his name. For months I had worried about the day when I would need to say his name and wouldn't be able to. In my phone I had entered him under the name "Blue

Couch," the location of my privately tutored, blowjob lesson, a moment never to be forgotten.

Each thrust released a memory of how I had tried to uncover his name, I clenched down as he fucked my ass hard, the way I liked it, trying to prevent the words from flowing out. I panicked. There was this overwhelming pressure to say his name, but I couldn't. Something had to give. I felt ridiculous! I had let this man access all my holes, and we had fucked so intimately, passionately, and roughly, but I could not ask him his name, why?

With as much force as a lodged piece of meat being expelled by way of a Heimlich maneuver, the words came out, "What's your name?"

He stopped fucking me. I was still looking away from him; I felt embarrassed. I don't know how, but I knew this moment was destined to happen. Months before, I had reached his voicemail. An automated voice message said, "You've reached the voice mailbox of," and then his baritone voice shouted out his name indistinguishably. With hope that others could decipher his name I enlisted their help, but no one could make out the deep, rumbling, grunt of a name.

One day my friend had called to further investigate. The construction worker answered, and my friend greeted him with, "Who's this?" Like he suddenly caught him in a trap.

"Who's this? You called me!"

"Oh, um, your number is in my phone, but I don't have a name. Can I put a name with this?"

"Who is this? I don't have your number in my phone."

"Sorry, wrong number." My friend hung up. That was my last phone call attempt made to solve this mystery.

After my announcement, he laid down in the bed next to me; I curled up with my head on his chest. I inhaled deeply, the smell of sweat and Old Spice rising up from his warmed body. He had one hand behind his head and his other slowly stroking his cock. He had a puzzled look on his face and said, "Joe. My name is Joe. You really didn't know my name all this time?"

I wondered if he was playing an internal reel of our previous encounters, searching for a memory, no matter how distant, of me crying out his name. I explained nervously, "Well, I guess we learned each other's names on the first date, but I forgot yours. Then things went kind of bad and you left, and I didn't think I'd see you again. But then I did, and it felt wrong to ask your name, because you remembered mine. The longer it went on the worse it got." It came out in an anxious tone that sounded like I was a little drunk and disorganized.

He laughed it off and sighed, "All this time you didn't know my name… ha!"

Suddenly, I couldn't hold anything back, there was a freedom in my confession. The words started running out of my mouth. "I tried to figure it out by checking our old emails. But you never signed them. Same thing in text. My friends told me to check your wallet when you went to the bathroom, but I didn't want to invade your privacy. I even once had a friend try to call and ask you, but that really didn't work." As the words left my mouth, internally I wondered why it had seemed so much easier to do all the research, instead of just asking his name. I suspect he wondered the same thing.

He rolled over on his side, looked me square in the eye and asked, "Anything else you want to know? Now's a good time to ask."

I laughed, still slightly uncomfortable, and kissed him. I ran my hand down his chest, around his dick and down to his balls. As usual he rose to the occasion. He buried himself deep into me, I called out, "Ah, Joe! Keep fucking it, Joe!"

Sexually, we were a perfect match. There was nothing that we couldn't try together and every time we hooked up it was amazing. After three years, we'd had sex hundreds of times, which meant that we had hundreds of hours of pre-and post-coitus conversations. Through those talks, he learned about my conservative hometown, family, career goals and current work drama. I knew that his family was what he called "big 'C' Catholic," primarily to explain their anti-gay views. This version of Catholic guilt resulted in him living two lives, the life he actually lived and the life he shared with his family. In real life he worked in construction. He was closeted at work, due to the hyper masculinity of his work environment. Outside of work he had a few gay friends who he saw on the weekends. He had lived with a couple of boyfriends in the past, but had rented two bedroom apartments and always presented his partner as a roommate—sleeping in a separate room. He refused to come out to his family.

Three years is a long time to get drinks and dinner, have conversations, mind blowing sex and overnights together, and keep it casual, no strings attached. One time after a somewhat romantic night of sex, with less pounding and more kissing and bodies pressing into each other, he said, "What do you think about this being more?"

"What does that mean?" I asked.

"Like my boyfriend. Like you text me good morning, instead of I want you inside me. Or, at least good morning first."

"Would you tell people about me?"

"Our friends."

"We don't have friends, I've never met anyone in your life," I said. Despite the amount of time we had spent together, I had never introduced him to my friends, and he had not introduced me to his. From the perspective of our friends, the unknown individual (he or I) was seen as mysterious, somewhat questionable in existence, maybe mythical, who was only referenced in the occasional retellings of our primal encounters.

He rolled over onto me, his chest pressing into mine; he nuzzled his face up next to my cheek. His beard lightly brushed my face as he spoke to me. "I mean we could tell our own friends about it. I could meet some of your friends. That'd be cool."

"What about your family. Would they ever know?"

"You know that's complicated. Why do they need to know?" He rolled away from me.

He knew as well as I that our relationship would always be a secret. He was very close to his family, always wanting their approval and always choosing to conceal his truths. Through much conversation, he saw my point. I would not be with someone if I felt hidden. I had done too much hiding in my life already.

Joe stayed in my life for six years. He was always kind and made me feel sexy no matter how my body shifted. He saw me at the start of my transition with hormones, when the hair grew in on my body and fell out from my head, and the binder's camouflage remained until it was made irrelevant by chest surgery. He saw my body continually change, my voice crack and then deepen, and my libido reach a welcomed plateau. In time, the blue couch was replaced but not upgraded, leaving a clear image in my mind of the moment I learned how to give an exceptional blowjob on a wonderful guy, who allowed me to pursue any and all of my desires.

THE PAST IN
THE PRESENT

ISHMAEL DICKINSON

"I love you, Harris. I always have." Leo sipped his shot of Casadores Reposado and took a drag of his cigarette. "I want to marry you. Let's get married and move to New York." He leaned back onto the bright yellow and red mural, fitting perfectly between outlines of figures—and cocks—evoking Keith Haring.

Tequila, Leo and I were a profoundly sensuous combination, but I had not consumed so much in the backroom of the Powerhouse that a marriage proposal did not paralyze my libido. What happened to the dirty talk and group sex that this backroom is famous for?

"I love you Leo, but we haven't seen each other in a year!" I leaned over, put one hand on his pec and the other around his neck so that I could feel his soft, thick, long hair. We kissed. I probed his mouth with my tongue, tweaked his nipple, and then slid my hand down his abs and into his lap where his cock was resting on his leg, like petrified wood, under his black Dickies.

He pulled away and locked eyes, "Let's go to my place. Will you fuck me, Harris?" I grabbed his hand, pulled him off the bench, and we flew out the steel door to Dore Alley.

I slumped into her large, gently worn, brown leather armchair and inhaled the familiar smells of my therapist's office—her collection of classic psychoanalytic texts and fresh flowers. This week white gardenias were spilling over the precast concrete mantel under a ray of golden light penetrating the magnolia tree outside her bay window. The southern exposure always kept her office on the warmer side.

"You know…that I choose to sit in your beautiful Presidio office and privately confess to you my joys and my pain is a great tragedy of American capitalism. Especially since Google knows all my life's filthy details anyway."

I watched Joan press her lips together in sync with her narrowing bespectacled eyes and nod slowly. As her impeccably coiffed straight brown bob swung gently back and forth, the creases of her mouth pointed to the floor, and her crisp white wool suit held the rest of her long, narrow body motionless.

"We need a real life infrastructure," I continued, "of collective caring and love out there for everyone—all my poor, queer friends—to engage. Together. Therapy is so isolating…and expensive—even with your generous sliding scale."

"In the meantime," Joan countered, "while the revolution germinates, Harris, take advantage of this time to reflect and reset. I know you appreciate the social and political contexts of your therapy and your life, but why don't we pick up where we left off last week, hmm? Wasn't it an older gentleman here on business? Why do you think you're so enamored with all this anonymous sex?"

I stroked my mustache a few times and then liberated my mouth from the cover of my hand. "I think my initial foray into Craigslist, along with my visits to Blow Buddies with Seamus and Art, when I first moved out here was so mind-blowing that I keep looking for excitement and new formations in these anonymous meetings. I just wish the Internet hadn't made cruising so easy. And so alienating."

My heart pounded when I saw his email land in my inbox, from "MASTER SIR" on March 23, 2003. I opened it: "41 Los Reyes Terrace. Come to the flat on the second floor at 2pm. The door will be open. Let yourself in. Take off all your clothes and put on the blindfold that you will find resting on the table in the foyer. Once you are naked and blindfolded, say, 'Sir, your boy is ready for you.' I will lead you into the dungeon and begin our session. As we discussed, we will start with restraints and some light flogging and move into heavier paddling and caning along with some cock and ball torture. I will see how you are doing and from there we will proceed into some bondage with electric shock stimulation and hot wax, and then I will restrain and fuck you mercilessly in the sling. You know the safe word."

~~~~

"Then again," I continued, "I think initially I was acting out some anger about the unrequited love I had for my former therapist, but surely it's also alleviating some deeper rage. I think fucking cis men literally fucks with them in other ways whether they are gay or straight or something else."

I looked up at Joan who returned her gaze toward me, though it had been somewhere else. Is she listening to me? Is she feeling a hint of my turmoil? Or is she thinking about her next client or her lover at home? What is stopping me from asking her?

"The business man—he was rather bland with a little charm. You're right—he's the older, white, investment banker guy I met a couple weeks ago at his hotel on Nob Hill." Joan was now looking out the window again, apparently distracted by her own thoughts. "There's something that feels very freeing for me about anonymous sex," I said. "Of course, I never would have imagined or wanted this for myself as a woman. But as a man, I still get to see a side of men that I was not able to see before—like a tenderness and a vulnerability there that I never recognized."

"You know, Harris, you mention your rage, and I can't help but notice that this man—or the scene—sounds a bit like the man who raped you before you began to transition."

Joan noticed my discomfort, as I clenched my crossed arms to remind myself to stay in the room.

"He was a married, investment banker you met in the bar at the Four Seasons, right?"

"That's true," I said, "but this banker guy had a really gentle way about him. When I got to his room, he was getting off the phone with his wife. He seemed genuinely sad that he could not have sex with his wife anymore. And, now he's having sex with a trans guy? I don't know what to make of that, but at the end of the day I just really like to have sex now. A lot."

Joan kicked her legs up on her ottoman, crossed them, and pushed her glasses up on the bridge of her nose. She was listening to me. She had heard about so many different tricks at this point: older, younger, white, black, Latin, Asian, skateboarders, businessmen, cab drivers, construction workers, social workers, scientists, queer, gay, bi, trans, straight, married, recently divorced, vanilla, foot fetishists, tops, bottoms, big guys, leather daddies, bears, twinks, hippies and punks. When I told her about the San Francisco Opera diva who taught me how to deep throat cocks, I wondered if she knew him.

"There's this really cute guy I met last month. He's young—maybe 25—a white, skater kid that comes in from Vegas to see his rich, divorced sister once a month. He's tall and lanky with long, blond hair—the kind of guy I would get crushed out on as a teenager. We fucked in the most random places. A hotel hallway, the park on Russian Hill, the beach. He is almost as hot as the young, quiet black kid from San Francisco State who I see every once in a while. The one who loves to fuck trans guys in the ass."

Joan's eyes were wider now though her pupils were so dark that I could not tell if she was focused on me or something beyond me, through me. She leaned her head to the left as if she had a thought.

"What is it?" I demanded.

"I just wonder what you think about all this physical intimacy you are enjoying? I know a lot about these other men now, but where are you? Beyond the thrill and the pleasure, what does it mean to you?"

I felt a heaviness like my body was melding into the leather chair. I was suddenly flushed with heat and the room started to feel like it was spinning. Why does there have to be more to this than pure pleasure? I took a deep breath and closed my eyes for a moment. I thought about my old therapist. How I'd left her so abruptly.

"Well, it does seem to take away from my capacity for emotional intimacy. It's like I don't believe that's possible or maybe even desirable for myself. I've tried with a handful of people since I've lived here. More than that really. Nothing seems to take."

I thought about the blank stare on the twink's face when I informed him that I was trans. He'd been chasing me around San Francisco for so long. I was the first trans guy he had ever met. How was that possible in this city?

"Cis gay guys get weirded out by me. Trans guys are too busy navel-gazing and documenting their transitions. The only trans woman I've been with was for a couple of BDSM sessions, and the cis women I've dated want a monogamous relationship, or a really butch-femme kind of deal, or someone who is totally emotionally available. I'm not there."

I felt my throat close up, forcing me to swallow in the way one does when they are about to cry, but I hadn't cried in years. I took another long, deep breath through my nose and slowly let the air out through my mouth.

"Maybe, the most interesting fun—the best energy—is when Seamus and Art and I pick up a guy at the Powerhouse or the Hole in the Wall and have sex together in the backroom or in the alley."

"I think it's really fucked up that you can't commit to me because you want to fuck other guys. That really hurts, Harris."

It was one of those warm, blue sky, sun-soaked September weekdays to sit in a crowded Dolores park and settle our score. The only problem was that we had an audience on all sides: hipsters and hippies everywhere drinking tallboys, playing drums, and smoking weed. "Doesn't anybody ever work in this city?" I directed my indignation toward the gaggle of twenty-something year-old, blond, white women burning sage on a blanket next to us. "I'm sorry. I really like you, Ted, but I need to have these other outlets. I really like to fuck cis guys. I need that for myself and I thought I was pretty clear about that part of my life with you."

"What's wrong with our sex?!" Ted raised his voice, and the gaggle of women next to us stopped laughing. "We can have more sex," Ted explained. "We have great sex." I could see his eyes watering through his bright red, Warby Parker frames. It reminded me of the last time we sat in this park together. Happier times. When he helped me redirect a political campaign that I was working on. Ted is masterful at messaging.

"Yes, the sex is great! That's not the point. Well, maybe it is the point. I also want sex that comes without everything else."

"I don't understand that. You're being a dick."

"Yes, that is also the point. I am a dick—so, let me have this outlet for my dickishness." Ted jerked his head backwards and his mouth fell open and made a breathy sound of exasperation. I was even surprised at how cold I sounded.

"Sorry, Harris." His voice wavered. "I'm done." Ted shook his head full of tight brown curls that framed his now very red cheeks. He hoisted himself up and sashayed down the hill into a sea of blonde locks and man-buns. I pulled my phone from my pocket to see if my new trick had emailed.

No messages.

Summer Body

Julian Shendelman

1.

Remember that Valentine's day episode of Friends
Rachel plucks a polaroid out of Monica's hand
Scotty Jarret, wearing a sweater—except he isn't

They squeal and toss him into the pyre and
the stench of burning hair lodges in my head
Spent years nauseated until I grew my own
a garden I planted in my sleep
the chia pet I never ordered
the bridge between my scalp and ass

Every partner pets me like a dog
searches my belly for fleas
to crush between the fingernails
of the pearlescent sloping hands
of his slick arms, bare shoulders, pristine back

So when the opportunity presented itself
I fucked my clone
(it is worth noting that the biggest difference
between a clone and an identical twin
is context, or the lack thereof
which is to say
I didn't like him
but he paid for dinner)

At his apartment
I kneel and admire the length and depth
welcome him into me
wrap my fingers in the thick carpet of his spine
drenched with sweat and remember
Scotty Jarret and my swimming father and realize
I too am a sweaterman now
and the sweaterman above me cums and rolls over

2.
Sprawled beside the neighborhood pool
I let the sun slurp the water off my skin and
sweat like oiled rotisserie chicken
Beyond me, the end of the cul de sac
a trail of flip flop dents from my childhood home
to the pool I kissed in, pissed through my swim suit
in the deep end, bobbed for licorice in the shallows
sucked down chlorinated water until
flapping home again, steam in my wake

I used to go with my father
co-chair of the board at This & That
underinsured hourglass draining at the toes
swam with my hands
buried in his back hair and held tight
dove until the pressure built in our ears
skimmed along the wavering cement
We watched the garbage that collected there
abandoned leaves and vagrant bandaids
like floating members of a drowned country club
Long dad-toes, nearly prehensile
propelled us from the smoky lair
busting through the ceiling into
unforgiving wind and shattered water

gasping for air
thirsty for time

The gauzy summers of little girls on his back
like "a little piece of grit to build a pearl around"
something to turn over in my mouth
and harden, a marble with a date stamp
or something slippery behind my lips
a polaroid to keep in my pocket
a portable poolscape to sink in

PART III
GAY/QUEER CIS MEN

I Reserve the Right to Love Whomever I Want

Mudhillun "Moo" MuQaribu`

Introduction

T he year was 2003. Lawrence v. Texas and Goodridge v. Department of Public Health were being decided in favor of the queer community in the supreme courts of Massachusetts and the U.S., respectively. California, Pennsylvania and Kentucky were enacting nondiscrimination legislation that explicitly included gender identity. I was a super-duper senior at the University of Michigan in Ann Arbor, one of the two liberal "islands in the Midwest," as we liked to brag, the other being Chicago. It was a very PC campus, which easily rubbed off on me. Indeed, there was even a noticeable queer presence (and accompanying consciousness-raising) that I was able to tap into as a super-duper newbie queer completing year three of a sexless coming out journey. This was the beginning of my process of sloughing off some of my Detroit- and Islamic-perspectives and norms, which, in turn, allowed me to imagine all the possibilities open for exploration if I could just get over my fear of sex and tap into the freedom it enabled.

Templates of Gendered Desire

Enter Riley and Jordan, two androgynous "pocket gays" who tickled my fancy. Jordan was a cisgender male undergrad and a sissy in all the right ways: slim, slight, high-cheekboned, sharp-tongued, petite, short-haired-though-long-on-top, dirty blond, expressive. Meanwhile, Riley was a short, quiet, dark-haired, dark-eyed, mysterious, trans male townie—also petite, with a spiky buzz-cut and full, inviting, rose-colored lips and diminutive enough to blend into the background if not attended to. Both were white and from relatively typical Euro-American ethnic backgrounds. Both were very small in relation to my 6'2" wiry frame: an important coup I'd pulled off in late adolescence, having been a bag of bones, the runt of a brood of 11+ kids for at least 5 years until my younger siblings made it 14+. Riley and Jordan were idols of mine for all the man-hours they were putting in at the office and at the forefront of "The Movement" on campus. Furthermore, both were, in some ways, gender-nonconforming in presentation and unapologetic about it, which attracted my (then) sexually repressed desires.

I imagined ravishing Jordan by tapping into his compact, flexible, former-gymnast frame spurred, in part, by his ability to make himself heard despite his small stature. In my mind it would be like all the stereotypically loud and aggressive straight porn I'd ever been exposed to. Riley, however, I saw as a bit more subtle, more of a quiet personality, more delicate. With him, I envisaged a much more tentative, tender and mindful experience. Unfortunately, or perhaps fortunately, I never acted on my puppy dog, newbie desire for either of them, engaging only in the stereotypically cinematic and cerebral sex in my imagination. Instead, I found myself using library organizing time and volunteering otherwise around the campus LGBT office as a way to procrastinate my sexual identity formation, a coping mechanism free of any actual physical sexual exploration to deal with my fear, internalized homophobia and ignorance of gay sex. It was my time of being a pensive gay instead of a practicing gay.

At the time, I started sharing and reworking the narrative of my coming out in panel presentations on- and off- campus with other volunteers. One person, Rochelle, had experience in identity formation that included aspects of more fluid bisexual and lesbian identities. Hearing Rochelle's coming out story and how she conceptualized and presented herself made a very strong impression on me. Rochelle proclaimed to the audience that, above all else, transcending labels and experiences was who she was: "I reserve the right to love anyone I want."

I found Rochelle's exclamation to be liberating. It wasn't just that I could forestall foreclosure on an already stigmatized identity, it was that I could create a dynamic identity that didn't require foreclosure in the first place. With a few tweaks involving the metaphor of an "identity box," and a joke of warning listeners not to be surprised if I jumped out of the neat, convenient one society usually provides us queers for presenting ourselves to others, I was off to narrating my own identity tale in the same reserved yet liberating manner as Rochelle. I never made my disparate desires for

Jordan or Riley known, but I held out hope that I might experience them in one way or another one day.

SEXUAL MATURATION

After college, I relocated to the Mid-Atlantic. Largely separated from the community of campus activists, I put away many of my progressive notions and settled into the "monoculture" that was (cis) male and gay communities.

When I finally did start having sex in the community, I was what some would have proudly called a "gold star gay," having had no prior penetrative sexual experience with those assigned female at birth (AFAB). It wasn't something that I paraded proudly or misogynistically; rather, it was just something I was aware of as a fact of my history. In fact, I still had some wacky, leftover desire to "out-fuck" straight guys with women. Somehow, being able to please a woman "on her terms" was, for me, some bizarro badge of street-cred akin to the common gay desire to bed a straight guy. In retrospect, it's hard to tease out the internalized homophobia from just plain ole' curiosity or latent bisexuality. However, I've always taken the "on her terms" part as a mark of pride, as far as learning the lessons of consent and mutual fulfillment from queer circles and women's studies classes.

Fast forward, a little over a decade to mid-2015. My newfound interest in HIV prevention via PrEP (pre-exposure prophylaxis, a program involving a daily oral pill called Truvada and quarterly medical monitoring visits) led me into advocacy and back to communities of progressives. I had just stepped up to help moderate a popular (and growing) PrEP-focused, queer inclusive sexual health group on Facebook. The (aspirational) ethos of the group was fact based, sex positive, poz friendly, trans-masculine-friendly and (cis and trans) lady-friendly, although the main participants were cis gay dudes, many of whom were HIV negative.

One of my fellow moderators was a trans dude I'll call Bill. Not unlike Riley or Jordan in stature and features, Bill tickled my fancy such that I found myself crushing on him after a while, enthralled with his Movement-cred, experience and smile. His total package reminded me of my desires from that earlier era. I idolized Bill for the work he was doing in the community and came to value the consciousness-raising that came from working with and learning alongside him. Meanwhile, I was choking on making my interest known to him because, at times, I felt ashamed of my ignorance and afraid to make a mistake. Thus, history came to repeat itself.

AARON

With the era of Grindr and Scruff in full swing and trans-gay/bi visibility growing in mainly cis-gay/bi spaces, I found myself coming across more and more trans guys online and them coming across me too. I must have also picked up a few pearls of wisdom from Bill about presenting oneself to and interacting with members of other multiply marginalized groups. Embracing the sex positive and gender expansive ideals of our Facebook group in my life elsewhere (as well as the relative safety, distance and anonymity of the queer social media at my fingertips), I began signaling to others on Scruff and Grindr that I was open to the possibility of connecting with trans guys if they were open to the same possibility with me. I chatted with a few online, and then I met Aaron.

Aaron was an observant Jew navigating the new terrain of male identity in his religious community and in his soon-to-be profession as an educator. He was on the shorter side of average height for a guy (though visiting the gym regularly ensured that he wasn't petite like my earlier crushes), had his original equipment above and below the belt, displayed closely cropped, rascally curls of ginger that spilled into a light dusting of a scruffy chin-strap beard covering cherubic cheeks, full lips that curled and pouted, yearning to be kissed, and juuust the right endearing ratio of assertiveness-to-awkwardness.

I remember our first few face-to-face meetings. Aaron was in the process of exiting a relationship that was crashing and burning and needed a no-fuss bed buddy/stress reliever during the homestretch of his teacher-training program. Meanwhile, I was trans curious but hyper-aware of the concept of "Schrödinger's Rapist," among many AFAB people. Indeed, my only experience dating and hooking up was with other cis guys who, like me, often made decisions without factoring physical safety into the equation so consciously or viscerally. I also feared saying the wrong thing, not being "progressive enough," or damaging him by not being able to "get it up." It was a selfish quest to procure progressive points or feed the fear of identity foreclosure from earlier self-iterations rather than having a real desire for the individual in front of me. I suppose, in retrospect, it was good that I hadn't actually had much prior experience with women to taint my approach or overstock my self-confidence.

By our third meeting, Aaron was comfortable enough to come over to my place for Netflix ("and chill," as it turned out) and watch the new season of "Orange is the New Black." As the first episode stretched out, the personal space between us on the couch shrank, overlapped, and then disappeared. Sitting next to him, a knuckle on a knee, a thigh against a thigh, his head near my heart, our occasional touches, at first, were tentative and ambivalent. I remember worrying if I would be able to perform, questioning whether I could be attracted to front holes, that maybe this was just me trying to live out a PC wet dream. I soon dispensed with those fears, allowing myself to feel the occasional electricity of our contact, hoping he would notice the boner I was popping.

Starting but not finishing the second episode, I turned to Aaron and announced that I needed to get to work "eventually." He stared right into my eyes and, without a single word, transmitted a welcoming signal. Finally! I burst out in laughter as I begged off, asking him twice "What," then more laughs and a third general entreaty, then finally asking, "Can I kiss you?" All I needed was his "yes," and boyish smile, and I went to town.

We remained there in casual congress on the couch, neck-nuzzling, hand-holding, tress-tousling, crotch-crashing, head-handling, and lip-locking for about 10 minutes before repairing to the bedroom. Aaron asked permission before opening my pants, sliding a non-latex condom on me, and beginning to fellate me. Before long, I asked if I could perform intercrucial sex on him. "Can I thigh-fuck you?," I phrased it, after "frott" registered a quizzical "Hmm?!" from him. A new condom, our tops and bottoms came off, and a little of that led to full-on, Aaron-riding-Moo and Moo-fucking-Aaron-in-his-front-hole-missionary sex, complete with nipple-nibbling, man-moaning, "come to the edge of the bed" calls, tongue-tag, perspiration-n-panting, and all other manner of alliterative anatomical exploration before the inevitable alerts of 'I'm gonna cum,' quick, catchup, clitoral cosseting, energetic ejaculations on both our parts as well as post-climactic contractions and cuddling come-downs. Athletic, aggressive, loud, tender, revealing, mindful, passionate and mutually satisfying: It was all of my porn-style and pensive sex fantasies with Jordan and Riley, but better. It was magical and freeing and soon became a regular rendezvous between the two of us, either in my cramped bedroom when my roommate was out, or asleep or in Aaron's huge, sparsely furnished bedroom at his co-op on campus at the local Ivy League university.

In my enthusiasm towards this new facet of sexuality, I shared my experience with a close sibling. Unfortunately though, their response was very cautious, to the point of pouring cold water on the joy of sharing my new experiences. My sibling essentially yucked my yum. It dampened my enthusiasm and motivation to share, but not to continue seeing Aaron.

REFLECTION/TRANSFORMATION

I really appreciated the opportunity that Aaron was affording me, a newbie once again, to exercise the right I'd long ago reserved to love whomever I so desired. In addition to being liberated, I found it a transformative experience. Accordingly, I became much more apt to identify as queer rather than as merely gay and to acknowledge my own and others' gender rather than to leave it unspoken. It's even impacted my relationship with my racial identity because it turned the tables on the notion of privilege in a way that even my women's studies coursework hadn't. For those reasons, it's spurred me to become more of an ally to and an advocate for/with folks in trans communities. I do that by first listening and learning as respectively and compassionately as possible, becoming aware of my privilege and fragility around gender identity, plugging into efforts underway to stand up and make space in the community, making mistakes sometimes, and helping out as best I can in my everyday life.

Since connecting with Aaron I've met and hung out with other trans guys. While admittedly I still have limited experience in this department, I can say that, compared to cis guys, so far none of my trans buddies have bottomed anally, though they've been willing to top. I've also noticed that safer sex strategies seem to be more salient and the effort to build trust seems fraught for obvious reasons, but that also makes sex feel more meaningful.

The whole experience has certainly taught me that honesty is the best policy. If you don't know something or how to do something (like if you've never had the experience), then just ask and don't fake it. The same is true if there's something you like or don't like done to you. Knowing what you want is important because it makes sex better, even if it means you compare preferences with quite a few guys before you bed one down. Given differences of anatomy, assumptions don't always translate, but it can be an eye-opening and exciting learning curve.

Sadly, Aaron fell off of my radar screen (several times) given the demands of his undergraduate education program and several projects I had on my plate. However, I'll always be grateful to him for his patience, wisdom and service in "breaking me in." I'll (GREATLY) cherish for a lifetime the memories we made together, and I reserve the right to love whomever (else) I want.

WHAT DEFINES A MAN[*]

YOSSEF AHARON

As far as I can remember, I've always been gay. I have warm fuzzy memories of gazing appreciatively at men's underwear ads in the magazines my childhood barber kept. I kissed my sister's best girlfriend when I was about twelve, during "Truth or Dare," but that's about as much as I've ever done sexually with a woman. I came out as a gay man at sixteen in a bumbling but good-enough process to friends and then to my family.

I wasn't aware that trans folks existed until my sophomore year in college, when a friend came out as a trans woman. Then, in my senior year, I was in a Queer Studies class with a classmate who presented as male but didn't actually come out as a trans man until several years later. Our professor was also transmasculine, and even though we used female pronouns for both of them there was a clear sense that their gender identities were not quite the ones they were assigned at birth. This was at a small private liberal arts college on the East Coast, with lots of fancy urbane kids who could be intimidating to a kid from the South. A big draw to the school was its reputation for being very queer, though in retrospect it was more LGB than Queer or Trans affirming. These were the first times I directly encountered the T in my sheltered life.

Here I was, at this liberal college with its reputation for being a very open-minded space, and as knowledgeable as I thought I was, I remember often feeling incredibly naive. When I arrived there I didn't quite understand the difference between cross-dressing and being transgender or the nuances of gender identity, and I'm not sure I could've effectively explained the basic difference between sexuality and gender. This naiveté felt shameful at times, because everybody else seemed to have grown up in much more worldly and liberal environments than I had, and felt so much farther along in their understanding, even though I started going to queer alliances very early on in life. Living through this discomfort, I learned a lot and realized eventually that this sense of naiveté was mostly my insecurity and didn't always reflect the actual truth. I feel fortunate to have had a supportive and mind-exploding experience in college, because it was the first time that I became aware of my many assumptions about people, including sexuality and gender. It was the first time I stopped to question, "When we talk about men and women, what are we talking about?" In a philosophy class we read an essay about Essentialism, the idea that there are universal traits that define certain categories, and while this article was specifically about sexual orientation, it also challenged the idea of a gender binary and the notion that all men and women share universal traits.

Part of learning includes fumbling, and both during and after college I have asked questions or used terminology in ignorance that others found basic or even offensive. These experiences, despite being uncomfortable, pushed me to think critically. While it's not great to learn through feeling shame for misspeaking or not knowing, I have learned to think before I speak, to consider many sides of an issue, and to avoid making assumptions as much as possible. I've also learned to be accountable when I'm wrong. This world is vast and definitions of identity are constantly expanding and morphing, and it's impossible to always know or to say the right thing. When it comes to trans identity or sexuality, I do my best to embrace "not knowing," to be open to listening to what individuals are telling me about their own experience, and I try not to get shut down by shame if I misstep. I can easily get in my head trying to say or do the right thing, and sometimes this causes me to end up getting in my own way.

My sexual attraction in some ways transcends normative notions of gender, even though it also follows a pretty normative gay mold. I like big hairy daddies who are bottoms. The guy I'm dating right now is bearish and traditionally masculine, but one of the things I really love about him is that he's extremely expressive and talks openly about his feelings, which is *not* a traditional masculine trait. Gay men often talk about holding attraction to different types of guys: bears, twinks, etc., and this makes me question what we're *actually* attracted to underneath that label. Cuddle-ability? Personality? Kindness? Certain sexual proclivities? Furthermore, are people attracted to a "man" or a "woman," or are we attracted to certain traits of a person that don't have to do so much with genitals, per se?

The first out trans man I met was at a coffee shop in Denver that I used to frequent quite a bit when I was in grad school. I had such a crush on this pierced tattooed punk rock barista and got turned on every time I went to order a latte. When I became aware that he was trans it didn't cause me to question my sexuality, but it absolutely caused me to question what it would be like to have sex with him. What came up for me most in thinking about dating or having sex with a trans man was insecurity around not knowing how to interact sexually with a trans man's body; not understanding what his anatomy might look like. Looking back, I was making an assumption that all that trans men's bodies looked alike. The nail in the coffin was the strong fear of making someone feel like an experiment, or a fear of embarrassing myself by not knowing what I was doing.

There's a *Sex in the City* episode, where Samantha has a threesome with a gay male couple who want to try having sex with a woman. They figure that if they are ever going to have sex with a woman they should do it with Samantha, because she's hot, she loves gay men, and she's adventurous. The three of them are in the couple's bedroom and they start kissing and stripping down. Samantha is in a silky nightie, and I think they're in their underwear. The camera focuses on one of the guys as he's kissing Samantha's body, going lower and lower. Everyone is moaning…and then the action suddenly stops. The guy who has been going down on Samantha has hit a block, sits back up and stares at them unsure of what to do or say. Awkwardly he asks, "Anybody wants to go get ice cream?" and that's the end of *that* adventure. This scene perfectly captures my feared first attempt at sex with a trans man: I would not be able to get or to stay hard, I might not ultimately like the differences I find, my not knowing might feel embarrassing for both me and the trans guy I was having sex with, and through this clumsy encounter I worried I would further stigmatize my partner.

As I reflect on these fears I realize how much they were tied up in my own sexual practices and confidence level, which makes me realize how much I've changed over time. Early on in my sex life, I was mostly having sex with men older than myself and I was frequently put into a bottom role. It's only a bit later in life that I discovered my inner top and became confident in topping. However, when I was mostly bottoming I didn't really know what to do sexually with a trans guy and the thought of a strap-on really never appealed to me. When I bottom, I understand the sensations and pleasures that I'm (hopefully) giving my top's cock from my own direct experiences of topping or masturbating, and this understanding comes with a sense of sexual prowess. I get that topping with a strap-on might be very hot for somebody, and I'd be willing to give it a try, but I don't bottom very often, and when I do, I like the idea that I'm making a guy's dick feel the same way that I feel when I top. I guess I haven't been ready to step out of my comfort zone yet in this specific way.

Even as I'm writing this I'm questioning all of these assumptions that I'm making, like assuming that because a trans guy's strap-on is an insensate prosthetic, he's probably not enjoying himself. I shared this assumption with a gay trans guy friend of mine, and he told me that he really gets off on topping with a strap-on: that when his cock rubs against it just right he can come, and that also, energetically, he can feel the responsiveness of the guy he's topping, which is a huge turn on for him. He says the guys that bottom for him enjoy his collection of different dick sizes to choose from and pointed out that he never has to deal with erectile issues. Another trans guy friend of mine also talked about the advantage of having different sized dick choices. He has one cock he calls The Punisher, which is this big fat dick he takes out when he gets the urge to really ram a guy. He usually goes with the average size strap-on, but sometimes The Punisher needs to come out and it's super-hot for both top and bottom. Talking to my friends helped me see the appeal and got me a little curious about giving it a go sometime with the right top.

So much of the time preferences boil down to what's familiar. I've seen many cis penises in my life and I know what to do with them. I understand generally how they respond and how to touch and please a guy's cock. However, the cis guy I'm seeing right now has a difficult time reaching orgasm, so I'm having to relearn how to have sex with him, and how *his* penis and the rest of his body works. Sometimes it's frustrating for me because I feel insecure that I'm not doing a good enough job. That said, I'm also having a lot of fun exploring his body, like how he loves having his balls played with, which isn't something I've necessarily ever focused on for extended sessions. My fella cannot get enough of it, and it's so much fun to make him moan and to see his toes curl. This has been a good reminder that challenges of the unknown can also happen with cis guys, and that if you really like someone you can find ways of having sex with them that are connecting and hot for everyone involved.

I finally demystified sex with a trans man a couple of years ago. This handsome guy is someone I had met over Facebook who lives across the country from me. We were both part of a sex-positive group for gay men on PrEP. I didn't realize this guy was trans when I first started talking to him, initially around some travel advice. We started flirting, and at some point he came out as being trans, and I didn't feel the old sexual insecurities flare up because I wasn't sure that we were ever going to meet. We continued to flirt online, and as it turned out he had connections on the West Coast and came out here every so often. The idea of having sex with him, or maybe even more than sex, all of a sudden became a reality. I decided to be open and honest with him, to welcome a new experience, and to try to get out of my own way by not overthinking the situation. The first time we had sex, a big part of what made the experience so damn positive was that he was extremely open to talking about sex, took a sexy and playful approach to these discussions, and he had already had sex with other cis gay men who had not had sex with trans men. From those experiences he was aware of some of the insecurities that might come up or questions that I might ask. Also, he was able to tell me what he enjoyed and didn't enjoy in a way that gave me some specific ideas of how to make him feel really good. In discussing his likes/dislikes I had also gotten to share my own preferences and limits so he knew how to really get my gears going. Separately, I did my own research. I educated myself on trans anatomy and watched some gay porn with cis and trans men. I work at an LGBT Center on the West Coast with people from all over the gender spectrum, so at this point in my life I knew a little bit more than I had before when I was crushing on the guy at the coffee shop in Denver.

One major comfort in thinking about having sex with this guy was that it felt safe to tell him my concerns about not getting hard, or going down on him and getting weirded out. He wasn't going to shame me and we had established mutual respect. I remember feeling nervous about fucking his front hole and wasn't sure if I'd like it or not. Even worse—what if I liked it too much? Not in a way of making me question my sexuality, but in a way that could be fetishizing. I would occasionally get into my head worrying about what might go wrong, but talking with him kept my mind open and encouraged me to maintain a spirit of curiosity versus fear and insecurity.

The day arrived and this man showed up at my door, came inside, and was adorable! We started making out, and he says "Pause- I'm going to give you a quick tour of what I've got going on." The tone was light and sexy, and I was excited to dive in. He was very confident and seemed quite comfortable in his own skin, which was extremely attractive to me. We'd planned a meal at a local diner afterward, so there was a plan B if things didn't work out.

Once we started, I went for the gold. It was all extremely hot and new. It turns out that we had great chemistry! After spending a good long time eating his ass, which I love, he turned over and there was a giant wet spot on my bed, which was not something that I've ever had happen before. I was so proud! "Look what I helped make happen?!" Turns out I loved fucking his front hole. It felt like a completely new ballgame, with different muscles and positions. Some of my sexual confidence in my top skills were thrown off because what works really well for anal sex might not work so well for the front hole, and I wasn't always able to revert to my normal techniques. He was able to show me the ropes without saying anything in a shaming way. I listened to him, followed his lead, explored, and we both had a lot of fun. The experience was a huge triumph for me over fear of the Unknown, and a rewarding experience in stepping outside my comfort zone to embrace being open and vulnerable.

Looking back, a central lesson is to practice going for it without overthinking the situation. This experience also highlights for me how much of a difference the specific connection with a person can make in terms of sexual or romantic chemistry. Chemistry with another person transcends gender identity or genitalia (though the bottoms enjoying my friend's Punisher strap on might argue otherwise). If it bombs with a trans guy, or a cis guy for that matter, there's always the option to stop. I might show up at some cis guy's house that I met on an app and immediately realize that it's not going to work. I've also had times where I've started having sex with somebody, and for whatever reason one or both of us stopped to say, "This isn't really doing it for me." It's uncomfortable to do that, and in my younger years I sometimes went through with it anyway because I was afraid to speak up and hurt the other person's feelings. Now I see this as a vital skill and hope I'll feel able to do this with all my partners.

I'm in my late 30's, and one of the tenets that I've learned and embraced is that the more I let go of caring what others think about me, the more powerful I feel. I've enjoyed my 30's decidedly much more than my 20's, and a big part of it comes from listening to my own wants and needs and not trying to fit any certain mold or living my life to please others. I try to stay true to myself.

If asked my preference between a choice of having sex with a guy who is trans versus cis, I might instinctively answer that sex with a cis guy feels much more comfortable and familiar. However, reflecting on my first experience of sex with a trans man reminds me of how rewarding (and hot) it can be to explode those assumptions about what gender means or how cis versus trans bodies work, and to try something outside my comfort zone. While I may not have known all the right moves or positions, that giant wet spot was an excellent reminder of how much fun it can be to explore unchartered territory.

Interview-turned-essay, conducted by
and in collaboration with Avi Ben-Zeev.

Like Chocolate? Try Lemon Ganache*

Dwayne Treat

When I arrived in San Francisco fresh out of Alaska in 1980, I went to the Castro because it was the center of the gay universe. I was eighteen, in a work shirt and leather boots, so the preppy gay Castro clones sent me to Polk Street, where the hustlers and street kids were. I had sex with them, we took drugs together, and just had fun. I had little understanding of what I was looking for. I wasn't a hustler, nor was I a street kid. All I knew was that I needed to explore. My first foray at South of Market was to a sex club called the Gloryholes—there were about 200 glory holes there, neon lights, and you'd go and get your dick sucked for hours. When I found the sex clubs and leather bars at South of Market, I found my people. It was there that I felt comfortable for the first time.

Half a dozen years later, I was comfortably out as a gay leatherboy in San Francisco. I met this wonderful self-described leather dyke and former lesbian separatist named Miriam, and we had a not-so-brief affair. Miriam was short, rubenesque, very busty, and had long, blonde hair. It was strange for both of us. We weren't sure what was going on but we went with it. I think we believed that because we weren't on our normal tracks that our baggage wouldn't get involved, but it did, eventually, and we went our separate ways. Well, some years later Miriam became Joe, and in retrospect, our relationship suddenly made sense.

Fast forward 20 years, I was poz, longtime clean and sober, and in my early forties. I became part of a sex-positive cis gay men's community called Flesh and Spirit, a body-based spiritual group moderated by Kirk Prine. Kirk wanted to expand our horizons and open the group to trans men. As a first step in this process, he decided to invite a trans man called Shane, a tattoo artist in the Castro, to meet the group. When Shane walked into the room, I saw a bearded, broad-shouldered, muscular fireplug of a guy. He looked to be in his mid-thirties, had a buzz cut and was of roughly average height. Shane shared his experiences with us, and then we broke into pairs to process the idea of a trans man as just another kind of man. I paired off with Shane and shared with him my experience with Joe (formerly Miriam). That was the point at which it dawned on me that I am drawn to male spirit, regardless of the body.

The other cis gay men's responses to Shane ran the gamut, from curiosity to discomfort, but at the end of the evening, it was clear to all of us that a trans man is a...man! It's kind of unfortunate that trans men and their allies have to do this type of education—especially in environments that otherwise pride themselves on being open, affirming, and body positive – but at the very least it's nice when it happens.

My first sexual experience with a trans man wasn't until I was in my late forties. By then, I had been to several tm4m (trans men 4 men) events and had also seen a Buck Angel film at the Frameline Festival. Little did I know that this would kick off a three-year-long journey in which I would end up dating and having some super-hot play with a trans man.

We first met at Boot Camp, the 15 Association's annual run (gay men's leather sex weekend). My friend, Ralph, tied up this hot trans guy called Lev, and three of us took turns "torturing" him. Lev caught my eye immediately—he was in his twenties, short and sturdy, dark-skinned and clean-shaven, with an alternative look about him. It took a while for the two of us to play one-on-one, because I thought he was standoffish, and he had no idea I liked him. Later in the fall, we met again at Delta, another 'leather run' on the East Coast, where we shared a cabin with Ralph and a few other guys we knew from Boot Camp. Being in the same cabin allowed Lev and I to get to know each other better. I learned that he was feeling unwell and out of sorts, and as a Dominant Daddy and massage therapist, I knew a trick to get him to feel more comfortable. I didn't tell him any of this. All I said was, "Do you want to play?" Although Lev is versatile and would later spend half the run elbow-deep in various bottoms, I implied that perhaps I'd tie him up and do mean things to him again.

Before our play date, Lev asked me what he should wear, and I said, "Wear a jockstrap!" I was making the assumption that trans men would only be comfortable in gay men's spaces if the parts that made them different were covered. Lev looked disappointed and said, "A jockstrap? As opposed to nothing at all?" My response was, "Oh, naked is an option? That's even better!" My assumption about his comfort said more about me and where I was at rather than about him. I took Lev down to the whipping dungeon and threw him on one of the bondage tables. Instead of the torture he expected, I surprised him with a 90-minute massage. With the sounds of whips, yelps and moans in the background, I got to use my touch to bring him back into his body. At the end of the massage, after I wiped him off and sat him up, he said, somewhat dreamily, "You ate my brain!", which made me feel very satisfied that I'd gotten him out of his funk and turned him into a puddle. It was rewarding to see Lev enjoy himself for the rest of the run, whipping, fisting and fucking a variety of men (none of whom were me…yet) to his heart's content.

The following year, Lev contacted me and told me that he was going to spend the summer in San Francisco. We made plans for a date. After dinner at his place, sitting on the couch, I admitted to Lev that my skill levels with a trans guy's body were very limited. He was utterly unfazed and proceeded to give me the guided tour of his body. In the process, I learned that his reason for being out of sorts the last time we'd met was because he'd developed an anal fissure as a side effect of a medicine that he was on. Lev was still feeling cautious about playing with his ass, but I welcomed the opportunity to address the trauma and coax his hole open. I'm particularly skilled at playing with butts and was excited to play with him in a capacity in which I felt competent. Playing with Lev's ass in this way moved him from the category of "unfamiliar and possibly scary trans man" into the category of "sexy gay man." By the end of the session, we were both pleased to discover that his ass had transformed from scared and tight to open and hungry for more. That evening sparked a deeper intimacy between us that took us from being acquaintances to something more.

This was a prelude to our spending the summer fucking and dating and fucking some more. Lev returned home after his stint in San Francisco, and the next time we saw each other was at the following year's Delta. We were overjoyed to be reunited, and I couldn't wait to get into the dungeon and tear his clothes off. One particularly memorable scene that year was when I tied Lev up to one of the bondage tables, abraded his nipples with sandpaper paddles, and that made his dick hard. I was so excited to see his dick peeking out that I commented out loud in the middle of the dungeon. The person next to us, a seasoned leatherman, walked by, looked over my shoulder at Lev's hard and protruding dick, said, "Interesting!" and then walked away.

It was a warm day, and all this play made Lev very sweaty. His armpits smelled like the testosterone musk of a young athlete. It's clearly not the parts that identify the man. Testosterone, yum!

Many gay cis men who say that they can't have sex with a trans man are afraid that trans men would have "female" smells. First, the idea that women (or "female" genitals) smell bad, like fish, is a very misogynistic concept. Second, trans men smell like men! They have the testosterone level of a nineteen-year-old guy that comes out of every orifice of their bodies and can even be a little addictive. There's nothing feminine about trans men. In fact, sometimes the cutest twenty-year-old man in the Castro is actually a forty-year-old trans man. It's the best of both worlds, an actual mature adult with a cute little body. I'll take it! Cis gay guys take note, it doesn't matter if you're a top or a bottom, if the connection with a trans guy feels good, then don't overthink it. Just go for it. My friend Ralph says that his rule for dessert is to always eat chocolate unless there's something with lemon. So don't be so strict about the chocolate rules, because the occasional lemon ganache could rock your world.

Interview-turned-essay, conducted by
and in collaboration with Avi Ben-Zeev.

Boy Drag*

17

ə

I grew up in the 1970s, in a fairly rural area of California. My mom was a Teamster and my father worked on an assembly line in a factory that produced American cars. I am the first person in my family to ever attend college. Growing up, as early as fourth grade other kids began to identify me as gay, long before I had any kind of consciousness of my own sexual identity. Around seventh grade, I had an epiphany of, "Oh, that's what people were talking about." Looking back, this period of not knowing was perhaps a sign that my gender expression and sexual identity would change and develop over time.

After my "Aha!" moment in seventh grade, I sought out a girl who lived down the street from me, and who came out as lesbian when we were both in the fourth grade. Once I started to realize I was not like all of the other boys in school, I approached her and said, "So you're a lesbian right?" She said, "Yeah." I confided that I might be gay but that I was not 100% sure. She was very kind and helped me to piece together who I was.

People viewed me as being more "feminine" in my presentation, including my body language, vocal intonation and style of clothing. Today, I present more masculine, even bearish, but it feels like "boy drag" to me a lot of the time—a costume I'm putting on. More recently, I began doing bearded and non-bearded drag, and it's fascinating to watch people's inter-action with me based on which drag I'm in. Clean-shaven drag is something people can more easily wrap their mind around, perhaps because it feels less threatening. Bearded drag makes people far more uncomfortable perhaps because it blends characteristics of both masculine and feminine—it isn't one or the other. When I'm in bearded drag, I get a lot more avoided eye contact. What I find really staggering is the kind of permissiveness that people feel entitled to—people will come up and touch me without wondering if that's ok. Doing drag is a pretty recent thing, and it has taught me a lot about gender as performance. It has also helped me see that putting on a pair of combat boots, a tank top, and having my chest show is also drag—but no one blinks at that kind of everyday "masculine" boy drag.

Most of the men that I would encounter growing up, were in their 30s, 40s and 50s. At the tender age of fourteen, I was hooking up with much older guys. Unfortunately, most of them were men who did not have a good understanding of developmental appropriateness, didn't know how a fourteen year old communicates, or cared about what my boundaries might have been or that I was still figuring them out. These early formative encounters taught me to distrust and fear men. On the one hand, I desired men and wanted to be close to them, but on the other hand, men also meant probable danger.

There can be a huge power differential in inter-generational relationships. Older folks in our community need to be incredibly mindful of the position we are in and to be intentional around communication. It's important to be mindful of power differences because exploiting them is not ethical. Unfortunately, I encountered a lot of men in my formative years who weren't particularly ethical or had my best interest at heart, and that felt especially painful because it was my introduction to our community. More than anything, I just wanted to be told that I was ok. Sure, I was fourteen and horny and wanted sex, but mostly I wanted validation because I wasn't getting it from my family, school or society. I desperately needed to know that I was ok, and I needed my mentors, my elders, to communicate that to me.

Reconciling desire with safety and trust was incredibly hard, and it wasn't until about now (I'd say in the last four years), in my late forties, that I've made peace and have come to realize that there are some really genuinely beautiful, wonderful, kind men out there in the world. It also helped that my college sweetheart was a guy who was a women studies major. His desire to understand the world through a feminist lens rubbed off on me, so I went into gender studies. Getting a sociological perspective on men and power helped shed light on some of my questions and also lead me to my academic pursuit.

My parents were incredibly unsupportive, but I was super fortunate to have a neighbor who lived up the hill and who became my "gay mom." She was a therapist, and provided me with great resources, including *One Teenager In Ten*, and overall helped me to get a sense of myself as a queer man. This issue of sexual identity, to be honest, is still something I go back and forth on. I am not straight by any stretch of the imagination but what kind of "gay"—where exactly I fall on the Kinsey scale—that really changes from day to day, but is rarely on one extreme.

I can be attracted to women, but maybe because I present more as gay, women don't give me the time of day. Women want to hang out but I rarely ever get a sense that they might feel, "Oh! He's attractive." I've had sex with women, twice in my life, and I really enjoyed it. The opportunity has not arisen that much. I spent a lot of the 1990s actually kind of secretly being attracted to a lot of the butch dykes I knew. They were totally hot with their short hair, curls that looked like side burns, Levis and big boots. It was weird being a gay man, with mostly dyke friends, having these secret crushes. It was never something that I explored. I didn't feel that I could, or perhaps, I just didn't know how. What I've come to learn is that my desire boils down to presentation and energy. When I see a masculine person who looks potentially a little dangerous, has an edge, a swagger, I am hooked. The actual genitals are not of huge consequence. It's a certain combination of masculine and feminine energy that I can't quite put my finger on, but I know it when I see it.

Sometimes sexual identities are so circumscribed, especially among gay men; it's really maddening. I don't tend to go out a whole lot, or socialize, particularly when it involves self-defined groups because I will fail at knowing all the rules. I'm a big hairy guy so it might seem logical that I'll do bear stuff, but in bear culture there are hierarchies and "rules" around what a bear should be—you need to look and act a particular way, and there is much gate-keeping. This is really rampant among cisgender gay men and there's also quite a bit of gynophobia. Here's my response: If that part's not for you, that's fine, but what I don't quite get is what exactly is prompting you to have such a strong visceral reaction.

We live in a misogynist society that devalues what's perceived or constructed as feminine. For gay men, in particular, there's all this self-definition around what makes us different, which is that we like other men. It seems kind of silly but somehow this quest to self-define as a community ramps up the misogynist element that already exists in our culture to global proportions. I find a lot of gay men far more sexist than straight men by virtue of this need to self-bond. Also, we really need to look at our internalized homophobia. As a culture, we associate gay men as being feminine and therefore not "real" men. So by rejecting the feminine, some gay men feel like they have more access to power. It's complicated but worth thinking about.

I was aware that trans folks existed since around the age of fifteen, because my gay mom was a known figure in the queer leather community, and I spent a lot of Christmases at her house. She knew a wide variety of people, was very involved and still is in queer community, so I was lucky to have access to trans and gender non-conforming folks from relatively early on in life. Having a trans lover, though, has been a more recent experience for me in the last five years or so. My first sexual experience with a trans gay man was through an app. When he showed up, I was nervous about saying something or doing something stupid, or of not being mindful and being insulting or hurtful. I was very cautious of not wanting to invade boundaries or use terminology or language that was inappropriate. I just wanted to make sure I was ok, that I was appropriate, and he caught on to that pretty quickly, and was like, "Hey! Relax, just be you..." He thanked me for being so diligent about my approach but encouraged me to let my hair down a bit. His attitude was very helpful.

In some respect it was like any other experience where there's a person you don't know, and you are going to their home or they are coming to yours. You don't know who this person is or what to expect, what history they have or what baggage they are walking around with, what triggers or excites them. Are they even stable, or high? Luckily, this trans man was more take-charge, which I really appreciated (although I don't have a problem doing that). He was a guy that liked sex and probably had a fair amount of it, so he knew the drill and how to navigate this experience with a neophyte. He communicated off the bat about what he liked to do, showed me how he liked to be touched, and what felt good. He also asked me what I was and was not interested in doing, which I liked. It was refreshing! It wasn't a long a conversation, and quickly our clothes were off, and...sex was hot!

Since then I've had sex with other trans men and I appreciate that, in general, trans guys tend to be more communicative. In the cis gay male world, we make a lot of assumptions about what kind of sex a guy wants, so we usually just go for it. Trans guys don't have that luxury and communication seems key to being safe and to having a sexy time. A trans guy needs to know when he answers the door that I'm an appropriate person to be coming into his home, and that I'm not only knowledgeable about what I'm walking into but respectful and excited about the experience I'm about to have. That said, I've also been with a couple of trans men who were younger, into drugs and alcohol, not as communicative, and not as great at disclosure or discussions around boundaries. I was the one to take the lead in those conversations because I am older and of the mind that it's important to have skilful communication around boundaries.

I am the older man now. I have white hair, wrinkles around my eyes, and younger men are looking at me, thinking, "Daddy." And I am like, "Crap! How did this happen?" This might sound a little hokey but I think we, middle aged and older guys, have the responsibility of stewardship. Our young community members need modelling and demonstration of what good communication looks like: how to negotiate boundaries, how to engage in difficult discussions about identity and, how we as a community support, embrace and bolster each other, rather than create more divisions.

Interview-turned-essay, conducted by
and in collaboration with Avi Ben-Zeev

Love me Some Scruffy Men with Innies and Outies*

18

AJ Chase

A s a kid, I didn't know what I was, but I was smart enough to know that there are things you don't talk about. I knew that I liked my mom's boyfriends who had facial hair better than the smooth guys, but then I learned that men don't compliment other men on their facial hair in society, that you keep it on the inside, privately. In the 80's, gay guys were supposed to like dick, pretty guys, country or leather. That wasn't me and it was not acceptable to discuss these desires with friends. Kinsey came up with this idea that you can be attracted to the very end of the completely heterosexual spectrum (1), or the completely homosexual spectrum (6), and then there's the gray area in the middle. Well, I'm clearly a 5. I don't find most women attractive, but neither am I like, "Pussy, I can't go there," the way gay guys joke about in bars and clubs. I'm like, "Yeah, whatever dude, OK."

The first time I heard about trans men was when I was twenty-two years old. I'm forty-nine now, so you do the math! I was out with friends at the Lone Star Saloon in San Francisco when I spotted this cute little blonde haired blue-eyed bearded bartender. He was running around, filling everyone's cups and stuff, and he and I were making eyes at each other. I was a hell of an introvert, and some of my friends were laughing because I was actually flirting in front of people, which was so not me…Then he stopped by, I got a kiss, and my friends were laughing hysterically at this point.

I'm like, "What?"

"Dude, if this is going to go any further, you know, there's probably something you need to know!"

"What, is he married?"

So finally they tell me he is trans, and I'm like, "Oh, Ok!"

Up until then, I had led a really sheltered Southern Baptist childhood. I never smoked marijuana, never heard about the wide variety of things that occur in society, and it just kind of struck me that my friends' hooey was malice. What's so funny about this guy being trans? Looking back, I think it was actually not cool for my friends to be outing him in public, because what if I had become an asshole about it or something. Prior to that day, it had never occurred to me that there was anything other than boys who grew up to be men, and girls who grew up to be women, and that was the entire allotment of gender in society.

Just a few blocks down from Castro on Market, there's a bookstore with lots of queer selections. I was there one day flipping through this photography book about trans men and thought, "This is kind of cool," and, "Oh, hey, I know this guy!" It was the cute bartender. Other than that, I had no further experiences with him.

The first time I had sex with a trans guy was when I was living in New Orleans. I was thirty-one years old. Late one night, I was horny, and this little bearded guy cruised me on an app.

"Hey, yeah sure, but there's something you should know, I'm HIV positive, on medication."

Little scruffy dude says, "Oh, OK, I'm cool with that."

So he comes over, and we're making out on the couch. He starts unbuttoning my pants, and playing with me, so I start unbuttoning his pants. Before I could get any further, he puts his hand on mine and says, "There's something you should know."

I'm thinking, "OK, what is there for me to know at this point?" and so he tells me that he's trans.

"OK."

"You really OK with that?"

"Yeah, I've never done that but I don't see a problem."

I play with him digitally, and it's kind of cool. I have no idea what I'm doing, but it's fun and as far as that went.

When cis gay guys ask me for advice about getting with a trans guy, on the one hand, I like to keep it general. I can offer some basic tenets but it all depends on the individuals involved. That said, my advice is, just be honest about what you're looking for and don't treat him differently because maybe his body parts do or don't match yours. You're not falling in love with a body part, so if you're interested in having a relationship with this guy explore having a relationship with him. When you take your clothes off have a short discussion to get on the same page. Ask him what he likes his body parts called.

I've heard a lot of nomenclature. Some trans guys prefer "front hole" and some embrace calling it their "pussy" because they claim that word back. So when I talk about safer sex to a trans guy, as we're getting it on, I say something like, "Should I use a condom to fuck your front hole?" or whatever comes up, as long as I'm being descriptive, accurate and honest. I just roll it up into the part of the discussion I have to have anyway because I'm HIV positive.

Don't be afraid of this kind of conversation, guys. It's easy and it works. When I'm about to have sex with a man, especially a trans man, I can make a lot of assumptions about what feels good to them, etc., so instead of going with my assumptions, I ask what they like and how they want to be touched. I will say, "Hey, dude, I dig your body parts, but let me know what you want." So it's good to ask for communication, but be brief about it because you just want to have passion and go for it and not walk on eggshells too much.

Society, in general, is becoming more open to gay and trans people. BDSM communities, or however you want to label them, are definitely becoming more open too, because they acknowledge that even though society tells us that our desires are perverted or evil, or any of the various labels that they've given us throughout the years, it doesn't necessarily mean that we can't make ourselves happy in consensual sexual relationships.

Society is finally getting to be more sex positive, but sometimes people get confused. My best friend and his wife are a straight couple. They're very monogamous and jealous but they've welcomed my husband and myself into their home, and they acknowledge that we have a relationship that is very different from how they were raised. They say that it's cool that my polyamorous lifestyle works for me, and that they love me. One time, I got a random text from my friend's wife, "If you're fucking a guy that has a vagina does that technically make you bisexual?" I told her the same thing I tell everyone else, "No, I'm still very much gay." I have always been and still am attracted to men with facial hair. It's just that some of the men I'm attracted to were born with innies and some were born with outies.

Interview-turned-essay, conducted by
and in collaboration with Avi Ben-Zeev

Soft Masculinity

19

Matthew Florence

Before moving to San Francisco I used to equate the term transgender with women who were assigned a male gender at birth. It's not that I couldn't conceive of men who had been assigned female at birth. I just didn't really know any at that point. What I was familiar with were butch lesbians, both as friends and because of a documentary a friend had made about them. Personally, I was uncomfortable with aspects of maleness, but when it came to female butch identity, I thought: "If someone had the possibility of living life as a masculine female, then why not?" Of course, discomfort with masculinity or not, living one's truth is about living that truth, fully.

Arriving in San Francisco—otherwise known as Sodom and Gomorrah, according to my fundamentalist Christian family—I became exposed to men who had transitioned into their true selves from being assigned female at birth. These men were more involved in the lesbian community, though, and were usually partnered romantically with women or other trans men. So I was taken by surprise a little the first time I encountered a trans man who identified as a gay man.

Perhaps the surprise was due to how that encounter happened. You see, I was in the back room of a bar that allowed men to be the pigs that we are. Drinking, smoking, fucking, with only first names exchanged, and even that kind of "intimacy," only sometimes, and after the fact. In this carnal scene filled with earthly pleasure, I spotted this really hot, tall guy, and we immediately started making out, no words exchanged. I reached my hand inside the rim of his pants to get to the center of his Tootsie Roll, but to my surprise, he blocked me. His gesture felt playful though, so I proceeded to try again, and a gut instinct told me that the center of this roll wasn't the traditional one. I don't know what gave me that intuition. There was nothing in his mannerism, looks, or anything that said he was transgender. Sometimes my ability to read people is just really strong.

Calling myself a gay-identified bisexual at the time, I wasn't afraid of pussy. I liked it, in fact. What made me drawn to the gay male world was its masculine energy. So I wanted to let him know that I was okay and wasn't going to scream in terror for having touched genitals that weren't the traditional cock. I approached his pants again, but I did so more gently. He removed my hand once more, muttering, "Um, I have a boyfriend, and our rule is that we can only fool around with people from the waist up."

"Ah, I was wrong," I thought, but I still felt compelled to tell him about my intuition, so I said, "That's funny, I thought that maybe you were transgender, and that's what was going on."

He stared at me for a long minute, with a surprised look, and then acknowledged, "Yes, yes, I am." He explained his ruse as having been rejected once guys found out he had a pussy. I told him I was fine with that part and asked if it was okay for me to put my hand down there. This time he let me.

That was my foray into the world of gay trans men. At the time, they used to call themselves Tranny Fags, though I'm not sure if that term is still used. As someone who now identifies as "queer," I resonated with taking back pejoratives. I also really liked that trans men approached sex in a different way than my encounters with women up to that point. Yes, they often had different parts, but they were definitely part of the wonderful bacchanal of the gay male world. Part of the reason why I preferred having sex with men over women is that I liked uncomplicated sex that still prioritized connection, but perhaps with fewer strings than a lot of the women I knew tended to want.

A funny thing happened along the way. I realized there was something else I liked about gay trans men. I'm Black and a feminist, and unfortunately in the traditional gay male world, that sometimes means that I don't always fit. For so many white gay men, they are white men first, with all the attendant privileges thereof, who also happen to like having sex with other men. You would think that gay men would automatically align themselves with other oppressed people, but that is certainly not always the case. Of course this is not always true, but generally speaking, gay male culture tends to reinforce these attitudes. On the other hand, and I can't speak for all, the gay-identified trans men I've met have had a more radical and inclusive look at life, an intersectional perspective on issues like women's rights, #BlackLivesMatter, and more. Perhaps it's a result of being so far outside of the mainstream, or maybe it has to do with having been socialized, to a large extent, as female. I don't know, but that inclusive social justice perspective helped me feel an affinity to trans men that I didn't expect.

Today, I've come to understand my own sexuality as revolving around a desire for a soft masculinity. What I mean by this term is a masculinity that is not overly privileged, not about power and control, but comfortable and in control. I find this type of masculinity very attractive, in its many manifestations, among cisgender men, cisgender women, trans men and genderqueer individuals, so my dating is not exclusive to any one group. What I do know is that gay trans men often have a sensibility that makes me feel comfortable and at home.

SEARCHING FOR MY
SEAHORSE HUSBAND

SHEEDU AL-NEMMEH

KELLY AND LOSING MY VIRGINITY

As an adolescent, I didn't have many friends until the last semester of my senior year of high school. Just before going off to college, I got a job making pizzas in order to put aside some money. With that job came my first real group of friends, and they liked to party, which was unfamiliar to me.

This was around the time that Kelly joined our crew. She had just returned from her first year of college. We spent the summer at raves, in Goth and S&M clubs, partaking in drugs, drinking and bonding. These were the places that would allow underage kids like us in.

I believed I was asexual, with no real interest in or experience with sex. To me, Kelly was just a friend. She felt differently. As we rolled on ecstasy, she grabbed my hand, intertwined our fingers, and rested her head on my shoulder. I was young, naive, sexually unconscious and unsure, but I accepted her advance and we became a couple.

Two weeks later, I left for college in Las Vegas, and we decided to continue dating long distance. Every night, we called each other from our dorm rooms to talk about school, life ambitions and personal growth. Though I never expressed an emotional attachment, she missed me and came to visit over Thanksgiving weekend.

I had gotten a small suite at the Paris Hotel for us to share. I was still underage, but I came prepared with a bottle of vodka purchased by an older college friend. I met her in the lobby of the hotel and helped carry her bags back to the room. In the privacy of our room, with vodka and all the alcohol we could find in the hotel mini bar, we started mixing drinks and taking shots. It wasn't long before we got hammered!

As my drunkenness increased, so did my courage. I kissed her and a spark ignited. We started making out, I momentarily paused to flip through porn for ambiance, then feverishly returned to making out. We passionately started tearing the clothes off our bodies, discarding them on the hotel room floor, then sprinting to the bathroom to climb in the shower. I had never done anything like this before, could hardly imagine this was actually happening. But it was! I was drunk and kept going. As the hot water ran down our bodies, I sucked on her nipples. To this day, I remember how beautifully big, soft and pillowy her boobs were. I knelt down, she opened her legs, and I ate the fuck out of her pussy. By the time we got out of the shower, I was half drowned from the constant cascade of water.

We toweled off quickly and took another shot of vodka. I threw her onto the bed, her petite body bouncing as it hit the mattress. I returned to eating her out. She was delicious! I could have happily kept my head between her legs for hours, sucking up her juices. I climbed on top of her to kiss her, our bodies pressing into each other, exploring the soft spots, the places that were burning, and the tender bits.

When every nipple had been sucked, every square inch of skin had been touched, and our bodies merged into one, I felt ready to enter her. I dove down to taste her sweet juices one last time before pushing my penis, cautiously, into her tight vagina. I remember feeling her full bosom push into me, as I pushed into her. She allowed me to slide in bare, without a condom, because she was on birth control. Her tight pussy squeezed my penis, pushing me to within an inch of an orgasm. I quickly jabbed her with my penis, did a couple of thrusts, and pulled out quickly. This was my first time! If I had stayed in, I would have only lasted for a minute. Repeating this strategy of quick entrances and exits allowed me to last for a full five minutes. It was amazing!

We dated for a few more months. For me, the relationship had felt more like a friendship. I enjoyed her company, we shared friends, but the sex felt disconnected, like I was having it with a friend. This became increasingly obvious to me, when I realized that I needed to be drunk to have sex with her. I didn't know it then, but I do now—I don't fall in love easily.

OPENING

After that relationship ended, I resumed questioning my sexuality. I stopped looking for love, or sex, or whatever, and focused my attention on school. I returned to thinking I was asexual and practicing celibacy. My only sexual outlet was porn. I was indiscriminate, watching both gay and straight sex scenes. The gay scenes provided some clarity to my inner curiosity of what sex between men could be like—something I had questioned since having a casual crush on a frat boy who was openly gay.

Two years later I moved to San Francisco to attend art school. I befriended a fellow student called Tatum, a loud-dressing, nouveau riche, East Coaster, who stood well over six feet tall out of heels. Tatum was a trans woman. I respected her authenticity and strength. We became very close friends and then roommates.

While living together I saw her date a string of terrible men, who hid her from their friends and fetishized her. She became increasingly depressed. At night, she would talk about how hard it was to find a man who would show her generosity, empathy, honesty and character.

When I looked at Tatum, I saw a woman who was genuine, sincere and fierce. She boldly lived her truth. I believed she deserved to be treated with kindness and compassion, because that is how one behaves as one human engaging with another. She was not accustomed to this humane treatment and started to believe that I was the man for her.

One evening over dinner, as we sat silently eating together, Tatum put her fork down and asked, "Will you be my boyfriend?"

Tatum was eight years my senior. I had only been in one previous relationship, leaving me inexperienced in these situations, and uncomfortable with these types of conversations. I had low self-esteem, which made me feel like my opinions were less relevant. In fear of losing my closest friend, I accepted her advance.

In the beginning, I was perplexed by our sex life. I had assumed that as the "male" of the relationship, I would be the active partner and she would be the passive partner. Also, I assumed she would have a vagina. Much to my surprise, neither proved to be true! Tatum was a top, and only a top! Until I met her I had never been penetrated. She was well endowed and it took a year of gentle stretching and patience to finally take her inside me.

Tatum and I stayed together for six years, but our relationship went south. Our sex was infrequent, at most four times a year, due to her hormone treatments and my low libido. Towards the end, she became abusive and I walked away from that relationship.

FIGURING IT OUT

Again, I began to question and explore my sexuality. I had always supported the gay community, growing up non-judgmental and meeting a variety of people from different backgrounds in my youth. I had curiously watched gay male porn but, to figure out if I was gay, I needed to probe deeper. Was I a bottom? Could I ever top again? I wanted to identify and learn more about my sexual desires.

After leaving Tatum, my sex drive surged! I went from two lovers to multiple partners in a period of months. It was easy to find sex in gay male community, but to find a partner or someone to date proved quite a challenge.

Gay men preferred casual encounters and non-monogamy, which was unfamiliar to me. I experienced culture shock by the way gay men dated, like how they could have anonymous sex after knowing someone for moments. The best-case scenario was having a couple of dates with a guy, then no more contact. I came from a heteronormative background, in which people met, dated, had sex, moved in together, built relationships and got married. I struggled to find something worthwhile with gay cis men and continued to struggle to fit in.

While exploring sex with men, my mind began to reflect on what I knew to be true about my desires. Memories of Kelly came up, the smell, taste and texture of her pussy, how I used my fingers to get her off. These were hot images but I knew by now that I was not attracted to a woman's body—the curves and soft skin did not arouse me—that I was indeed, sexually incompatible with women.

I also knew that I liked men's bodies, mostly because of the body hair. I loved to rub my palms along the furriest of arms, stomachs and legs, and I very much enjoyed feeling a man's body hair against my body. I loved the scratching sensation of stubble on my legs or face during intimate moments. I finally realized that I was aroused by men's bodies—their roughness, rigidness and hairiness. These were the bodies I lusted for.

I dreamt of finding something in the middle. I desired a strong, firm, hairy, masculine body that also had some scrumptious anatomy up front that differed from mine.

This led me to search for a trans man lover. I already knew that I liked the complexity of trans bodies, and having dated Tatum I learned not to make assumptions about what a trans person's anatomy would be or what they'd want sexually. Trans people are all unique individuals, living authentic lives.

Honestly, I found trans guys sexy and still do. But I wondered if I could say that and not sound like I had a fetish. If I said I found men sexy that would have been acceptable, but it felt dicey to voice a more specific desire.

I like how trans men's features are male, with prominent brows, square jaw lines, face and body hair, deep voices and strong bodies. To me, trans men are more rugged than the highly groomed pretty gay boys that dominate the city. Despite this ruggedness, trans men somehow maintain an edge of softness, maybe around the eyes or the lips.

At that point, I became open to having a "boyfriend" or "partner" that differed from cultural expectation. I thought it would be fun to disrupt the norm of "gay = sex between two cis men." I could imagine being in the world with my boyfriend and no one would know our hidden histories; they would see us as we were—equals.

A CASUAL ENCOUNTER

Three years ago, the Friday of gay pride weekend in San Francisco, I had my first encounter with a trans man. I met him online, we trudged through the basic getting to know you questions, and then discussed meeting up in person. When he asked whether I had any FTM experience, I assured him that I was comfortable with his anatomy, had been in a relationship with a cis woman and then a trans woman for 6 years. Truthfully, I let him know, I had no real experience.

He accepted my response, and we scheduled our first date for the San Francisco Trans March After Party, at a bar named El Rio. We stood on the crowded patio, sharing stories about ourselves, our jobs and friends. The conversation flowed, as did the beverages, and our chemistry built. We left the crowded, smoky patio that was filled with a sea of trans folks, queers and allies for the quieter bar next door. That bar was less crowded, dimly lit, and allowed us to get closer and have our first kiss.

Later that evening, we went back to his place in Bernal Heights. As he walked me through his house, he shared about the home improvement projects he had been doing. I got turned on as I imagined him using tools, knocking down walls and doing renovations.

We continued drinking at his house. He wooed me, and I was enthralled by him; he was the epitome of a true masculine man, with natural mannerisms no different than those of a cis man. He presented himself as blue collar, which in the gay male world was a fantasy persona, but for him, was real. Throughout the night we continued drinking and talking until we decided to go to bed together. I was too drunk to do anything sexually. We cuddled in bed and I fell asleep in his arms.

In the morning, I woke up with my usual hard on. I rolled over and started running my hand across his hairy chest. I lay there worried as he slowly woke up in my arms. I had never had sex with or even really known a trans guy before this—I was nervous! What if I didn't like the sex, or worse, what if I couldn't stay hard?

I decided to try. I ran my hand from his chest, down his thick happy trail, then under his boxer briefs, and down to his pubic region. Briefly touching his t-cock, then retreating swiftly to his chest. I did this several times, but could not follow through to sex.

He made me coffee the only way I like to drink it—in a pour-over cup. We continued on with light conversation about what we had in store for the day.

I left there thinking that he was a great guy, we had chemistry, and an amazing evening. For me, it was obvious I wanted to see him again.

Sadly, that was the last time I saw him.

MORE SEARCHING

After that night, I began looking for a trans male partner online, searching Adam4Adam, Craigslist, Scruff, the dreaded superficial Grindr and even OKCupid. As I scanned the profiles, I noticed that many of the guys were in polyamorous relationships, mostly with women or gender nonconforming people who had been assigned female at birth. I continued my search, for what now seemed like the rare, gay trans man.

On OKCupid, I found a match!

Once I finished reading his profile I sent him a message immediately. He took nearly a week to get back. We continued to talk in this pattern, me promptly replying, due to my personality and upbringing, and him responding slowly.

After more than six months we finally met for a drink at a bar near my place. We had good conversation, so I bought a second round, but he declined the drink. We continued talking about our passions, lives so far, and especially our sexual and dating history. He specifically wanted to know if I had "FTM experience." I was honest and told him about Kelly and Tatum, and said that I did not have any "real experience."

We moved onto a game of pool. My competitive side wondered, "Should I let him win?" As the cis-male in the equation, I felt that I should be the more dominant and protective partner in social settings. Well, so much for that idea! He was an amazing pool player and dominated the game. In the blink of an eye, he kicked my ass. I was turned on by that! I had actually found someone who was just as competitive as me. His win was amazing. I was awestruck!

He walked me safely home. Saying good night with a kiss outside of my apartment building. As I walked into my house I thought about what a great night it was. We had so much chemistry, I felt a connection.

A week or so later he texted me, "Want to go out tonight?"

"Absolutely!"

I was excited to see him again and brought my last bottle of black-berry-infused whiskey I had made for my 30th birthday. We spent the night walking around Ocean Beach, sipping on the bottle, and getting to know each other. We walked along the water's edge, I dipped a toe in, and discovered it was warm.

Impulsively, I stripped off my clothes and jumped in. I convinced him to shed his clothes and join in the fun. In the moonlight, he removed his shirt, then his binder, and I realized that he still had breasts. I had noticed before that his chest didn't look as flat as other guys' chests, but hadn't given it a second thought.

We splashed and played around in the ocean, the swirl of the water and the sensation of sand on my body aroused me. We swam to each other and started making out, our bodies pressing together. I felt his breasts against my chest and I stayed erect! This proved to me that we could have sex, regardless of whether or not he had breasts.

We left the beach and returned to my house, showered off the salt and sand, and climbed into bed. I enjoyed giving him head and fingering his hole, rimming his asshole, sucking his nipples, biting a bit and our passionate make-outs. He told me that he came multiple times, but I felt uncertain, and that was unfamiliar. When having sex with cis men you know they are cumming or have cum; with an FTM guy it was less clear.

I put a condom on and slid inside his front hole. I wanted to be gentle, to take my time feeling his body shifting to let me in. The sensation of heat and pressure of the internal walls of his front hole against my penis was incredible. I slowly thrusted in and out, feeling his body contract and relax in sync with my body, gently bucking my way to a new personal record of eight minutes of intercourse.

After that we had a few more dates, but things started to come to light that made me uncomfortable. First of all, I discovered that he was still living with his ex-girlfriend. Then, one time I visited him and he had his period. This turned me off, but probably not for the reason you'd expect. The problem wasn't the period, but that he was unsure if he wanted to continue to transition or revert to being female, so he was only taking the minimum dose of testosterone. Without judging his decision, I knew I preferred to be with men who were certain about their male identity. I didn't want my partner to change his mind.

MURKY WATERS

In my experience, dating cis men has been more transparent but has not led to partnership. It also feels difficult to find a trans male partner. I've had several unfortunate experiences where the person I was interested in was already in an open relationship, and was really only looking for a quick hookup when they took their T-shot and became horny. Sometimes, I questioned whether I was just a novelty for them, or a fetish or fantasy. In moments when I felt rejected and insecure, I expressed my frustration by questioning their gender and sexuality—unfairly, I thought some of these trans men might still identify as women who wanted to have sex with women.

Despite these more frustrating moments, I continue to be overwhelmingly and shamelessly attracted to trans men. However, I feel like most cis-dominated gay male communities do not support this perspective. Some cis gay men have called me bisexual for dating FTMs, because they do not see trans men as men. That seems ridiculous! The trans men I have encountered were a lot more masculine than the cis gay men I've gone on dates with. Questioning whether trans men are men feels like cis-gay-male misogyny and a community-endorsed fear of the vagina.

For me, it is less about anatomy and more about energy. When people care enough about each other, it will work out. The gay community preaches acceptance and understanding, but often is filled with hypocrites who don't accept or understand. Regardless of the gender my future husband was assigned at birth, I hope that he will treat me as well as I will treat him.

I fantasize about being with a trans man who retains his original plumbing and is a versatile bottom who can confidently bend me over and fuck me. I have met some masculine trans guys, but so far, most have been complete bottoms. My ideal match would be a masculine trans man, open to monogamy, and would be willing to switch sexually. He would be interested in bearing children, and I would proudly call him my "seahorse husband." In this fantasy we'd build a family with a kid or two and live happily ever after. I know that's a lot to ask, but one can dream!

At the beginning of this essay I was a teenager, uncertain about whom I was attracted to and unclear about what role I wanted to play in bed. Now, I know I am queer, identify as sexually gay, and date a spectrum of people. I'm no longer a loner. Although I am the only gay guy in my group of friends, they support me and accept me no matter what. I've been open and honest about my past relationships and sexual experience with cis and trans men and women, and my friends have been unfazed. Ultimately, I found acceptance where I thought I would never find it. The greatest gift in the world has been to realize that I don't need to fit in to be happy. I just need to be myself.

Spirit and Flesh*

Rev. Daniel Borysewicz

I 've learned over the years to be open to where the universe wants me to go, or at least to try to be. I learned about being of service from being in recovery—that willingness to help others is a way to get out of my own head.

Growing Up, Death in the Family, and My Mother's Beef with God

I grew up in upstate New York, outside of a small city called Utica, in a Roman Catholic household, and the youngest of three boys. By the time I was twelve, it was only my mother and me. My brothers left home, my maternal grandmother died when I was ten, and my father died from Hodgkin's lymphoma. We stopped going to church because my mom was mad at God because "he" took her mother. Death in my immediate family at a very early age had an impact on my life and is one of the reasons of why I was drawn to becoming a hospice chaplain.

I started working when I was in high school, then dropped out halfway through my senior year because I was bored and more interested in getting high. I ended up joining the Navy, following in my father's footsteps and not in my brothers' who were in the Air Force. (The Navy would take a high school dropout but the Air Force did not.) I worked as an aviation electrician on helicopters for four years, got out, and came out as being gay. This was in the early 80's.

Boy Scouts and Sexual Identity

When I was eight years old, I had a realization that I was not like other boys. I was in the Cub Scouts, and we were about to go on a winter camping trip in snowy upstate New York. The plan was for me to go with a friend, a boy who lived on the next street over, and to get a ride from his dad. When I got to his house, it became clear that he wasn't going to go because he wasn't feeling well. He was lying on the couch in the living room, with an Afghan pulled up to his waist and no shirt on. I remember to this day, looking at him and thinking: "Oh my God, this is such a beautiful sight!" I didn't feel sexually attracted per sé, because I was only eight, so perhaps it was more sensual than sexual. I was feeling like I was witnessing something incredibly beautiful and also being sad that he wasn't going on the trip. I can still see this image very clearly in my mind's eye.

Once I left for the trip, I was happy of course. I wasn't going to dwell on it, but obviously I still do. I'm dwelling to the point where I still remember this image very clearly. My spirit was saying yes, you are attracted to this beauty, and that there is something here that shows who you are and that you want to see more of. It was my first sign that I was attracted to boys.

In high school, I thought of myself as bisexual and had a few girlfriends. It wasn't until I got out of the Navy that I actually started having boyfriends, but I also still occasionally dated women. It wasn't until after I got sober in 1993 that I stopped having sex with women. Today, I identify as queer. I'll have sex with women but I won't date them. I'm not attracted to feminine energy. Right now, I predominantly date trans men.

FIRST ENCOUNTERS

The first trans guys I met were in Tucson, Arizona in 2007. I was working for the Southern Arizona AIDS foundation doing HIV prevention work and met Mitch and Harry, two volunteers at the local LGBT community. They had been lesbian girlfriends and then started the process of transitioning to becoming men. Eventually, Harry identified as a gay man while Mitch identified as a straight man. I was totally blown away by their story.

Getting to know them helped me to better understand the nature of a "true" homosexual—a gay man/lesbian woman who is attracted to their same gender (regardless of gender assigned at birth or how someone presents)—and that's how Harry could go from being a lesbian attracted to women to a man attracted to men. Harry's gender might have changed, but he was still attracted to "same." I know there are a lot of nuances, that gender or sexuality is not cut and dry, not black and white, but thinking about Harry and Mitch as gay versus straight helped me early on to wrap my head around some of these issues.

The first trans guy I became involved with was in Phoenix. I was invited to a transgender and allies pool party. This guy and I got to the party at the same time, and it was lust at first sight. We liked what we saw and spent the rest of the evening swimming in the pool, floating around, chatting and flirting. We ended up going home that night, and I was like, "Oh my God, this is what I have been looking for all my life!" Don't get me wrong; this was not me thinking that he was the "best of both worlds." That's offensive and never came into my consciousness.

There was intimacy. He hadn't had top surgery yet, so I got a chance to learn about his boundaries. He explained to me what his body dysphoria was like, his breasts were no-man's land and that helped me to begin to have some kind of understanding of trans experience. He was willing to educate me about what parts on his body were okay to play with and what parts were not. It helped that I'm a guy with street smarts and a quick study. He was the only trans guy that I actually ended up having sex with in Arizona before I moved to the Bay Area, which is another reason why I wanted to relocate there.

When I talked to some of my cis gay friends in Tucson about being with a trans man, they questioned whether I was bisexual. At the time I identified as gay, so I said, "No, I'm not bisexual!" I thought, "Whoa! Just because he was born with a vagina, doesn't mean he's not a man." My friends had so many questions about this trans guy's body…

"Does he have a dick?"

"Yeah!"

"How big is it?"

"Why, do you want to suck it?"

These invasive genitalia-focused questions made me crazy. Just because someone's genitalia is not the same as what a stereotypical male genitalia is supposed to look like, you don't get to treat them this way. I learned early on about the discrimination that was happening within the gay community, and it taught me about the injustices that were happening. We are marginalized people, yet we're marginalizing people within our own community.

MY SEMINARY BOYFRIEND

After getting my GED while in the Navy, and many years later an undergraduate in Anthropology and Queer Studies from the University of Arizona, I got inspired to pursue a Master's of Divinity degree at Pacific School of Religion in Berkeley. This path was not something I could have foreseen, because up until then I identified as a Pagan and not as a Christian. If anything, I initially intended to pursue a Master of Arts in Ethics and Social Theory, but then became aware that there was a joint program where you could do both programs at the same time. The details of this path make for a longer story, but suffice it to say that I followed spirit and found my path.

In seminary I ended up meeting a trans man who would eventually become my boyfriend. I learned a lot from him as far as how to talk to folks in the trans community. He was able to provide me with a lot of information about asking the right questions, to wait to find out what someone calls their junk before you give it a label. He also showed me how much fun I can have with a trans man. In fact, after being in the Bay Area for six or seven months, I had sex with a cis guy, and I was like, oh, this is okay but not quite as great.

When I had sex with my seminary boyfriend, at some point we paused, and he asked me, "Do you really just want to have sex with women and are using trans men as surrogates?" I told him I didn't think that was the case. Several years later, I had sex with two cis women (after 20 years of only having sex with men). They were both kinky. One of them was androgynous and queer and the other was straight and slender. During sex, the slender woman was straddling my face and calling me "Daddy," and all of a sudden I remembered the question my seminary boyfriend asked. I thought, even though I have had trans men straddle my face in the same position, in no way was this experience with this woman the same. Her smell, taste, energy and high-pitched voice were all very different from a trans guy's. So no, it is not the case that I was having sex with trans men because they were easier to bed than women. There is no correlation between the two. Trans men are men. They smell, taste and have a masculine energy just like cis men.

I LOVE HAVING SEX WITH TRANS MEN

I love sucking cock but I love, love, love, eating pussy. It's one of the things I've enjoyed most over the years. I've come to recognize that I am very empathic, very sensitive to energy, and sexual energy specifically. I love the gradual buildup of sexual energy within female-bodied persons, and especially with trans guys. I love the fact that trans men can have multiple orgasms, and if they do, that we're both going to have a wonderful time. With cis guys, it's like a one-time deal more or less; the sexual energy builds up quickly, crescendos, and then is gone. With trans guys, It's a gradual buildup of sexual energy, and it keeps building and building. I just suck up that energy. I love giving pleasure and also feeding off of that sexual energy. I would consider being monogamous with a trans guy but not with a cis guy because I would not want to give up having sex with trans men.

BEING TRUE TO WHO I AM: A KEY TO BEING AN ALLY

About five years ago I went on a coffee date with a trans guy I had met online. On those online dating sites, people will see a picture of me and probably assume I'm a butch daddy bear. So here we are having coffee and he says: "You're much swishier than I expected you'd be." I started laughing and said: "Yeah, you're right!" If he had said the same thing to me five years earlier, I'm not sure I would have had such a lighthearted response. I would have been offended. But because of the work that I've been doing on myself, becoming open to some of my own issues, my own internalized homophobia, and learning to integrate masculine and feminine aspects of myself, I was actually in a much better place. "Yeah, this is who I am! If you don't like it then I'm sorry…" I believe that becoming a whole person helps me to be a better ally for my trans brothers and sisters. We are all human beings who are trying to just get along. Obviously this guy had his own stuff he was projecting.

Something that also helped me to become an ally for the trans community was dealing with my own issues around femininity, and especially in regards to transphobia toward trans women. Once I got to know trans women and actually connect with them, it helped me to understand their experiences and to look at my own baggage. Unpacking all of this stuff within me really helped me to become a much more whole person, and I owe a lot of it to my engagement with the trans community. Doing this entails working with shame. It is a central piece that comes up for all of us, and dealing with it helps make us whole.

BODY IMAGE: LEARNING FROM TRANS GUYS

Being a big guy, something I've struggled with most of my life is body image. In summer 2013, I had gastric bypass surgery and lost about ninety pounds, twenty, which I've gained back. There was a period of time where I thought "Only if I'm skinny and sexy then people will want me." I've come to realize that being a big man is who I am. If you want me and want to have sex with me, you need to want me as I am. If I decided to lose weight, it's about me wanting to do that for myself and not for other people.

There was a long period of time where I thought that I had to look a certain way to be attractive to guys. In the Bay Area, there's a much larger pool of people who are attracted to someone like me. I realize that I don't have to be desperate and have sex with just anybody who finds me attractive. I'm not going to do that anymore. I need to be interested in you and find you attractive, because I deserve better than a pity fuck.

One of the things that I've learned from dating trans guys is that I don't like having anonymous sex anymore. I very rarely have casual sex because I want to at least get to know the person a little bit first, and more than just their name. Trans or cis, I want to go out for coffee first. I also don't want a crazy person showing up at my house. For trans guys, it's safer that way, but now I feel that way for myself, too. More than anything, I like some level of intimacy because sex is not just about getting off. If I want to get off, I'll just jerk off, and I do that all the time anyway. So if I'm going to have sex with you, I want to at least engage with you, even if it's a short conversation. Anonymous sex brings up the desperation I used to feel so many years ago, when as long as someone wanted to have sex with me it didn't matter if I was attracted to them. Fear of rejection by those I was attracted to also played a part in these feelings of desperation. I felt like I needed to go for it because I didn't deserve better. Ultimately, that kind of sex was not fulfilling me emotionally. I've learned to become more of a whole person and to honor myself. That's a theme that comes up for so many of us within the queer community—we still don't recognize the fact that we need to honor others by honoring ourselves first. With trans men, I sometimes feel that we help each other heal.

SALVATION WILL COME FROM GENDER FLUIDITY

My personal work on body image, internalized homophobia and shame has provided me with the courage and personal insight to create a workshop, "Flourishing Beyond Shame," to help others look at their own shame regarding gender and sexuality. I have been offering it to communities and conferences since 2011. Healthy shame can provide us with a painful feeling of humiliation or distress caused by the consciousness of wrong or foolish behavior. Unhealthy shame, or "false shame," as I call it in my workshop gives us a sense of feeling flawed, defective and unacceptable as a person based on the external influences and pressures from the values and morals of another person or group of people. In this workshop, I provide people with opportunities to reflect on their personal understandings of how stigma and shame can affect gender and sexuality and become a hindrance to living a flourishing life.

A trans woman once told me that when the world needs more balance, more trans people will come into it. The proliferation of gender fluidity is perhaps our salvation. As a hospice chaplain, I talk with people who are on the journey towards the end of their life and some of them are concerned about their "salvation" after death. I believe that the salvation for humanity is for each of us, cis people, to walk alongside our trans brothers and sisters to gain a deeper insight into our own gender identity and how fluid gender presentation truly can be for each of us as *Homo sapiens*. When I look into the eyes of another, I see the image of the Divine. When I look at a transgender person, I believe I am seeing a true representation of the Divine on earth. It is my hope that other cis people will come to see our transgender siblings like I do, as Divine siblings who will help bring balance to the world.

Interview-turned-essay, conducted by
and in collaboration with Avi Ben-Zeev.

BROTHER OUTSIDER

J. JAMES KEELS

GrowlR listed you as >1 mile away, your text
had punctuation, didn't use emoji,
you used *discreet* correctly and
that compelled me as much as your thick beard. Your furry belly.
You reminded me you were trans*, just in case I hadn't read your profile
or noticed your handle,
or paid attention to your photos.
No doubt because
many men blindly send dick pics, throwing a fistful of darts at a board to
see if one sticks,
while writing
sup? looking? u hung?

Your bookshelf contained my undergraduate years;
we discussed Audre Lorde's <u>Sister Outsider</u>, you said
you had read it as a lesbian, but now
you needed to read it again, because –

and you led me to the bedroom after crating your dog because you
wanted him to feel safe.

I spent the first part of my life hating men.
Conflicted, because my desire
was overwhelming, yet my primal fear
the air in a car during July, windows rolled up, the hot seat burning my
bare legs,
the black plastic dash too hot to touch.

The men who drugged me, or who expected
something
after driving me home, even though I was only fourteen.
My brother, who bellowed threats, had fist fights on the front lawn outside
my bedroom.
The boys at school, whose looming shoulders barred my access to the locker
room
so I wore my gym clothes under my jeans to avoid being sucker punched.

My only friends were lesbians. Not the *really* butch ones,
they scared me too –
but the ones who would cry at kd Lang songs, and smoked Marlboros,
bursting into grin when discussing a new femme they were dating,
who drove me to school on the back of their motorcycle, and warned the
jocks
not to fuck with me,
and who later took me to prom.

Kissing you then, touching the scars where your breasts
had once been, I wondered if
you knew those men, too. I wondered if your desire was anything like
mine.
Those men frightened me, yet I longed to give them my body,
taking theirs in my mouth like a holy Eucharist.

Did you also desire them, even as a lesbian? Or did their gender appeal to
you, the belt buckles
they wore, the Wranglers with
Skoal rings in the back pocket,
their easy swagger and sense of masculine entitlement.

You are not that man now. Nor am I.
We explore – our parts
somewhat different.
Our chromosomes have only one x in common.
Yet our histories, I suspect, are similar.

I have butch swagger,
I can summon it on odd Friday nights in the Castro, though I know
it is really just drag.
My torso that of a hairy ape, you grab handfuls and tug –
my fingers explore your thick beard, less
wiry than mine, I wonder your grooming secret, searching your medicine
cabinet while I pee
and write down the name of the beard oil you use
the one I smell all over me,

making me hard again.

We can rewrite all this, you know.
Make it *ours*.
We can be the very men we envision,
rejecting the fistfights, and booming voices like echoes from
far away landscapes, now barren and dusty
favoring an even tone, strong and resonate.

We can keep the swagger, because, *fuck* – it is *so sexy*.

We can also be soft
and sweet
and loving
and kind
while flexing our might
and our muscle –

forging deftly ahead.

PART IV
COUPLES

LOVE, TRUTH AND NAKED YOGA*

23

AARON AND ALLAN

AARON'S STORY

GRANDPA, LEATHER AND WILD PIGS

I was born in small town in Finland. My Grandpa was my favorite adult. We lived in the same house, so I was lucky to get to see him every day, pretty much most of my childhood life. Grandpa and I would get up early, while everyone else was still asleep, have breakfast and hang out, and then take bike rides in the woods and go for outdoor adventures, including to see the wild pigs, which were super cute and wonderfully muddy.

Grandpa was a leatherworker. He made wallets. I hung out with him at his shop, the sweet smell of leather filling the air, sitting on his table as he sewed. As a bonus, I got to pick up the leather scraps off the floor and make stuff from it. Grandpa impacted my sense of masculinity and attraction. He was warm, kind, silly, always spoke his mind, a bit stubborn, and the social center of our small town. I was his little sidekick, which I loved. He was a big man, with massive big legs like tree trunks that probably seemed especially huge from my small child's vantage point. When I see a guy walking down the street with big thighs, I immediately swoon a bit.

AMERICA, TRUTH AND BOOK BURNING

I was about ten when my family moved from Europe to Georgia. While it was hard to leave my friends, my grandpa, and learn a new language, I did really like the warm weather. I loved dressing in shorts and a t-shirt and walking around barefoot pretty much all year round. It was a welcome change from my cold and constantly rainy hometown. Before I became a teenager, I was a pretty happy kid, bopping about in local parks, climbing trees, and generally being a tomboy. My grandpa would come visit. And I'd go back and visit him and my old friends. Old and new friends—we'd do adventures. Life was good.

During my teens and twenties, however, life was not so good, and that's an understatement. Gender norms started rearing their ugly heads. Life stopped making sense to me. The way I dealt with my gender (and life!) was to disappear. I was confused and felt lost. But I didn't know why. I didn't even connect my lostness with gender. I didn't get all the social intricacies and norms of what being a teenager was supposed to be. And I didn't know that trans guys existed. I knew something was off but I couldn't put a name to it. And, of course I couldn't research it because I didn't know what to research. This was before the age of the internet.

Still, I had constant daydreams of being a guy and doing stuff with other guys, going out on adventures and such. As I grew older, these adventures became more X-rated. I was living in my head most of my teens and twenties, so my first sexual attraction to a "real person" came later in life. Don't get me wrong, I had a rich inward life and loved having sex, but it was all fantasy and in my head. I didn't know what to do with my rich inner sexual life. I was afraid to tell anyone because I thought, "Oh my God, they will put me away," so I kept my "twisted" fantasies to myself and jerked off to them, sometimes quite elaborately. I did scenes with me, myself, and I. When I was a kid, I'd take rulers and spank myself, pretending like I was student and principal all at once, or a pirate and pirate's captive, a hiker and a horny park ranger. Very fun! But also lonely.

Outwardly, I directed all my energy to being good at school. (And Judo. Judo rocked. My eighty-year-old teachers were amazeballs. And they could beat anyone.) I thought learning would lead to "truth." I loved intellectual growth and was fascinated by the subject matters. I thought that if I just studied hard enough, I'd figure out the "who am I" and the "who am I in relation to other humans" questions. I wanted definite answers, clarity, a tangible system of rules I could rely on, because I couldn't reconcile my inward life with the external world. So I sought out math and physics. Surely answers would lie there!! And surely they would take up so much time that I could avoid having to face the socially awkward me.

I wanted to find Truth with a capital T. I wanted to dig deep. At the end of undergrad, after a lot of physics, math, philosophy of math, I realized none of them got me closer to truth of life. There was a moment when I realized that a lot of math is actually subjective. I felt so betrayed, I actually did this ritual where I burned my math books. I was done. In retrospect, I wasn't fair to math and physics—I was looking for something that math and logic could not provide. They are useful in some situations, but they are not the source of truth, love and connection. It was like looking for a donut in a toolbox.

COMING OUT TO MYSELF AS TRANS

There was a distinct moment when I realized I was trans. It felt like a truck just ran over me. I was thirty and in the Lesbian Avengers, not because I identified as a woman sexually attracted to women, but because people who kind of looked and behaved liked me were more likely to be found there. One day a trans guy walked in to do a presentation. He was a very nice guy and an engaging speaker, and as I sat there listening to him, all of a sudden my heart swelled and all the connections I was never able to make swiftly clicked in. "Oh my God, this is who I am!" Right afterwards, I took him aside and asked him all this logistical stuff (like where I would get T). I knew with 100% certainty that I was trans and that I'd finally found the answer I had been looking for. Truth revealed itself so fast. After trying to find it for thirty years, it was unleashed by a real live person rather than a thought process or theoretical system.

In my elaborate sexual fantasies I could be a guy with guys. I could have a bigger hairier body. In my twenties I'd watch BDSM porn and "play along." I'd tie myself up, take out some rulers, tree branches, paper clips, clothespins, and have a truly fabulous time. "Can you take it?" I'd say to myself. "Oh yes, please, please Sir," I'd answer. Then I'd say, "Well then, one more." I had lots of fun and orgasms galore and knew my body inside and out. But, I did miss sharing that with another person.

In my twenties I did have sex a couple of times with a guy who was a close friend of mine in grad school. He confessed that sometimes when we were having sex it felt like I was trying to draw him into a different world, one far from the here and now, and he felt like I was somewhere else. He was right. When he said that, I actually felt seen. I said, "Yes, that is true. I am trying to draw you into my fantasy life, a world that often seems more real to me than the 'real' world." Essentially I wasn't able to have honest, present sex in the form that my body and being took pre-testosterone.

It wasn't possible for me to see myself or the other person fully, or to be seen fully by the other person, so sex was kind of fraught. There was most definitely an element of pleasure and fun in sex, and I really liked my friend, but not being fully me prevented our dynamic from working.

Once I came out as trans to myself, I started feeling full blown desires for others. It was amazing. And wonderful. I actually thought, "Now I get why there's all this fuss about sex." I remember going to an FTMI meeting. There were a bunch of trans guys sitting around a table, and I went, "Oh my gosh, they are all so beautiful!!!" Look at those sideburns. The beards. The hairy legs. The broad shoulders. The ease and joy and excitement that shined from their very cores. I kept going to meetings, not only to learn, but also to flirt, flirt, flirt, and get naked with these beautiful men. I was a kid in a candy store. I became extremely sexual. Trans guys and cis guys. Lots of guys. I remember meeting this cis guy at a grocery store, he was super flirty with me, and I was super flirty back. I could feel this intense yearning in my body, like, "Whoa, okay, this is what these love songs and shit like that are about."

DISCLOSURE: BE TRUE TO WHAT YOU NEED

The biggest difference of having sex with trans and cis guys for me has been the level of disclosure. With trans guys, there has been an ease and naturalness to the dynamic. With cis guys, I had to deal with disclosure: when and where. Do I "come out" before we make the date? When we're on the date? When we're naked? It took me a while to figure out how to disclose in a way that was right for me.

Earlier on, I didn't want to make a "big deal" out of being trans. I'm a guy, you're a guy, so what if we have different histories and bodies—everyone does! The guy I'm with will find out once we start getting it on and he'll deal. But, that's not how it always happened. Early on in my sexual adventures, a bunch of guys and I were on a bike ride, and this guy and I decided to go to his apartment afterwards—oh goody. We started to get naked, kiss, make out, touch—oh goody. And then I casually mentioned I'm trans. He said: "Well I did have sex with a girl in high school one time, so maybe I can do this…" Ohhhh! So not the reaction I was hoping for. What made him think it was ok to compare me to a woman when I'm obviously not one? That experience felt too naked to me. I want bad news when I have my clothes on. From then on, I decided that all disclosures happen early on in the date, so I know who I'm dealing with—when I'm still clothed, literally and otherwise.

Here's an example of how disclosure has worked well for me. One time I was camping on Fire Island with friends, a cis guy was there and we started flirting. I decided I would disclose early while our clothes were still on. But I still firmly believed that it wasn't a big deal and wasn't going to make one out of it. I also wasn't going to kill the mood, so I said playfully, "Hey, just so you know, my parts are going to look really different from yours." For a split second, he had a "What the hell are you talking about?" look on his face, but then he said: "That's cool, I'll show you mine, if you show me yours." (I don't think he ever got what trans is or that I'm trans. For him it just stayed at "our bodies are a bit different"—which was actually quite liberating and fun. And fun we had!)

Disclosure, for me, is about what I need. There's no right or wrong; it's a self-assessment of what will make me feel at ease. It's not about the other person. They can take care of themselves. They may or may not have their own things to disclose, which they can choose how to do. And disclosure is not always about being trans. There are many other things to potentially disclose or "share": your sexual preferences, BDSM, emotional needs and desires, physical needs/desires/limits, need for sleep, etc. etc. Endless things to share. I hate it when being trans is made out to be this BIIIIIG thing that if you don't disclose exactly how the other person wanted you to disclose then you're lying. That is big baloney. No one else is expected to immediately disclose their childhood relation to gender and the exact size and shape of their genitals. There are so many guys who have been awesome when I've shared that I'm trans. There are a lot of amazing guys out there and a few of them have issues, which I think they should disclose!

MEETING ALLAN

We met in a naked yoga class. I had gone through a break up a year and a half earlier with someone I was really into and was just starting to feel like I was open to dating and being in a relationship again. So I went to naked yoga. I looked it up online and the website said that it was trans friendly. I thought, cool, but I was a little nervous and wondered what it was going to be like. The teacher was awesome and didn't bat an eye. He just extended a warm hello like he did to everyone else. Awesome. I decided to go inwards, make this about yoga and not about flirting, and to gently allow myself into this space of nakedness. After class, I talked with a guy, and we exchanged emails. Then I left yoga and the next day I get TWO emails: one from the guy I gave my email to and one from the guy who eavesdropped on us and memorized my email on the sly. The eavesdropper was Allan. Allan's note was super direct: "Hey we partnered at yoga last night. I think you're really cute and I'd like to get to know you more." Mmmh, a little stalky. But I loved his directness. So I agreed to meet up with him.

A week or so later, we met up at a café and we connected really well. We talked about friends, art, life. But, when we talked about what we liked to do sexually, that's when we actually had a moment of pause, both of us. That's the funny part of the story. He went first, and said something like, "I like to fuck a lot." I shared that fucking had not been a big part of my sexuality, but that BDSM is really important to me and that I've been part of the BDSM community for the last fifteen years or so. He said, "Oh, I'm pretty vanilla." And then we looked at each other and went: Mmmmhhhh. But, since we liked each other, we decided that we were going to have another date anyway, just to see what happens.

Then on our next date, I still needed some clarification on something that was puzzling me before I could get naked. Allan had told me that he was really attracted to trans guys, and I thought it was cool, but it also made me want to ask him questions: What does that mean to you? What attracts you to trans guys? If I was going to hear something like, "Well, because you're halfway between a woman and a man," I'd be done. There are definitely wrong answers to these questions for me. But, he said something like, "Well, you know what? I feel like my gender is not totally binary and I feel more at ease with people for whom gender isn't totally binary, or have a more complex gender." I thought, "Yes, I can see that, so okay, we can proceed and see where this goes." As it turns out, sex was really good! Afterwards, I told him: "You're not that vanilla!"

We have learned that we both actually like a lot more than we thought we'd like, which is really amazing. For me, it's been fun to do more fucking and love it. And Allan truly is not vanilla! Early on in our relationship, I came over after a particularly hard day at work, and Allan suggested he tie me down and clip one of those big paper clips on my parts and then grind away. I said: YES! Please. Turns out that his HOA was meeting right outside his door in the hallway that night. And they got quite an earful! Hee hee. Allan proudly told me that the next day. I was impressed—not only is Allan not as vanilla as he had claimed to be, he is also totally sex positive and A-OK with the entire condo knowing we were having scream-ing-our-heads-off sex that night.

When I think back on the night we first met, though, things could have turned out quite differently. I'm tremendously grateful we went on that second date. We could have so easily parted ways that first night, assuming we had no sexual overlap. I'm so grateful I felt open and curious and adventurous that night. I've not always been that open. There have been times where that kind of initial seeming incompatibility would have stopped the dating right there. But for the grace of the universe, we were both open and curious that night. Without that, I wouldn't have met the sweetheart of my life. What a loss that would have been! How inconceivable now, to not be with the sweetie of my heart. The man with whom I am building community, family and love. Wow. How one brief moment of deciding to try or not to try can have such a big impact on life. It really taught me to not get myself stuck in my own boxes. And, that even though there's me and there's him, there's also "us"—and that "us" changed us both, and we both have a lot more range than we thought. We now do switchy, topsy-turvy, BDSM, fucking, and even romantic lovey mooshy sex. And sometimes we giggle and make up funny animal stories.

I LOVE AND APPRECIATE ALLAN

One of the things that I love about Allan is that he values direct communication and makes a big effort to do it. When we have a difficult interaction we both try really hard to stay with it until we know what's at the root. He does it, even when it's hard. That's probably the hugest gift a person can give me—to not run away just because of an argument or difference of opinion. Allan listens to me and speaks his truth and kindly makes space to hear what I have to say. We're not perfect. By any means. This stuff is hard! But we keep trying and keep coming back. Instead of thinking about difficult conversations as conflict, we sometimes think of them as sharing. Sometimes quite intense sharing.

Allan, I love that when we wake up in the morning, from the first moments you open your eyeballs, you say hilarious things. You make me laugh the first thing in the morning and that's amazing. And you draw the funniest cartoons. You are just one of the sweetest people I've ever known, and not just to me but also to your friends and family. I love how you care about relationships and actually put energy into them. I love your creativity, how you speak truth and…that you're a sexy and horny animal. You have the cutest butt, I just want to dive my head right into it, and touch and lick you all over. Your belly, your thighs, your cock and yummie balls, your hairy chest, smelling the nape of your neck, and kissing you, my kissy monster. I like watching your graceful dancer body move. I want to grow old with you. We're going to be two old horny silly loving grandpas (uncles in actuality, but that's a technicality).

ALLAN'S STORY

BOY CRUSHES AND DREAMS OF A BIG CITY

I was born in a small town in upstate New York, the youngest of five kids. I had a good childhood; I went skiing and hiking regularly with my family and friends, which I enjoyed thoroughly, but part of me craved the cultural opportunities of a big city. I was learning to love movies, theater and music, and the town I grew up in simply didn't supply much of that. I became very involved in high school musicals as a teenager. I saw that as my ticket to a bigger world.

As far as sexuality is concerned, I definitely had crushes on boys in school but I didn't identify these crushes as being gay. It was a strange disconnect: having feelings that I was not going to name, or perhaps did not know how to name, because there was no context for them; pre-internet, pre-awareness. My only opportunities at that point would have been to go to the local library and look up some sort of pathological model of homosexuality, right? So part of me yearned for a big city, not only for the cultural opportunities it promised, but also for the social opportunities. As soon as I graduated from high school, I ran off to NYU, where I loved being part of this huge and sometimes overwhelming mix of people and opportunities.

BOY SCOUTS, BONERS AND FEIGNING HETEROSEXUALITY

My first sexual encounter was with a friend when I was thirteen, and he initiated. It's still vivid in my memory. He came for a sleep over at my house. We were sleeping in twin beds, and just before going to sleep he started to ask questions about masturbation: did I know what it was and had I done it? Talking about this gave us erections, and he invited me to his bed where we did the Princeton Rub.

I got another lesson in masturbation in the Boy Scouts. We were in a tent, maybe three or four of us, and we started talking about jerking off, and the most experienced kid did a show-and-tell with a demonstration, and the rest of us joined in. I've since heard from other guys that it is like a coming of age ritual and more common than I realized.

I enjoyed these experiences a lot but I didn't equate them with being gay. I thought that I just needed to meet the right woman. I had a plan based on family and social expectations that then became my own expectations. I had other sexual encounters with boys my own age in high school, and as a senior I had a few that were intense, like "Wow, I'm really, really enjoying this." I was able to have these experiences, love them, and want more of them, and *still* say to myself, "I'm straight and I'm going to get married someday to a woman."

My last gasp of feigning heterosexuality was when I was 20 and joined a fraternity in my sophomore year. I lasted a year. I made new friends but didn't feel fully integrated socially or sexually. In fact, I realized that I wanted several men in the frat, and that scared me. This was an environment where there were "fag jokes," drunken weekends, and talk about sex with sorority sisters—not with each other. It wasn't me. So I started taking theatre classes and eventually realized I needed to get out of the frat. I felt like an exotic bird. I didn't want to be exotic. I wanted to be with my own people.

COMING OUT AS GAY

After coming out, a college friend said, "Congrats, now that you're finally out, I'm taking you to a bathhouse." That provided a very fast exposure to sex beyond schoolboy experiments. I did nearly everything anatomically possible in one night! I also started to have deeper and more meaningful relationships with men. My first serious relationship was in college with a fellow student who appeared very confident and sure of himself. That was quite attractive to me. After a date or two, we spent an afternoon in his bedroom, and it was absolutely transformative. Several hours of sex, eating, more sex, watching TV, more sex, sleeping and… repeat. It was absolutely enchanting, and I was head over heels.

I came out to my parents and the rest of the world when I was 22. I absorbed a gay identity and joined that tribe. What did I do in the late 1970s to come out as a gay man in America? I got my ear pierced, subscribed to *The Advocate*, and joined the Radical Faeries. It was all part of my personal search, but it also narrowed my vision of who I was.

ENCOUNTERS WITH TRANS MEN

Trans guys were invisible to me for a long time. Socially and politically, my world consisted of primarily cis gay white men. In my 20's, 30's and (well into my) 40's, there was no intersection between trans and cis gay men, and, in fact, I had very little contact with anybody who I knew was trans, until I started teaching in college and Loren Cameron's *Body Alchemy* was published. I remember thinking, "That's the hottest man I've ever seen." Independent of his genitals, his entire body was very attractive from a gay man's perspective. The fact that his genitals included a front hole was mesmerizing. It was that special combination that fascinated me. I was just bowled over. I didn't go further and say, I want to meet, date and have sex with trans men. Instead, I noted his incredible hotness, then filed it in the back of my head. I was in a relationship at the time, and it was very easy to go on with my gay life as though nothing had changed. My reaction to Loren Cameron's photos didn't rattle my identity or behavior, but it did rattle my psychosexual core.

My next point of reference for trans men was years later when I had a few trans men students in my classes (I'm a professor). One time, my colleague and I were discussing one of these students and my colleague said, "You know, he has a crush on you!" I didn't know. It was meaningful that a trans man was interested in me. I admit being flattered, but I was not sexually attracted to him and besides, he was a student and I don't cross that line. But I began to pay attention to my feelings for trans men and considered acting on them.

Part of my reluctance to pursue sex with trans men, even as I was sort of putting things together, was that I didn't know if I could perform sexually. I remember thinking, "I don't want to hurt anybody's feelings and I don't want to be embarrassed. I don't want to treat anybody like my experiment and yet I'm really curious." So, finally, I started making contact with a few trans men on a dating site.

The first trans guy I hooked up with was inexperienced with cis men and did not want to be penetrated. We got naked, did very little touching, and instead watched each other jerk off from across a room. I was really turned on, and so was he, as both of us were exploring. I was accustomed to erections as signs of arousal, but now I was seeing a swollen vulva and wetness from a man's body. I was electrified. I knew at that moment I was having a profound sexual awakening.

From that first good experience (I didn't see him again, though we swapped warm emails), I went on what I laughingly call a "tranpage." I dated and had sex with twelve trans men over six months. There were no strings attached, and my experiences were overwhelmingly positive. There was lots of hot sex and much learning on my part. There is no uniform way trans men relate to their bodies, or T, or fucking, or anything else. Sexually, I always topped, and for the most part I was also psychologically a top, but I wasn't always the seducer or initiator. Sometimes I "bottomed from the top," so there was a separation between the physical and energetic acts.

I was particularly attracted to the confidence trans guys exuded when they disclosed. From my perspective, disclosure is actually very sexy, especially when it comes from confidence. Someone who thinks, "I'm not disclosing because I'm afraid you're going to reject me, but because I'm taking care of myself," sounds like somebody who is committed to their mental, physical and spiritual health. That's super attractive.

Acknowledging and acting on my desire for trans men did make me wrestle with my identity a bit. Never have I questioned my sexuality; I'm way out there on the Kinsey scale. I've simply discovered that my attraction to the masculine spectrum is more expansive than I previously realized. Once I understood that in myself, it was joyous and liberating. Beyond the sexual, I felt an *emotional* attraction to trans men, and a growing desire to have a trans-cis romance.

It was during the "tranpage" that I met Aaron. He was number 13.

AARON, MY LUCKY NUMBER 13

Aaron was the only trans man I did not meet online. I went to a naked yoga class because I like yoga and being naked with other men. I didn't have any special expectations for the evening. When Aaron walked into the studio, I had an "Oh my God, who is this person?" moment. His face was so handsome and intelligent, and he radiated a fantastic energy. Then, when he took his clothes off, and I realized he was trans, I practically melted through the floor. After class ended, I hung around while he was talking to somebody else. I overheard his email address being spoken to this guy, so I emailed him the next day. Borderline creepy, wasn't it? LOL.

On our first date, Aaron was very direct in the questions he asked. I had never been confronted that way so early on, so I was a little nonplussed. I felt like I had to stand up and take notice, and I wasn't sure of where that intensity was coming from or where it was going. Since then, I learned how invaluable that style of communication is. And it isn't always verbal.

I'll never forget something that happened early in our relationship. We were enjoying a laid back Sunday afternoon of sex. My face was between his legs, and as I was licking and sucking him I started to cry. Boom—no advanced notice—the tears just rolled. I was falling in love with Aaron and overcome with how right it felt to be with him, this wonderful person and his body. It was a kind of homecoming, yet we were new to each other. He was moved by my emotions and held me close. We lay there silently, without need for words.

Early in our dating, it was a very big deal to me that we were in a cis-trans relationship. I felt the need to tell people who were close to us about this difference. I would always ask Aaron first if that was ok. I was trying to be respectful of both him and us. As I look back, I think, "Wow, man, that was really a big deal to you, wasn't it?" Now it's not really something I think much about, and our difference has melted into just who we are as people. Any conflicts or whatnot have nothing to do with gender, gender identity or gender assignment. It's more that we have different sleep patterns, desires around going out and traveling. You know, couply stuff.

MY OWN GENDER IDENTITY

My own gender identity has become more clear to me from my experiences with trans men, particularly Aaron. My body is reconciled but my psyche moves between masculine and feminine. When we started dating, I told Aaron that I felt myself to be quite trans. I was concerned that wouldn't sound right, that it would be insulting. My transness does not manifest outwardly. It is not physical, but more behavioral and psychological. It's internal and I have no desire to express it externally. I have come to realize I am somewhere in the gender galaxy other than resolutely masculine and feeling like a man, and I have finally come to terms with something that was very private. As a kid my role models were women, my fantasies were about women, but they weren't sexual fantasies. They were more "being" fantasies. Like my attempt to join a fraternity because I was trying to emulate my sister who had joined a sorority. On the surface, the fraternity phase invokes the wrong narrative, which I was denying my gayness, but the real narrative is that I was performing a boy version of the girl version.

This element of truth about my gender was so personal. I never spoke it out loud until very recently, and it far post dates the truth of being gay that I didn't verbalize it until I was in my fifties. My personal narrative of coming out as gay is much cleaner and more linear. Now I look back with some amusement at how long it took me to figure things out. My gender identity wasn't in any kind of conventional way fully masculine, yet the only thing I wanted to change in my body was to get it in better shape. Sex reassignment? Not for me. So what kind of creature am I? I'm most comfortable as a queer man, primarily masculine in identity, but with a feminine presence in there, too. And finally, *what is gender, anyway?*

AARON, I LOVE YOU!

Aaron, sweetie, one of the things that I love about you is your insistence of saying things as you see them and being real. You have worked on being this way for many years, so when you tell me that you value my honesty and directness, it means a great deal. It makes me feel good, like maybe I'm doing something right if somebody who has devoted so much time and effort to having this much integrity and honesty, says that I'm doing an okay job. I love your commitment to us, family, friends and community. I love the life we are building together. I love your art projects, your witty word play and your playfulness in general. You are my passionate, funny, warm, sexy sweetie, and I love you!

Interview-turned-essay, conducted by
and in collaboration with Avi Ben-Zeev.

I Won't Let You Slip Away*

24

Kris and Owen

Our Family

We have been together for almost ten years. We are not officially married, but at this point we basically think of ourselves as spouses. We are considering a courthouse wedding on our anniversary. The ceremony itself is not a priority for us, as neither of us is religious, but now that we have a foster son who will be with us for a while, we are thinking that there might be good legal reasons to do it.

Everything has changed so quickly! Initially, we had decided to be temporary foster parents for babies and toddlers, especially those who were medically fragile or had been drug exposed, before they found permanent homes. But then we got our first foster baby—a micro-preemie—who came to live with us when he was released from the NICU. He came home on oxygen and had so many needs. As we worked together, we completely fell in love with this tiny human. We figured out ways to rearrange our work schedules, to ensure that one of us would always be there for him—we couldn't leave him with anyone else yet. We strategized and problem solved together and found out that we are excellent baby daddies, and that this particular little guy fits in with us perfectly. It currently looks like he might be going up for adoption, and we didn't even have to consider our decision to start going through the adoption process to be ready for that possibility.

ORIGIN STORIES

KRIS

From the get go, I was a very gender variant child. My mom was the same way when she was young. She was a tomboy, who played with matchbox cars. Those toys were later passed down to me—that was one way my parents let me explore gender roles early. In so many ways I felt I was different from my peers. I was born early, resulting in me having Cerebral Palsy. Being immediately viewed as different has made it easier to question cultural and social norms about everything, including gender.

Initially, I came out as a butch dyke, but that label didn't really feel right. So, I started to move away from that identity, looking for something that seemed closer to my reality. Around then I had a fortunate meeting with a transgender person, Lucas, in high school. He started attending my school as a boy, and was later "discovered" to be female-bodied, which caused quite a scandal. Immediately, I felt fascinated by him. The way he was in the world made me think, "You are so much closer to what I think I am." Finally, I had a tangible identity, something that felt more accurate than anything else I had explored before.

When he first arrived at school, Lucas was not out—but I knew! He hadn't told me, but I was able to instinctually sense his truth. His gender fluidity and authenticity shone brightly in his eyes. He lived in a way that was true to himself.

Watching how Lucas lived in the world showed me how I had been trying to conform to a label or fit into a box of some sort, because that had seemed easier. This is how things were done in Chattanooga, Tennessee. It's a gendered place, where people expect you to behave a certain way and do things because that's the way they've always been done. I began to rebel against those expectations in order to pursue an authentic life for myself. I started to research everything about being transgender on the internet. Back then, there was a lot less information available.

My school friends were mostly queer identified, including Lucas who had been so inspiring to me, and I found other LGBT teens through word of mouth. We created a support group and reached out to others in bigger cities in the South. I found a couple of guys on Live Journal. One guy I was intrigued with provided a clear plan for transitioning on his page. After reading up, I realized that testosterone was an option. I came out as trans to my friends and family and hoped that they would continue to support me during my journey to be myself.

My dad was a huge support when I came out in high school. Shortly after I told him I was transgender, he took a road trip to Atlanta and bought every book he could find on the topic. He became my personal encyclopedia of trans history. To this day he knows more about it than me! He extended his unconditional love to many of my friends whose parents were not as accepting and open.

Through our LGBT support group and the beginnings of social media I connected with more LGBT teens in the South. Over time, I would merge my new friends from the big city, Atlanta, with my friends in Chattanooga, building my first queer community. For the first time, I felt a sense of belonging and knew I was not the only person in the world that felt this way.

OWEN

My family is very autistic. My younger brother has autism most clearly, but my mom and I have many of the same characteristics. We were a quiet, reserved kind of family. When I was a kid, both of my parents worked, and I was left alone to do my own thing most of the time. I appreciated having the freedom to explore the neighborhood and had plenty of time to pursue my own interests and study whatever I wanted. At the same time, I didn't get any strong support. My school life was very violent and horrible. My peers, as well as many adults at the school, taunted me about my social awkwardness and gender presentation.

When I was young in preschool and kindergarten, I strongly identified as a boy. As I got older it became more complicated. I sometimes identified as a boy, but sometimes neither as a boy, nor a girl, and sometimes as a tomboy girl. I always wanted my hair cut short and picked out boys' clothes when I had the choice, but usually didn't get my way.

Regardless of how my hair was cut or what I wore, people would ask, "Are you a boy or a girl?"

Upset by their question, I would reply, "No!"

By junior high, I didn't identify as a certain gender; I identified with mythical characters who were neither male nor female, or who could switch between male and female, which I learned about by scouring the Mythology section of the library. To try and obtain more information about my identity, I went to the feminist lesbian bookstore in downtown Madison, Wisconsin. I perused the transsexual section—the word transgender did not yet exist—to try and find examples of other people like me. But all that I found were books about lesbian separatism, womyn loving womyn, and transphobic ideas about male to female transsexuals stealing womanhood from "real womyn."

I had hoped that this store could offer answers for me because I felt queer, like somehow I belonged in this community, but I couldn't figure out how to make myself fit. I knew after my visit to the bookstore that a lesbian was a woman-identified woman who loved another woman, and that meant that I was definitely not a lesbian. I felt that I could not be gay, because other people didn't see me as a boy. This left me feeling trapped, because at the time the "gay and lesbian" communities didn't seem to include anything about gender identity. This meant that I felt isolated from the gay community while growing up. I watched the growth of Pride parades with interest and read a lot of gay history and fiction. As famous people like Ellen DeGeneres started coming out publically during my adolescence, I felt proud and excited, but kept those feelings to myself.

As an adult I moved to San Francisco, to some extent, to get even closer to the gay community that I still felt unable to enter. One day, I went to the library to look up transsexuals again similar to my earlier pursuit in the bookstore. This time I found Loren Cameron's book, *Body Alchemy*, and another book that described and showed pictures of trans men. My mind was blown! I suddenly knew that transgender was a thing and that I wasn't just an isolated aberration! This was the first time I heard about physical transition with hormones as well as surgery, and I immediately wanted to do both. I ran home and started calling everyone in my family, announcing confidently, "I am a gay man!"

Coming out didn't go exactly as I expected. I thought that my mom, who had also been a tomboy growing up, would understand right away, but she got upset and cried. Then I called my dad. I expected him to say, "You are as ridiculous as you've always been." But he didn't say that. Instead, he was supportive and encouraged me to be cautious with making any physical changes. The last person on my list to tell was my boyfriend at the time, who I expected to react with horror. His response was, "Well, yeah that makes sense."

I Love You, As Is

Kris on Owen

A few years ago, when I was just starting graduate school, my step father had become quite ill and was taken urgently to the hospital. My mother called and urged me to come see him, so together, Owen and I rushed back to Tennessee.

When we arrived at the hospital we were told that my step father's condition was serious, and the doctors encouraged us to gather up family and close friends to say goodbye. I remember how difficult it was to get everyone there, but I tend to take control in these situations and demanded that everyone show up for my step father's sake. Once everyone had gathered, we decided to take him off life support, since that was what he had told us he wanted, and we would all be there as he took his last breaths. As the machines turned off he shocked us all by waking up! He opened his eyes and said, "What are you all doing staring at me?"

He kept talking over the next few hours. Eventually the doctors and nurses decided he should be released with hospice care and we could take him home. That is when Owen became my super hero. He volunteered to go back to the house with my mom and step brother to receive and set up all the medical equipment. After my step father came home, Owen continued to provide the majority of the support. He would gently wipe my step father's face with a wash cloth, help him find ways of being comfortable, and help manage his daily needs. He was amazing! I watched in awe as he put his own needs aside in order to be there for our family. He brought us all closer together during a difficult time.

Owen on Kris

Before we officially "met," we had actually run into each other a couple of times. The first time was at a Thanksgiving dinner at Kris' house. I had been invited by my roommate because I didn't have anywhere to go that year. My roommate had assured me that I was welcome and that he would confirm Kris would know I was coming. Despite my requests, he brought me unannounced to the party. I was the uninvited party crasher! But Kris was kind and graciously took us on a tour of his house.

The part I remember best was his bedroom. As I walked in I saw a series of nude pictures. While looking at these photos I thought to myself, "Oh

187

my god! Oh my god it's him! He's so hot!" I could not pay attention to what was happening, I was so distracted. The pictures were from a school project about gender identity. Kris had taken a series of photos of himself on the theme of gender and transitioning. It was part of a larger project exploring the vastness of gender identities, and he clearly felt very happy and proud to talk about them.

According to Kris, we were introduced to each other one other time out at a club, but I must have been too drunk to remember! Apparently I ran off part way through our conversation, so we didn't end up connecting at that time. Luckily, we would get another chance!

The night we "really" met was at a party. I was in the kitchen sitting on the floor talking with some fascinating new acquaintances from New Zealand. I remember the door opening, a group of people walking in, and one of them was Kris. He caught my eye right away. I wondered to myself, "Who is this adorable guy?"

I assumed that he was the date of one of the people he had come with, so I watched to see how he acted with them. I noticed he kind of wandered away from the group—maybe they weren't together! So then I started thinking about how I could make this happen…How could I talk to him?

When Kris was standing in front of the refrigerator holding an unopened beer, I realized that that was it! That was my chance! I had been at the gay pride parade that day and had gathered the usual bits of junk being handed out on the street, one of which was a keychain bottle opener.

I leapt up from the floor and walked straight toward him, valiantly carrying the bottle opener. My heart was pounding with nervous energy. He was wearing black and white checkered clothes, and his hair had a little poof at the top, ridiculously cute. I forgot all about the New Zealanders.

We talked for hours, about nature, being transgender, scary movies, growing up in the Midwest and the South, and a million other topics. As the conversation went on we realized that we had met before. And, that we also had a crazy number of things in common. We had both grown up in the Methodist church before losing connection with Christianity as teenagers and had gone to the same small liberal arts college in Ohio, missing each other there by one year. The more we talked, the more we realized how many times our paths had crossed, and I grew increasingly committed not to let this guy slip through my fingers again. As the night's end approached, Kris offered me a ride home. I was so relieved to know our conversation wouldn't be over. I accepted the ride. Unfortunately, with other friends in the car, he had to drop me off first, so I couldn't invite him into the house. As he drove away I thought about calling him and asking him to come back. But I didn't.

My roommates explained to me the most basic protocols when meeting someone new. They emphasized, "Never call before three days, or you will be seen as desperate." I could not handle that constraint; I managed to wait a day and half.

We made a date to go for a hike, a long one up a mountain. I remember talking and having such a great time in such beautiful scenery. At some point, I stopped to move something—a salamander or bug—that was in the middle of the path, so another less-observant hiker wouldn't accidentally crush it with their boot or bike. Kris has told me that this is one of the first moments he started thinking he wanted to keep me in his life. For me, it was nice to know we were on the same page about not indiscriminately killing little life forms.

Everything felt right. He asked me if I wanted to go watch a horror movie at his place. I happily accepted. Then it got late and he offered to let me stay, and I said yes. For three days we kept finding ways to not say goodbye to each other. Then, finally, we had to get back to life and work, but from that moment on we found every minute we could to be together.

Two weeks after we met, Kris invited me to go on a work trip with him. He was working as a nanny to two little boys, and I didn't have a job at the time. I was nervous, but went on the adventure. The family had rented a large vacation home for themselves, and in the back was a private little house by the pool for us.

When Kris was done with his family obligations, we retreated to the privacy of this small home. We had been seeing each other nonstop for two weeks, getting closer and closer, but we had never gone beyond snuggling.

As we made ourselves more comfortable, I became very nervous. I had only ever been with non-trans, straight or bisexual men before, never with anyone trans or anyone who saw me as a guy. I worried I would not be into it, but then I was. We figured it out together. We were so attracted to each other, it wasn't about experience or know-how—it was about desire. Our first time was passionate, intense and sweet.

Less than two months later I moved in with Kris. Initially, we thought it was a temporary situation to help me out until I could get a job and an apartment of my own. But this is the San Francisco Bay Area, and by the time I could afford my own place we had gotten used to living with each other.

I got a job as a nanny, and Kris was still working as one. We were surrounded by all these little people all the time. This prompted conversations about our desires for the future.

Kris asked, "What do you think about kids?"

"No," I decisively announced.

"Wow. Really, I think I might want kids," he said.

This conversation continued on for most of our relationship. At times, Kris even expressed to me that it could be a deal breaker if I didn't want to have kids with him. Until recently, I wasn't open to that conversation.

When I think of Kris at his best, I think of how he is when he is with children. He is so supporting, loving and sweet, and really concentrates on what they need, physically and emotionally. He is so genuine when he is with kids, willing to let go of any concern that he has about being socially appropriate, to just have fun and connect. Whenever he sees a kid being bullied he will always stick up for that kid, even if he doesn't know them at all.

THE FUTURE: POLYAMORY?

KRIS' TAKE: OWEN IS MY BALANCE

Our relationship works because we have different abilities. I am the more practical one and keep Owen grounded in reality. He is the creative one, who encourages my imagination and pushes me to do things I would likely forgo if left to my own devices.

In our daily life Owen is my physical balance. When he is with me I have nothing to worry about. He is the one that stands on chairs to grab things and change the light bulbs. Intuitively, he knows how and when to support me. He's made nature more accessible, reduced my anxiety about the sloping floors of movie theatres, and gave me a hand when I nervously climbed the stairs to give a presentation. We are monogamous, but the conversation is currently about changing that status.

Before meeting Owen, I had primarily practiced non-monogamy. I'm more familiar with dating more than one person at a time, or dating a third person as a couple, and more types of complicated situations. But when I met Owen, I was satisfied.

I know from experience that an open relationship requires a lot of time, energy, negotiation and communication to make it work. At different times in our relationship I have felt unable to commit to the work, due to lack of emotional resources and tangible time. But I have always stayed open to seeing other people because I believe Owen deserves to have his own experience, and because I wholeheartedly believe that one person cannot meet every need in a relationship. We are very complimentary to each other; we both make it possible to exist in places that might be kind of tricky otherwise.

OWENS' TAKE: I'M WITH KRIS EVERY STEP OF THE WAY

I am forever grateful to Kris for helping me better understand myself and social situations. He brings my attention to social cues—something I didn't even know existed until my brother was diagnosed with autism—and helps me understand why people are reacting to situations in certain ways.

He also helps me notice my emotions. I'm bipolar, and experience many, often rapid mood swings. When I seem depressed, he is able to gently point it out with an offer to help however he can. In the moments that I am stuck thinking about how horrible the world is, he can help me realize that these thoughts are linked to my depression.

I try to support Kris' mental health as well. Over the years I've learned how to calm him when he is anxious, and help him see when he is over-reacting. I also try to physically support him, offering my help as needed. Together, we find ways to make life more accessible and pleasurable.

Before we were a couple, I had a history of dating people who practiced non-monogamy, then transitioned to monogamy after meeting me. This is not necessarily what I desired. After transitioning and passing as male, I felt a curiosity to explore flirting with, picking-up and building friendships and relationships with gay men. But then I partnered with Kris and that became less of a priority; but, the idea lingered. As a novice non-monogamist, I'm aware that I have no previous experience to bring to the table. I struggle terribly with communication, and absolutely abhor drama. Still, I am open to the discussion and exploration.

OUR LIVES MOVING FORWARD

Imagining our lives moving forward is so much different than it was six months ago. Now, we are envisioning life with a son and figuring out how to support him as our permanent child. Going through the foster care system has helped us get better at staying in the present moment, rather than worrying or fantasizing about what will happen next. We are learning how to balance our time together with our son, as well as how to have adult time for just the two of us. Even after all this time, sex is still pretty awesome! As for opening our relationship...the conversation continues, both of us aware of pros and cons.

Interview-turned-essay, conducted by
and in collaboration with Pete Bailey

Author Bios

Ə is a queer cisgender male writer and educator. He performs everyday boy drag, as well as bearded lady drag, in various Bay Area venues.

Aaron is a European-born trans man in his late forties. He loves biking, hiking, being an uncle, frogs, making art and hanging with his sweetheart in their house with lots of plants and acrobatic squirrels.

AJ is the name the author chose for himself, at the age of twenty-four. He is a gay cis man, forty-nine years old, born in Sacramento, CA, and has lived in various cities across the U.S. AJ is an analyst for a major government entity, and enjoys gaming and country dancing.

Allan is a white cis man in his late fifties. He loves his family and friends, travels, writing, and enjoys cooking and gardening with his sweetheart.

Brian George Bernstein is a freelance writer. Through his writing, Brian hopes to raise visibility of under-emphasized LGBT issues.

Buck Angel is a transsexual-identified man, born in in Los Angeles, California. Buck has been an adult film actor, director, and producer and is now a motivational speaker and activist. Buck is known for Finding Kim (2016), Sexing the Transman (2011) and Fucking Different XXY (2014). He has appeared on numerous media platforms, panels, and works tirelessly as an advocate for LGBT rights. He also produces bondage gear and sex toys. Visit him at, Buckangel.com

C. K. Mahdi is a culturally mixed Arab American residing in Northern California. They've received a bachelors in Sociology and Middle Eastern Studies, and a teaching credential in Special Education. They are the author of the novel, *Run Wild, Run Deep*.

Dwayne Treat is a fifty-five-year-old sober leatherman who resides in San Francisco. As an HIV+ gay man, he has ridden his bicycle twice from San Francisco to Los Angeles to benefit HIV/AIDS causes. Dwayne is happily retired and enjoys volunteering and serving as a mentor in his community.

Ishmael Dickinson is a recovering San Francisco resident and aspiring fiction writer, who has a day job as faculty at a university. He occasionally writes with a pseudonym to prevent his conservative family and professional colleagues from clutching their pearls, should they be confronted with the product of his imagination and life experiences.

J. James Keels holds an MFA in Writing from Vermont College and won the PEN New England Discovery Award. He has written for various zines and journals, and has self-published many chapbooks. He also has a BA in Sociology, Human Sexuality Studies, and LGBT Studies from San Francisco State University. Visit him at, www.jjameskeels.com

Jack Whacker has been an activist, artisan, sex worker and is now a 'boring' 9-5 professional. Jack believes that trans men are an asset to the gay community, and has been educating cis men and breaking their stereotypes about trans men, by bedding them for over 10 years. His main teaching: trans men are sexy! Contact him at b.j.dailey@hotmail.com

Jonah Elliot is a student and writer living in the American South with his two senior rescue dogs. He teaches foundational literacy skills to adults and works to provide incarcerated people and their families with access to books and other necessary educational resources.

Jules Purnell is a queer, trans, mixed-race POC residing in Philadelphia. They are a current Sexuality Studies MEd student at Widner University, and perpetually fascinated by sex and all its iterations. Jules teaches on kink, polyamory, consent, and safer sex. Find them at: julesmpurnell.com

Julian Shendelman is a gay trans man and community organizer. After 10 years of living in Oakland, he is returning to Philadelphia with hopes of having more time to write. Julian was a 2016 pushcart nominated poet, and his first published chapbook, "Dead Dad Club" was released by Nomadic Press in the spring of 2017.

Kris is a thirty-something year-old gay trans guy who lives in Oakland, CA with his partner, Owen, their foster son, dog, and two cats. He works in the field of pediatric occupational therapy and is continuously inspired by the resilient and amazing children he is privileged to work with. When he's not working, he loves being in nature, reading, exploring, and spending time with his family.

Luciano Sagastume is queer, trans, and Latinx, in his early thirties, completing a master's in the Mind, Brain, Behavior program at SF state. When not inundated with statistics homework and literature reviews, he works for trans health rights through advocacy, research, and supporting Bay Area community organizations. He's an Aries.

Matthew Florence is a writer, thinker, and creative type who hates mayonnaise. When he's not at the movies, he consults with nonprofits, writing grants and providing organizational development services.

Mudhillun (pronounced 'Moo-Dylan' like Bob Dylan) **MuQaribu** is an African American, able-bodied, cisgender, late-thirties, now-Pennsylvanian male from an Islamic family in Detroit. Mudhillun works in the education field, is a marathon runner, writer, and activist.

Owen is a forty-year-old gay trans guy who can't believe he's lived 4 decades already. He enjoys writing fiction and non-fiction, painting large canvases with lines and circles, drawing comics based on his dreams, camping next to crisp mountain lakes, and taking classes on art and science. Occasionally he has to take a break from these things to work for a living. He's currently writing a children's book, and discovering the joys of family life.

Rev. Daniel Borysewicz is a progressive hospice chaplain, spiritual guide, Reiki practitioner, social activist, U.S. Navy veteran, and an ordained minister in the Universal Fellowship of Metropolitan Community Churches (MCC). Daniel's mission is to connect people, ideas, and resources for mutual benefit and to be a presence in the world that brings the radically inclusive love of God to all people.

Sheedu al-Nemmeh is a thirty-two-year-old queer cis man who currently lives in San Francisco. Sheedu is a perpetual student who enjoys exploring diverse cultures, art, philosophy, and living life to the fullest. He hopes that his essay will contribute to efforts for ceasing transphobia, misogyny, racism, and body image shaming within the gay male community and society at large.

T is a trans man, just about to turn forty. He is a photographer, currently living in the East Bay, with his cis male partner of ten years and their cat.

Yossef Aharon is a gay, Jewish, cisgender, late-thirties, LGBT counselor, currently living in the Mid West. Yossef is a big animal lover, enjoys strong coffee, and likes his men scruffy, bearish and on the bottom bunk.

Xander is a queer, Jewish, poly, twenty-three-year-old trans man, who lives on the East Coast and works in the legal field. He loves to read, cook, and share time with friends. His favorite colors of lipstick are, hot pink, purple, and inky blue-black.

Now What?
A Handbook for Families with Transgender Children
Rex Butt

New Girl Blues...or Pinks
Mary Degroat Ross

Letters for My Sisters: Transitional Wisdom in Retrospect
Edited by Andrea James and Deanne Thornton

Manning Up: Transsexual Men on
Finding Brotherhood, Family and Themselves
Edited by Zander Keig and Mitch Kellaway

Hung Jury: Testimonies of Genital Surgery by Transsexual Men
Edited by Trystan Theosophus Cotten

Swimming Upstream: A Novel
Jacob Anderson-Minshall

Words of Fire!
Women Loving Women in Latin America
Antonia Amprino

The Wanderings of Chela Coatlicue
On Tour with Los Huerfanos
Ananda Esteva

www.ingramcontent.com/pod-product-compliance
Lightning Source LLC
Chambersburg PA
CBHW061522020726
47502CB00006B/2195